CHAOS

A Sci-Fi Alien Romance

Hattie Jacks

Copyright © 2022 by Hattie Jacks

All rights reserved.

No part of this book may be reproduced in any form or by any electronic or mechanical means, including information storage and retrieval systems, without written permission from the author, except for the use of brief quotations in a book review.

Editing: Epona Author Solutions

Cover: Kasmit

Proofreading: Polaris Editing

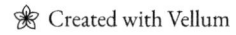

❦ Created with Vellum

Robin

If I had a watch, I could set it by the comings and goings in the surgery.

It's the only place on this whole alien planet I've seen so far, with its crumbling concrete walls, the scent of antiseptic, and sedatives. But I have seen some of what lives on this planet. They're big. They're most definitely male. They have huge wings, dark eyes, and long, sharp claws.

I don't know how many of them there are or anything else about this place. All I know is I was abducted in a spaceship by a huge lizard with stinking breath who found me huddled in my car at the deserted car park. I understand everything the aliens say because they did something to my brain, and I got blown up when the flying aliens rescued me from the lizard aliens.

My luck knows no bounds.

I start to count down under my breath. The surgery's first visitor should be coming through the double doors right about...now.

One door slams open and through it stagger three aliens. Young ones, by the pale color to their wings. One droops between the other two. The ruler of this little kingdom within a kingdom, Orvos, medic for the Legion of the Gryn, rises from his desk. Naked from the waist up, like they all are, probably due to the wings, his imposing, craggy features twist into a grimace.

"What now?" he fires out.

He's not got the best bedside manner.

"Drink, drugs, or fight?" he spits.

Or temper.

"Um, flight competition," one of the upright ones says. The injured merc, dangling in their arms, eyes rolling in his head, says nothing.

"Vrexing mercs." Orvos clucks. "Put him over there." He points to a ledge which, similar to mine, doubles as a bed and juts out from the concrete wall.

It has a crude mattress, covered with a fluid resistant material. I know from experience he'll get one blanket.

I pull my two blankets over me a little farther. Hard fought for and I'm not letting them go. They're all I have in this world.

Orvos bustles around the young warrior he referred to as a 'merc,' which I think denotes they are the bottom most rank in this legion. The hapless male is quickly sedated and his wounds treated. If he's lucky, he'll get a couple of hours rest before Orvos kicks him out, still drowsy, feathers slicked down, with an exhortation not to come back ringing in his ears.

He's just one in a long line of minor injuries which will troop through the doors over the next hours.

"How's my little human today?" Orvos, having finished with the merc, bustles over to me.

"Great!" I smile up at him. "I'm feeling great! Maybe I can get out of here?"

"Sit up," Orvos says.

Bastard.

"I'm fine just here, thanks." I smile warmly at him, hoping he'll leave me alone and let me out of the surgery, too. Some hope.

"Up you get." He reaches in, hooking his arms under mine and lifting me into a sitting position. Unable to help myself, I let out a little cry at the pain in my ribs and arm.

"You're not going anywhere, little human." Orvos gazes at me, his dark eyes impenetrable. "Not for a while."

Fuck. Fuck. Fuck. I can't stay here any longer. I'll surely go mad!

I try a different tack.

"But I'm so bored! The other humans will look after me. At least I'd have someone to talk to," I plead with him.

I could always talk the hind legs off a donkey. It was part of my charm. Part of my job. That's what my former boss said.

Former boss as in the boss I left behind on Earth. Former boss because I'll never have to let him touch me again. Because I've been abducted by aliens, not because I could have escaped his clutches any other way.

I give Orvos the benefit of my best, most impressive, most 'please discharge me' smile.

It doesn't work.

"Human females in my surgery are my responsibility," he rumbles. "Jyr would have my hide if anything happened to you. Your little body took a real pounding, and until you heal, you stay here."

He's referring to the blast which broke numerous ribs, my left arm, and my right ankle. We were in the process of being rescued by the Gryn when the spaceship on which we were captives decided to explode.

I seem to have gone from the frying pan and into the fire as far as aliens go.

From the disgusting confines of a ship full of scaly lizard

aliens who prodded us around like cattle to being at the mercy of a parade of huge, muscled warriors, most of whom are unhappy and injured, or occasionally drunk. And the constant smell which seems to be designed to remind me of the one man I should forget.

The man who took my pride, my self-belief, and more. Even the thought of him makes me swallow hard and shrink back under my blankets. It doesn't help that the Gryn have no females, other than the handful of found humans they have taken into their care. The only females I see are the ones I know from my captivity and who didn't get as damaged as me.

"You are to rest. Your breakfast will be here shortly." Orvos doesn't smile, but the tone in his voice has changed.

I don't think he likes much, but I've been here so long, I think I've become some sort of mascot for him. Not that he likes the visits from the other humans any more than he likes having his surgery 'cluttered up with mercs.'

Other than that, he doesn't talk much.

I wish my stupid useless body would heal. Diana and Jen have told me about life outside of these four walls, and as much as it sounds alien strange and terrifying, at least I could see it. See something else, other than Orvos and the endless parade of 'vrexing mercs.' Curiosity about my new home burns at me.

Hopefully Diana will come today. Maybe bring Kat, the human who was with the team of Gryn warriors who rescued us and scraped me up off the ground. She has the cutest little robot. I could spend hours with it. I don't see much of Jen these days, but then she was a bit of an enigma, preferring to spend time with the hulking, dark and dangerous Gryn we first met when we were all captives of the lizard creatures called the Drahon.

My breakfast arrives, and Orvos carefully places the tray on my lap. For a male his size and his temper, he can be nice when he wants to be. Maybe like the father I always longed for. A dad I could look up to, rather than run away from.

"Hey you!"

I wake from a light doze to see Diana sitting down on the edge of my bed. "Hi!" I attempt to push myself upright but fail. "Any chance of a breakout today?" I hiss conspiratorially.

Diana appraises me cooly and looks over her shoulder at Orvos, who is sitting at his desk pretending to ignore us.

"When you can sit up on your own, I will petition that great hulk, Jyr, to let you out. But until then, you're best off here, hun." She gives me a hesitant smile.

Diana is a strong lady. She's a Londoner through and through, while I was an incomer, drawn to the city from my rural roots in Yorkshire. Leaving behind the stone walls and emerald, green fields for the big smoke. Leaving behind my disaster area of a family and dropping myself into something else entirely. But I loved to hear her stories. She was some sort of antiquities dealer and has tales from her travels which raise the hair on your arms. Although nothing quite beats alien abduction.

And she doesn't take any shit. Not from the Drahon and not from the Gryn either, it seems.

Given I've seen the Prime, Jyr, the leader of all these enormous males, once, he's not one I'd challenge. He visited me along with his human mate Viv, a beautiful woman who was very kind and understanding. She made sure I had the extra blanket. Despite his formidable appearance, I'm pretty sure I could've talked Jyr round given half the chance. I can talk my way out of most things. That's what made me valuable to my former employer. But actually stand up to one of these big aliens? I learnt a long time ago not to do anything rash. Not where men are concerned.

"I'm so bored," I complain to Diana.

"I know, hun. But until you're well enough to deal with

these males, you have to stay here. They mean well, honestly, but they're rough around the edges and sometimes don't know their own strength."

Her words send a shiver through me. I've seen some of what she says in the males who come in with fight injuries, their naked torsos streaked with blood.

To distract myself, I curl my hand around hers. "Have you heard anything about your sister?" I ask.

Diana's eyes go cold for an instant. "Nothing. The Gryn have promised to look for her, and I know she's here on Ustokos. I just know it." She bunches her hand into a fist, but I don't let go.

My life might be boring, and painful at the moment, but at least I have no one to miss and no one to miss me.

"I'm sure they'll find her," I say, attempting to be strong for Diana.

After all, I can't be strong for me. I lost that ability a long time before I was abducted. I may as well try to do some good for someone else.

Vypr

"The weapons store is somewhere around here." Syn checks his vectorpad again, then he turns it the other way up, while I sigh in frustration.

To my left, Ayar kicks a rock and eyes the vectorpad with suspicion, but at least his weapon remains slung over his shoulder.

I look around at the ruined buildings. We're in the neighboring city, or what's left of it, to Kos, where our lair and eyrie are situated. Not that any city on Ustokos is unscathed. The great reckoning between organic life and the sentient AI, Proto, destroyed virtually all our cities and most of our technology.

What tech was left was untouchable. Proto was in it all and when it found you, it was death or capture. And if you were captured, you'd most likely long for death. It doesn't bear thinking about, not anymore.

Since the Gryn finally managed to destroy Proto and regain control of our planet, we're starting to rebuild little by little as our numbers are small. We're also discovering tech which has lain dormant for a long time. Our forefathers were once as sophisticated as we are backward.

Today, we're trying to locate a weapons dump Syn claims to have identified. Because this is a low level mission, only half of our Elite unit has been sent out, consisting of me, Ayar, and Syn. Syn because he knows tech.

Ayar because he can't be trusted on his own, anywhere.

I growl at Syn, wanting to hurry him up. We are exposed out here, and although the threat of killer bots is long gone, I don't like being this exposed. I glance at Ayar again. He shakes out his feathers a little. His skin sheens because I made him have a bath and a preen earlier. He is a magnificent male, and my heart beats a little faster for him.

He is my mate. From the first moment I saw him, trapped in the terrible machine, I knew he was mine. They say you always know your mate when you see them, and for me, it was Ayar. My beautiful, troubled warrior. The male I saved and love.

And protect, constantly. Mostly from himself.

"Got a lock!" Syn says, triumphantly.

"About time," Ayar grumbles. "I was promised explosions." He levels his gaze at me, and it's one I recognize of old. He's in the mood to fight.

"No blowing anything up today, you vrexer," Syn retorts. "We need these weapons. Especially after we got the last cohort through. The Guv's desperate for more laser pistols and rifles." He references our commander, Strykr, who has been given the unenviable task of marshaling some of the newer Gryn warriors into units like ours.

Maybe not quite like ours. We are the original Elite. Formed by Ryak, the lair head of security, who moved us all to the eyrie a cycle ago. Any other units will be a poor imitation.

With Strykr busy setting everything up, I'm hoping a command position might open for me. Maybe then Ayar and I might get a small barrack room to ourselves, rather than having to share with the others.

All of which means I could do with this mission going well, and not turning into a vrexing shambles.

"We know how important the weapons are, Syn. Any chance you could tell us the location and we can get on with our jobs?" I fire out at him.

Syn has had a downer on Ayar since he joined the unit. Most of the time, it doesn't bother Ayar. A lot of social interactions seem to go straight over his head. But it bothers me. Right now, Ayar stares into the sky, probably thinking about blasting something.

"That building, over there." Syn points north and springs into the air.

Ayar and I unfurl our wings and follow him as he rises over the shattered remains of the Gryn civilization and swoops low over the one building in the area which still possesses a roof.

When we land, I see why. It's more like a bunker. Thick walls and roof have protected it from the original bombardment which reduced this place to rubble many hundreds of cycles ago.

"How do we get in?" I ask.

Both Ayar and Syn turn to look at me, Ayar looking particularly baleful.

"Vrex the pair of you." I get busy with the various explosives I've become an expert on since Proto fell.

Before, when the skies were full of bots and laser weapons were out of bounds due to the tech contained in them, we used swords, daggers, and crossbows. Even now, I probably prefer this type of weapon for combat, if given the choice. But I seem to have found a new calling when it comes to explosives.

Having carefully rigged everything to blow the corner off

the bunker, I indicate to the others to get back and let rip with the charge.

A huge cheer comes from Ayar as the thing blows. He loves a good explosion, which is why I have to keep his contact to my stash of ordinance minimal, or quite a lot of Kos would be in even more ruins.

Given we're trying to rebuild, it wouldn't go down well with the senior Gryn if he did start damaging more things.

Dust settles and reveals a warrior sized hole in the side of the bunker. Before I can stop him, Ayar is inside, whooping loudly like a youngling.

Syn stares at where Ayar's feathers disappear, slithering down the hole. He looks at me, and I run my hand through my hair in exasperation.

I love my mate, but even I have to admit he's a liability.

Howls of delight echo from the hole as Syn makes ready to drop in, and I follow.

Maybe, just maybe, for once, this is a mission will go right for a change.

Ayar

Vrex, the explosion was good! Vypr knows how to make me feel good. He knows I love loud things, and it was very loud. Reverberating in my head and chasing everything else out. I could pant with joy. In fact, I do.

I also like dark places, and the bunker looked dark. I know I should check with the others before entering, but protocol is boring, and I hate boring.

Dropping down, it's dark and echoes beautifully as I roar out my enjoyment of being out on a mission with Vypr. I like being out with all of the unit, but as long as my Vypr is with me, I don't care either way.

Vypr will protect me. He always does. He was there when I opened my eyes after Proto caught me, and he's always there.

Always.

Could have done without him making me have a bath this morning though. I don't like bathing, and he knows it. I let out a couple more whoops to enjoy the echo and grumble a bit to myself. I like making a noise. I like growling, too.

Anything to be in the moment. Being in the moment keeps everything at bay. I can't, I don't want to remember what happened to me before. I get enough of the repetition every night, up until my head hurts so much, I want to vrexing tear it off.

But then Vypr is there, and he makes it better.

"Vrex it, Ayar. Where the vrex are you?" Syn calls from somewhere behind me. "We need to follow the schematic, not go vrexing about in the dark."

Syn doesn't like me much, not that I care. He knows his stuff and probably has his own agenda. Fine by me as long as he doesn't get in the way of a vrexing good explosion and my laser cannon. I trust him by now, given he will indulge me in a fight once I've annoyed him enough.

I like to annoy him because I like to fight. Plus my fellow unit members, Jay and Mylo, know I like to fight, and they have ways of avoiding it. Boring.

"Where have you been, you vrexer?" Vypr is beside me, laser pistol at the ready.

"I like it down here," I tell him as he wing bumps me affectionately. His free hand rakes through my feathers pleasantly. "It's dark."

"Keep sharp. Syn's not giving anything away about what's in this weapons store," Vypr murmurs in my ear, and I feel he's on edge.

He doesn't like the unknown. My Vypr likes things neat and ordered. I know he wants a command of his own one day, and I have to try not to vrex things up too much for him.

It's just once the red mist descends, whether it's a fight in the eyrie or a fight anywhere, I can't help myself. What's worse is often I can't stop myself from indulging in the destruction.

Because I love it. Seeing things come apart in my hands, it's like a balm to my soul. From utter destruction comes utter perfection. When there's nothing left, I feel free.

I'm sure I wasn't always like this, but to investigate who I was means I have to revisit those memories which ache inside me. Something I won't do, not even if Vypr asks me to.

"Where the vrex has that warrior gone?" Vypr hisses beside me. "Syn?" he calls out.

We pick our way down through a dark tunnel which gets wider the farther we go. There's no answer from Syn, and I have my laser cannon ready for the first sign of danger.

Somewhere, in the darkness, something moves.

Something cackles.

Something is alive but not alive.

It won't be intact for long. I let rip with a bolt from my cannon even as Vypr cries out for me not to shoot. The entire place lights up with the laser and it's then I see it.

Tech.

It lines the walls, console after console, and in the center, the one and only thing I fear most of all.

The machine.

This place has a machine. I open my wings and beat upwards, slamming into the roof above me. I flip over, scrambling, flapping, struggling, and doing anything I can to get as far away from the thing as possible.

Something metallic grabs at me, and I swipe out with my claws. I maybe hear it make a sound of pain, but bots don't feel pain, so I keep going, through the dark, through everything in my mad, fearful dash to put as much distance between me and the tech in the hole as possible.

Bursting out into the light, I've never felt more alive. I beat it. I got away.

I lie down, outside of the bunker, my chest heaving, wings limp. My head aches like it always does before the blinding flash which will render me insensible from pain for hours.

What did I get away from?

"Ayar?" It's Vypr's voice, quiet and steady.

I open my eyes. One of his arms is covered in blood,

streaming from the puncture wounds at his shoulder. His wing is similarly streaked with red.

Too late, I realize there was nothing metallic down there. It was my mate, my handsome mate, I sank my claws into in my haste to get away. Get away from nothing. From the things in the dark I always see.

"Vypr, I—" I stumble out. What can I say to him? "I've vrexed it up again, haven't I?"

"No, Ayar," he croons, a cool hand on my forehead. "I understand. You don't have to go back. We'll return to the eyrie, leave Syn to do the inventory."

What the vrex did I do to deserve him? My Vypr. My mate.

Before I know it, I'm on my feet and flying, hard. Because the sooner I get away from the horror, the sooner I can be myself again.

I might hate the Ayar I've become, the unhinged, the unpredictable, the feared. But there's no way back, not anymore.

Robin

"I'm thirty-six years old! I won't be confined to my bed like a child!" I yell like a child at Orvos as I attempt to push past his bulk and fail, falling back on my bed.

"I didn't understand a word of what you just said, but I've already told you, when you can walk the length of the surgery without pain, you can go." He folds his arms over his broad chest and gives me a smug smile.

He might not have any bedside manner, but he knows exactly what I can and can't do.

And I can't get to the sanitary facility at the other end of the surgery without stopping to alleviate the pain in my chest from my poor broken ribs. Not quite yet anyway.

"What about a trip out? With the other women—females," I correct myself and plaster on my best smile.

"If you think I'm letting a precious female out of my surgery before she is fully healed, you've got quite the imagination," Orvos replies.

I growl in frustration as he turns his back on me, huge, dark wings shuffling. He stops, hesitates, and turns back.

"But, if we don't get any overnight stayers, why don't you

ask the females to come here and keep you company? I'm sure I can find things to do elsewhere in the lair." He winces slightly.

Orvos isn't the type to give up his domain so easily. I guess it's a concession I should take.

"Okay." I give him a wan smile.

I spend the rest of the day Gryn watching, hoping beyond hope none of the parade of males will need anything more than superficial treatment and, fortunately, no one does. Although on one memorable occasion, impressive level clean up is required from falling into a vat of beer. That particular merc is discharged rapidly to sober up elsewhere.

Diana's coppery head appears around one of the doors.

"It's all clear!" I call out, waving frantically and letting out a pant of breath at the pain it causes me.

She disappears. The door is pushed open by her arse, and I see she's carrying a tray groaning with food. Plus she's not alone! My heart leaps with joy as I see Jen, Kat, and another human woman who I think is called Lauren, but I've only seen her once before.

She was in with me a while ago, I think. Along with a large group of Gryn warriors, big, brutish, and bristling with weapons. Orvos was not amused, and I was having a bad day.

"Hi!" I say as brightly as I can, desperate to make a good impression with all of them, to make sure they stay with me for a while at least.

I got to know Diana and Jen because we were kept captive together. Jen doesn't say much. She never did, spending much of her time with the dark, evil smelling male Gryn who had been held captive with us. I wouldn't go near him. Somehow, she liked him.

Diana is a different story.

"Wow, look how long your hair is getting," I say as she embraces me.

I tug at her hair. For some reason, when she was abducted, she had it dyed bright orange. Now it's growing out, and it looks like the roots are a gorgeous dark brown.

"Ugh, I hate it," she says, running her hand through her hair. "You've not met Lauren, have you?"

"We've met, briefly. You had a lot of warriors with you." I laugh.

What I don't say is that two of them had stared at me for so long, I thought they might eat me.

"Yeah, that's the elite unit for you," Kat replies. "Never do anything unless it can be done en masse." The others look at her, and she claps her hand over her mouth as everyone dissolves into laughter.

I feel left out immediately. This is what I'm missing out on, being stuck in here.

"What do you mean?" I ask, my natural curiosity getting the better of me.

"Sorry, sweetheart." Kat pats her rounded stomach. "We were just joking around."

Now I understand. She's referring to the Gryn taking us as mates. Something akin to a relationship but far more intense and likely to have resulted in her obvious pregnancy. The thought of getting close to any male, alien or human, again fills my throat with bile.

After what he did, my so-called boss. The thought of his sour breath on my face, his hands...

"Are you okay?" Lauren asks me, putting a hand on my arm, her kind face peering into mine. "You're not in pain or anything?"

"I can get Orvos if you are," Kat says.

"No. No!" I smile with bitter brightness. "No Orvos, please! I'm fine. Come on, tell me more about what's going on out on this whole alien planet I've yet to see."

"Well..." Lauren looks around at the others, and Diana

gives her a nod. "Jay, my mate," she smiles in a way I don't think I ever have "and I had a sort of marriage ceremony."

"It was so cute," Kat gushes. "When Strykr gave me my band, it was lovely, but the ceremony is just..." She squeezes her hands together with a sigh. "Plus you make the cutest couple."

"You've captured someone's attention too," Jen says to me.

I'm probably a billion miles from him but even so, the thought of being on someone's radar fills my feet with clay. My heart clenches.

"Jen?" Diana says as a sort of warning.

"What?" I look between the two of them.

"It's nothing. One of the warriors was asking after you, that's all. He's a bit of a loose cannon. We said you were not interested because you're still healing, and he got a bit... angsty," Diana says, holding her hands out flat in a gesture she probably thinks will be calming.

"Oh." I'm not sure what to say. I see so many males, coming and going. I tend to hide away under my blankets most of the day. I can't imagine when I might have caught anyone's attention.

But while I appreciate being protected by these women I've only just met, I'm a little peeved at yet more erosion of choice.

"I don't think it meant anything," Kat says quickly. "Ayar's mated to Vypr anyway."

"Oh?"

"Let me tell you, once you get out of here, you're going to have such an introduction to the world of the Gryn!" Diana laughs, breaking the tension which has started to fill the room. "They're a mass of contradictions, these males."

Which is the last thing I want to hear. I don't want anything complicated when it comes to men or males. Simple, easy to read, not unpredictable. If I had a choice, I'd have been stolen away to a planet full of females. Much safer.

"If Orvos has his way, I'll be here forever!" I mock wail, trying to keep things light, not to give in to the squirm in my guts about my future, given these women are so blasé about it all. "So tell me more about what's been going on." I reach for one of the sweet pastries Diana has brought in, changing the subject. "Tell me more about this planet because I'm going out of my mind with boredom in here."

Lauren starts to tell me about the technology she encountered on her adventures with the unit, which is new to the Gryn. Everything to do with tech, from tablets to spaceships, is something most of them had never dealt with until recently. The planet was decimated by a war to end all wars with some sort of sentient robot, which nearly ended all organic life on the planet. She's funny and engaging as she speaks, plus Kat has brought her little robot, Ike, with her, and he buzzes around shouting odd phrases, which gives us a giggle.

I could almost be back on Earth. I didn't have friends, more acquaintances. My job as an internet hack didn't really lend itself to much more than acquaintances, but there were one or two people in the office I could have a laugh with. Although it all changed when he came into my life. My new boss, the one who asked me to spend time with him after hours. The one who...

"Ustokos to Robin?" Jen takes my hand in hers. "You're tired. We should go."

I realize my eyelids are drooping. "Not yet, please?" I plead as they get to their feet and start clearing up.

"We'll come back tomorrow." Kat looks at the others. "At least some of us will, I'm sure."

Which means I'm probably going to be forgotten about again. Kat pulls me in for a squashy pregnant embrace. I can almost feel her happiness.

"We'll get everything sorted for when you get out. You'll be staying with Diana and Jen. They have a lovely room." She withdraws and holds me at arm's length. "It's a huge step. Everything is new, but you are going to like it here, I promise."

"I'm sure I will." I give her a smile I hope is genuine. "Just got to get used to all the males, and I'll be good." I give them all a thumbs up.

In return, I get some gentle hugs and promises to return as soon as they can.

Then I'm alone, and the place seems very empty. Not for the first time, with just my thoughts for company, I wonder if I can survive here.

Because if males are the one thing you fear, how do you make a new life on a planet full of them?

Ayar

I finish stowing away my laser cannon. The headache which has been threatening still hovers just behind my eyes. I should sleep. I haven't slept properly for days, not since I saw the little human in the surgery.

There was something about her I can't shake. Her bright blue eyes, so incredible; although, I don't know if she saw me. I can understand if she didn't. I'm a scarred warrior with an anger management problem, or so I'm told. I tried to ask the other females about her at Jay's banding ceremony, but they didn't want to talk to me.

It meant I got into a fight. I always get into a fight when I want something. But this time, all I wanted was to get to know her better. The pale female with the big blue eyes.

"You finished?" Vypr appears in the armory doorway, leaning up against the door frame. He folds his arms over his chest, beautiful and magnificent. His skin is free of scarring, and I love touching it. It's soft and inviting.

"I'm done," I say, and I mean it. I'm really done for the day. My panic at the weapons depot has left me with a level of exhaustion I don't normally feel.

Because I don't normally feel anything. I exist, hovering somewhere between sanity and insanity. I hate it, almost as much as I love him.

I fall in step with Vypr, wanting to be near him but knowing he prefers to initiate contact. We make our way out of the lower ground levels of the eyrie, where the weapons are stored and the training pits have the occasional pairing of mercs sparring, until we reach the atrium.

"You hungry?" Vypr asks me.

I am, but not for food. I hunger for something else.

"Yeah, I could eat," I reply. Vypr always knows best.

"You need some time and a bath before we eat with the others." Vypr levels his gaze at me, strong and masterful.

I thought he would be angry I vrexed up the mission for him. When we returned to the eyrie, he had to explain to the Guv, our commander, Strykr, why we were back early and why we'd left Syn behind. I didn't stay. I've heard all the excuses for my behavior many times over.

"Was the Guv okay with...me?" I ask him. "With the mission?"

"He wasn't too interested. It was Syn's mission really. Provided Syn gets what he wants, the Guv's happy." Vypr reaches out a hand and runs it gently down the edge of my wing. "You shouldn't worry."

I close my eyes at his touch. This is what I want, more than food, more than to lose the pain in my head. I need Vypr.

He's gone, launching himself up the atrium, and I follow, chasing him down, not prepared to let him out of my sight.

Our barracks are, thankfully, empty of Syn, Mylo, and Huntr, the other unmated males who make up the rest of our unit. Our ledges are near the back, away from the others, where we can be together, even if we don't mate when the others are present.

My stomach rumbles.

"Bath first, then food," Vypr tells me, sniffing at my feathers.

I look longingly at him. "Bath," Vypr says, his tone more forceful.

Sighing, I strip off my boots and pants and walk through to our small healing pool. To any other Gryn, the bubbling waters are a draw after a long day on patrol or mission. To me, the sound reminds me of the machine, and I don't like it, not one bit.

Behind me, Vypr starts to hum, the low, gentle noise filling the chamber and deadening the sound of the water. He stands behind me and slides his arms around my waist, head resting on my shoulder, his muscular chest pressed against my wings. "Bathe, Ayar," he says in my ear, his lips brushing the delicate skin there and sending my body into shivers.

He releases me reluctantly as I wade into the water, then follows me until I duck my body under the surface and dip in first one wing, then the other, flicking the water through my feathers in the way he showed me.

"Sit," he says once I've sluiced my wings. He puts a hand on my chest and presses until I'm sitting on a ledge just under the water, while he grabs a cleansing bar, lathers it up, and rubs the suds over my shoulders, down my abs until his hands disappear under the water, and he's cleaning all of me up. My cocks respond to his firm touch.

"Vypr," I breathe out, unsteadily.

He stands up on the ledge and towers over me, water pouring off him, off his erect cocks. I tremble, my mouth watering. My desire ramping up.

I wrap my hand around his members and groan out loud at how good they feel under my fingers. Throbbing, hard muscle begging for my touch. Every ridge, every node made for me.

"Do you want to pleasure me, Ayar?" He puts his hands

on the shoulders of my wings and delves his claws into my feathers in the way which has my eyes rolling in my head with need as I nod my assent. "Lick me," he demands.

I wrap my mouth around him, moaning as I suck at him, wanting all of him and knowing he'll deny me like always. Knowing he'll put my wants above his own.

He will mate me thoroughly, and I won't get the chance to show him how much he means to me.

Vypr

Ayar slumbers next to me like a youngling. All snorts, snores, and the occasional wing flap. I did my best to exhaust him because having seen the machine in the weapons store, I know exactly what he thought it was. I made sure he pleasured me, and then I mated him hard, like always.

I know he wanted to pleasure me to completion, but he didn't deserve to, not today.

I sweep his hair off his handsome, scarred face. He has no memory of the injury which left him with a dark scar running down his left cheek and left shoulder. It went deep enough to damage even his hard shoulder skin, something which rarely gets so badly injured. The rest of his body is similarly scarred. He murmurs and wrinkles his nose in a gorgeous way. I shouldn't love him more like this, but in between sleep and consciousness, he's the Ayar I think he always was, before Proto got to him and turned him into a creature who feels everything, all the time.

Ayar has no limits. It's one of the many things I love about him. It just means I spend a lot of time keeping him out of trouble.

And I can't always be there, which is why he ends up fighting. Even when I am around, sometimes he can't help himself, and I have to pick up the pieces.

A pair of dark eyes watch me.

"Awake?" I trace my knuckle down the side of his face.

He isn't always awake when he has his eyes open. Sometimes, I find him standing, staring at nothing. It's then the headaches begin in earnest and despite my pleas for him to see Orvos, it's the one thing, the only thing he won't do for me.

He yawns, stretching out his hard muscular body next to me. Gryn warriors are social creatures. Sharing of ledges, baths, food, and preening duty are not uncommon among males. I understand it was common even when we had females. It means there is little said or even noticed about my relationship with Ayar. The rest of our unit don't care in the slightest. In fact, they prefer me to be around to keep Ayar under control.

Because he might be unpredictable and possibly downright dangerous, but he's taken to the new laser weapons as if he's handled them all his life, and what he can't do with a laser cannon isn't worth knowing. If we're in a fight, we need Ayar at our backs. He will defend us all to the end of his days.

My honorable male.

Ayar smacks his lips and wraps himself around me.

"You want to get something to eat, my mate?" I run my fingers through the feathers at the base of his wings, and he makes a happy sound. "Or we can stay here." I want him to take his time, to recover from his earlier fright, even if he'll never admit he was frightened.

"Want to stay here." He ducks his head against me, covering us both with a wing. His stomach rumbles loudly.

"I believe your belly betrays you." I laugh at him, wriggling out from under his soft, scented feathers which smell so perfectly Ayar.

I scoop up his pants and throw them at him. "Get dressed, you vrexer."

He puts one arm behind his head and watches me as I pull on my clothes and boots.

"Vypr." He hesitates.

"What is it, Ayar?" I ask, slipping a dagger into my belt.

"I'm sorry," he says. "For today."

"Vrex!" I have him pinned against the bed, one arm across his neck, holding him firmly. "What have I told you? Never apologize for who you are. And never, ever apologize to me. You're my mate and there's the end of it." I release him, pulling him into my arms as I run my fingers through his feathers, and he goes limp against me. "I mean it. I'll get my command on merit, Ayar. Nothing you do or don't do will change that."

"I want you to have what you want," he says, quietly. "It's important to you, so it's important to me."

"And I want you," I tell him. "To be happy and well. That's what's important. The rest can go vrex itself."

Ayar grins at me, his eyes twinkling with his usual mischief, the good sort.

The sort where he's happy.

"Does stuff 'vrexing itself' extend to training tomorrow?" he asks.

I bury my head in his wings, inhaling deeply, drinking in his scent, wishing what he wants right now is what I want.

"Not this time. Put your pants on." I half-groan as I release him.

ONCE AYAR IS DRESSED, WE MAKE OUR WAY TO THE atrium in order to be able to descend to the food hall level.

The place is unusually busy. Mercs—young, untried Gryn

warriors—flit from side to side, hollering. I see Ayar shake his feathers mid-flight. All these warriors in one place will not be good for him, and he's going to need careful handling to avoid a fight.

He lands, and a merc wing bumps him. The merc finds himself involuntarily airborne again.

Okay, maybe if we can get through a meal without a major fight, it will be a minor miracle, given Ayar's dark mood.

"Leave us." I land next to the merc's friends who are already advancing on Ayar. Shaking out my feathers, I hold my wings high alongside Ayar, who seethes.

The mercs back off. They know better than to challenge a pair of warriors, plus Ayar has somewhat of a reputation. It's not a good thing.

"Var beer!" Ayar announces as we walk into the food hall.

I had no idea there was any sort of celebration going on tonight. Had I known, I probably wouldn't have brought my especially volatile Ayar. Before I can stop him, he's across to the barrel and has drawn himself a tankard.

"Hey, Vypr." Mylo, our combat expert sidles up to me with a tankard in his hand.

"What's happening? I thought the eyrie was banned from any celebrations for the time being."

Something which happened after our unit lost one of our spaceships to the Drahon and got it back. Despite our victory, the senior Gryn felt we still deserved punishment. No parties in the eyrie until they say. It hasn't gone down well, especially as the unit which caused all the trouble has been partying for Jay's banding ceremony.

"Syn's found some tech which has impressed the seniors. We've been given special dispensation for tonight." Mylo grins. "But be quick, that barrel is all we get."

He diverts my attention back to the beer, and I see Ayar filling another tankard, his first already empty. With his mood, the last thing he needs is a belly full of beer when he hasn't eaten.

"Food." I reach him as he's draining the last of his second tankard.

"One more." He grins in a way I know means he doesn't have any intention of stopping at this tankard, neatly sidesteps me, and grabs another.

"Vypr?" Syn calls to me from across the hall.

I need to speak with him, but it means leaving a male who can't be trusted next to a vat of var beer.

"Keep an eye on him, will you?" I ask Mylo who shrugs without committing. "Make sure he eats something."

I hope Ayar can be trusted for five minutes while I speak to Syn to explain our early departure and to find out what he's done which has impressed the seniors so much. If there's any way I can emulate his approval rating, I want to be there. It's time for me to progress.

Syn sits on his own. Huntr broods a few tables behind him, snarling at any merc which tries to sit near him. He's a male with his own issues, but then, he'll have to join the line behind Ayar.

"About earlier. We..." I begin to explain.

"Doesn't matter. Don't worry about it," Syn says quickly. "I wanted to talk to you about the machine we found."

The one which put the fear of the goddess into my Ayar.

"What about it?"

"Ayar recognized it, didn't he?"

"So what if he did? What else did you find down in that hole? Because it can't be some ancient machine which has impressed the seniors."

"Oh, some weapon or other. Kyt was very excited about it. He'd used one before," Syn says, dismissively. "I'm more interested in the machine."

"Look," I snarl quietly, moving into his personal space.

"The machine we found Ayar in nearly killed him. I don't care what you think it is, he's not going back to give you an opinion."

Syn doesn't move. He's looking behind me. There's the unmistakable sound of an Ayar related commotion, the splintering of wing on bone. With a resigned sigh, I turn to find out who my mate has vrexed off.

Mylo helpfully stands to one side as Ayar is deep in a scrum with at least five mercs. One by one, they're flung away from him. He's winning this round anyway.

I shake out my feathers and prepare to dive in in order to end things, when one of the dazed mercs rights himself and, pumping his wings hard, he and another Gryn crash into my mate, uncoordinated, and it's enough to dislodge him from the rest. He's thrown backwards, bouncing off the beer barrel and falling face down onto a table, which smashes to smithereens under his bodyweight.

"By Nisis!" I fire out, walking towards him as he lies in the wreckage, one wing flapping as he attempts to right himself. "Ayar!"

Before I get to him, he's heaved himself onto his feet. A ring of mercs surround us, many of them obviously wondering what the enormous warrior is going to do to the two mercs who floored him. Which is the last thing I want. We can eat later; it's time to leave.

Ayar turns towards me, a crazed, hesitant smile on his face, his hands on his stomach.

Blood spills from around the large splinter of wood impaled in his abdomen.

"Vypr?" He says my name as if it's the last word he'll ever speak.

Robin

"WHERE THE VREX IS ORVOS?" An enormous warrior barrels through the double doors, carrying a similarly sized male in his arms.

He's covered in blood, and his skin is pale, not the usual tan color sported by the Gryn. Sticking up from his belly is a large piece of wood. One wing hangs uselessly, the other is tucked under him. He doesn't make any sound at all.

The silence is terrifying.

I'm off my bed and running without even thinking, haring through to the rear where I saw Orvos bustle before I fell into a light doze.

"Orvos!" I call out, just before I almost run smack into the huge male.

"What the vrex is going on? That's a lot of noise for a little female."

"Warrior...hurt." I gasp, the pain in my chest hitting me for the first time.

"ORVOS!" A bellow comes from the surgery, and Orvos moves quicker than I think I've ever seen him, darting back into the main room. I follow at a slower pace, deeply worried.

But not for me, for the injured warrior, his wings flailing as he's lowered gingerly onto a ledge.

The injured warrior who has begun fighting both Orvos and his friend, quite impressively for a male who has lost as much blood as he obviously has.

"Hold him still, Vypr!" Orvos says through gritted teeth. "I need to look at his wound."

"You won't vrexing tranq me," the wounded male grinds out, attempting to lever himself upright and stopped, partially by his friend and partially by the huge splinter of wood sticking out of the lefthand side of his abdomen. "Don't even try, or I'll kill you."

He makes the statement as fact. Not that Orvos is bothered in the slightest.

"Just vrexing hold him," he says to Vypr, who has one arm over the male, and with the other, he gently caresses the warrior's long hair out of his eyes, staring at him intently.

Orvos moves quickly across the surgery to grab the bottle of what I know, all too well, is a type of sedative he gets you to inhale. He caught me out several times with it while I was injured. As he heads back to the pair, the injured warrior makes a break for it. With an almighty effort, his wings are free, and he slams aside his friend and heads blindly towards me.

I should duck or do something, but I'm rooted to the spot as, still looking over his shoulder at Orvos, he hits me, and we go tumbling to the floor. My chest and arm spike with pain, but I'm more concerned he doesn't cause himself any more damage as he ends up on top of me, all feathers and limbs.

The male who, despite being bloody and seriously injured, smells absolutely divine. Like hot concrete after rain and an underlying spice I can't quite place. A pair of dark eyes, filled with agony, stare down at me, and they soften very slightly as he inhales a shuddering breath.

Time slows down. Our separate pain intertwines. I lift my hand to touch his cheek.

"You—" He's jerked backwards off me before he can finish what he was going to say.

Orvos shoves the sponge soaked in the sedative liquid under his nose, and the male goes limp. With seemingly little effort, he tips the enormous creature into his arms and hurries past me, through to the back of the surgery.

"Are you okay?" Vypr asks, holding out a hand while his eyes remain on Orvos.

I let him help me to my feet. My breathing is a little difficult because my chest took a beating from being jumped on, and my wrist aches.

"I'll survive. You'd better go with your friend." I look up at the big male.

And by up, I mean I really have to look up. He has to be close to seven feet tall to my average five-foot-six. He's smeared with blood, but I can't help but notice his handsome, chiseled cheekbones, dark eyes framed with long eyelashes, and his wings—they're darker than the others'.

"My mate," he says, quietly. "Ayar."

When he says the other male's name, a pain spikes through me, but it's not physical. *These are the males the girls were talking about!*

"Orvos is an excellent medic. He fixed me up just fine," I say. "Go, be with him."

Without hesitation, I put my hand under his wing and into the small of his back, giving him a gentle push towards the rear of the surgery. He stumbles forward, his dark eyes turning to me, almost black with the emotions churning within him.

I can't believe I touched him.

Vypr recovers himself and, without another backwards look, he strides through, all bristling feathers. I clutch at my chest and sink down onto the nearest ledge, my breath rasping at the shock of what just happened. My body and mind slowly start to register the impact of Ayar and the proximity of Vypr.

I'm trembling, stupidly, and as I look down at myself, I see I also have some of his blood on me. The fact he could move so quickly when injured and his desperation not to be treated are all puzzling. I want him to be okay, not just because of the look in his eyes when he saw me under him but because of the look in Vypr's eyes. The complete terror he might lose Ayar.

I don't think I've ever felt that way about anyone in my life. I left my life back in Yorkshire when I was sixteen and never looked back. Youngest of five siblings, I doubt my useless, dropout parents even noticed I'd left. Neither showed me an iota of love or interest, and my siblings even less.

Love. It's an alien concept to me. As alien as this planet. The one I've yet to see.

After two attempts to stand on legs which seem to have lost all strength, I hover for an instant, caught between wanting to check on Ayar and wanting to rest my aching body. Why I'm invested in his wellbeing, I'm not sure, and I'm not certain my interest will be welcome.

All I know is, his terror was mine as he stared down at me, and somehow, we had a connection I can't even describe, other than he knows what it's like to be completely helpless and to rage against it all.

Vypr

Ayar lies on the medi-chair, limp and lifeless. Orvos fusses around him, using various things I don't recognize to stem the bleeding from his abdomen.

Watching my mate get forcibly tranqued might have been worse than seeing him injured. I know just how much Ayar battles with the nightmares, the reason he would never come to Orvos. Enforced sleep means he's stuck in his own mind and can't get out.

"What's happening?" I fire out at the medic. He'd ignore me otherwise. "How is he?"

"Vrex you, Vypr, if you don't keep quiet, I'll throw you out. Let me get this thing out of him, and then I can tell you how he is."

It's only then I notice the long streak of blood down Orvos's arm. Ayar must have caught him when we were wrestling with him earlier.

"Vrex it, Ayar," I mutter under my breath as Orvos activates something on the medi-chair, and I am eternally grateful Ayar is tranqued because being trapped in the chair would be one of his worst nightmares.

As Orvos works, Ayar lets out a long groan.

"He's not tranqued enough!" I leap forward, pulling the medic away to make sure if Ayar can see anyone, it's me.

"Vypr!" I'm pulled away. "He's fully tranqued, just fighting it like he fights everything. He's fine. Let me work. I won't warn you again."

I step away from my mate reluctantly, and Orvos moves over him. It seems to take forever for him to remove the splinter, and all the time, I'm on edge, watching every move, every possible twitch from my mate.

But he doesn't move or make a sound again. Remaining motionless, something he never is. Even sleeping, Ayar is always in constant motion. My heart clenches in my chest. Life without Ayar is...

"Take him back through to the surgery. I've done all I can for tonight." Orvos holds his hands under a part of the chair, and the blood covering them is vaporized.

Ayar has a large white patch covering the injured area, and I wonder how I could have missed seeing Orvos place it there.

"Your mate will be fine." Orvos places a hand on my shoulder. "He's made of tougher stuff than you think."

I gather Ayar's limp, heavy form in my arms, muscles screaming at me from my earlier desperate flight to bring him from the eyrie to the lair. With infinite care, I lift him, and with Orvos following me, I carry my mate through to the surgery. The medic directs me to a ledge, and I lay him down. His face is too pale, and my heart hurts as if it's straining to help him.

Orvos hands me a covering, and I wrap Ayar up in it. I know he loves to be held, but the ledge is too narrow for us both, and my stomach clenches with the need to see his dark eyes meet mine again.

"Can I stay with him?" I ask Orvos. "I want to stay, and I

won't cause trouble." The surgery is Orvos's domain. I have to abide by his rules.

"The only troublemaker awake in here is that one." Orvos nods behind me, and I twist to see the bright blue eyes of the human female Ayar knocked to the floor.

Her face is hauntingly beautiful; although, I don't know why I notice. Maybe because her mouth is pinched around the edges as if she's in pain. Golden hair frames a small, delicate face, her jewel-like eyes enormous, her tiny body swathed in blankets. She gives me the hand gesture all the humans use, a wave.

"How is he?" she asks, sitting up and swinging her legs over the edge of her ledge. She's wearing a simple, short gown, and her legs are bare.

For some reason, my eyes are drawn to the pink skin on show. It looks soft, almost inviting.

"Ayar will survive, and thrive, like he always does," Orvos intones. "You can stay if you keep quiet and make sure the rest of your unit keeps out of my way," he tells me. "Don't disturb my other patient either."

He swishes away to the back room, and I turn my attention back to my mate, carefully brushing his hair back over his head and making sure his feathers aren't being crushed.

"His other patient is me," a quiet female voice says next to me. "I'm Robin," she adds. "Interned for the duration, so you can't disturb me." She tries a smile, but her nervousness is apparent, her hands twisting together.

"Vypr." I hold out my hand in the greeting I've been shown by Strykr's mate, Kat. "Pleased to meet you."

Robin takes my hand and shakes it. Her skin is soft and warm. Her gaze, all blue eyes, is warm too, although it's also filled with concern.

"What happened?" she asks, looking over at Ayar as she sits beside me. "How did he get hurt?"

I should tell her to vrex off. That this has nothing to do with her...

"I should have been watching him. It's all my fault," I blurt out.

Robin

Vypr's shoulders slump as he tells me he thinks Ayar's injury is all his fault. It's as if he's been defeated. Tiredness lines his handsome face, and his hand rests on Ayar's shoulder as if he can give the unconscious male some of his strength.

"I'm sure it's not your fault. Accidents happen all the time. Look at me." I give him what I hope is a reassuring smile.

It doesn't seem to help. Vypr's brow draws lower. "We should have known the Drahon would pull a trick like blowing up their own ship. You did not need to get injured," he says.

"You were there?"

I don't remember much other than running through the ship following the fluttering feathers of one huge warrior. Next thing I recall is waking up, wracked with pain in the surgery, Orvos on hand with his never-ending parade of sedatives. Unbidden, a shudder runs through me.

"Both Ayar and I were there, trying to rescue you, mistress," Vypr says, seriously. "I am sorry you got hurt because we were not swift enough."

Oh shit, it looks like I've just made things worse. He was feeling bad enough about his friend before I came and shoved my big foot in it.

"Call me Robin, please." I smile in exhortation and hesitantly put my hand on his arm.

For all these males fill me with a sort of dread, a feeling I'm unable to shake even though the man who did those things to me is far away, I can't stop myself from wanting to help.

Because once I got free of my family and found the world outside our tiny village, it was full of broken things which needed fixing. Somehow, I ended up working as a journalist for an online news agency, specializing in investigative pieces, I was doing what I could to make things better, exposing things which were wrong and ensuring justice where it was due. An odd choice of profession, but I like people, I like talking, and I love listening. And I have enough curiosity to make all the cats in the world quake.

Which is why when he took over the internet news agency I was working for, I couldn't walk away from the job I loved.

Who am I kidding? He wouldn't let me walk. Not when I 'owed him.'

It takes all the effort I can muster not to shiver at the thought of his voice telling me what to do. Instead, I concentrate on the sadness in Vypr's face and give his arm a gentle squeeze.

"Orvos isn't letting me out of here anytime soon, so if you need to talk, or if you want someone to sit with him while you, you know…" I leave the sentence hanging. "I'll be here."

Vypr lifts his eyes from Ayar to meet mine. Their darkness drives into me with the intensity of his stare.

"Why?" he asks, anger flaring from deep inside him, anger I know isn't directed at me, despite any fears I may have. "Why would you do this?"

"Why wouldn't I? Think of it as one patient taking care of another and my way of proving I don't bear any grudges."

Vypr moves his dark gaze back to Ayar, a look so filled with love it makes my heart flip flop in my chest. Not that love is something I ever think I'll experience. I've never experienced it up until now, and I'm not even sure what it means.

I was a damaged, broken thing, trying to fix the world instead of fixing herself. I was a walking Alanis Morissette song.

"Thank you," he murmurs, taking Ayar's viciously clawed hand in his.

I guess I've just found myself a new job.

Ayar

Vrex! I hurt. Not all over. Not like I've spent all day training in the fighting pit with Strykr. A different type of hurt, concentrated in my belly.

I don't like it.

I don't like the foggy feeling in my head either, the aftereffects of a tranq, along with a metallic taste in my mouth. When I open my eyes, I'm staring at a high ceiling which isn't our barrack room.

"VREX!" I attempt to sit up, to get to my feet, to get out of the surgery and away from the medic, his tranqs, and his machines.

"Whoa!" A sweet voice penetrates the fog and my failure to sit up. It's a voice I heard in my dreams.

The voice which kept the nightmares at bay.

Maybe I'm still tranqued. Maybe this is still a dream. I try again to sit up.

"Vrex! That hurts!" I groan out loud.

My belly is on fire. It burns at me. I look down to see a large white bandage stuck to my abdomen and a tiny, pink, clawless hand on my chest.

"Female?" My eyes track up her arm, over her long hair, which is the color of a sunrise through Ustokos' clouds to a pair of bright blue eyes which study me with interest.

"Where's Vypr? Why do I hurt so much?" I grimace, one wing rowing in the air at nothing as I try to decide if I want to attempt to get up or lie still and let the pain wash over me.

"He'll be back soon. He's been sitting with you for the past two days," the female says. "He's gone to get something to eat and have a bath."

The way she says it, I know she's talking about Vypr. If he hasn't had a bath for two turns, he'll be very grumpy.

"I'm Robin," she adds. "Fellow inmate."

"Where's Orvos?" I can't help but growl.

Robin's eyes widen, and a scent hits my nostrils which I don't like. Bitter and nasty, it chases out the good smell. The smell of her.

"Are you in pain? Do you need him? I can get him for you." She lifts out of her seat.

"No!" I reach out a hand and, despite the pain, I grasp her tiny wrist.

Her delicate, perfect bones feel as if I could crush them in my grip. The touch of her skin is incredible, soft, and it releases another flow of her delicious scent.

"I don't want Orvos. He'll just tranq me," I hiss.

Robin stares at me for a beat, then she laughs quietly. "You don't like the sedation either, eh?"

I huff out a breath. "Vrexing Orvos. That's his answer to everything."

She laughs harder. "Don't I know it!"

I become aware she's moved her hand from my chest and now it holds mine, her thumb rubbing circles on the sensitive skin between my thumb and my index finger. It feels good. I like it.

"Have I really been here for two turns?" I ask, finally dropping my head back and allowing myself to relax as she continues to gently move her fingers over my hand, rubbing and soothing.

"You don't remember getting here? Flying straight into me, knocking me to the floor?" she says, her eyes dancing at me.

"I didn't hurt you, did I, mistress?" Suddenly, every inch of me wants to protect her, and as quickly as I feel it, it's gone.

"My name is Robin." She smiles. "No, you didn't hurt me. You were just scared. I understand."

"I don't get scared," I growl. Her eyes widen, and I check myself. "Robin," I add with my best attempt at not being frightening.

Females don't like to be frightened. I don't like to frighten them. Even though I do.

"Of course you don't." Her frown is replaced by a smile so incredible, I could look at it all day.

I inhale as deeply as I dare. Her bitter scent has gone, and it's replaced with something which is almost ambrosia. Like my Vypr only deeper and just as delicious. It invades every part of me.

Every part...

"Ayar!" Vypr appears through the double doors, and I attempt to lift myself up to get to him.

I want to be in his arms, feel the press of his skin on mine, even if we don't usually do such things with an audience.

But somehow, something within me seems to think it's right with Robin, that she should see us together. Vypr strolls over, his wings and hair still damp from his bath. His scent is fresh, sweet because he's been eating the pastries the humans have taught our cooks to make, and I know they're his favorite.

"It's good to see you awake." He slips his arms under mine and gently pulls me into an upright position, nuzzling his head into my feathers, marking me with his scent.

"It's good to be awake. No thanks to the vrexing medic." I eye the empty doorway to the rear of the surgery. "If he comes near me again with the tranq, I'll rip his wings off."

"If I need to tranq you again, you'll not know about it," Orvos says, appearing as if from nowhere. I wish he'd stop doing that.

"And you can only sneak up on me because I've just woken up. You'll not manage it again," I snarl.

Robin stifles a laugh.

"How come none of my threats worked on you, Orvos?" she asks, batting her eyelashes at him.

Suddenly, instantly, I don't want her looking at him. Or anyone.

I growl.

"Oh!" She turns the beautiful blue orbs on me. "*That's* why. I don't growl as well as this one."

Her hand is on my arm, warm and soft.

I like her.

I SIT UP, WINGS AGAINST THE WALL OF MY LEDGE and fold my arms over my chest. It still vrexing hurts, but I'm enjoying the havoc I've caused, so I accept the pain.

"If you keep him here, Orvos, his behavior will only get worse," Vypr says, "especially if you tranq him again."

The smell of the tranq is strong, but given the entire bottle is spread out over the floor, and not on the vrexing sponge Orvos tried to shove under my nose when he thought I was taking a nap, it's not having any effect.

Unless you count the effect on Orvos. The medic is so vrexing mad, he's turning purple.

"Don't vrexing tranq me," I snarl out.

"How else am I supposed to check your wound? You won't even let me look at it," Orvos says through gritted teeth.

"You don't get to come near me," I continue to growl. "Not ever."

Orvos throws his hands up in the air. "Impossible!" He whirls around, grabbing a sweeper, and begins to clear up the remains of the tranq bottle.

"I'm not discharging you until I've checked your wound." He glares at me. "So you decide what you want to do." He sweeps the destruction into a neat pile and storms off into his back room, where he knows I won't follow.

I know exactly what's in there. A machine.

"Ayar!" Vypr shakes out his feathers. "Why did you vrex him off again? You want to get out of here, don't you?"

I admit, I miss our barrack room, and our nights together. I miss his warm body next to mine. I don't want to stay in the surgery.

Vypr sits down on my ledge next to me, running his claws through my feathers, then cupping my chin in his hand. "Well, don't you?"

"Yes," I admit, grudgingly. "But I'm not letting that vrexer anywhere near me," I grumble.

"Hey." Robin sits down on my opposite side, giving Vypr a quick smile. "I've had some first aid training. What if I check and re-dress your wound while Orvos watches? Then, if he's happy, you can leave."

I'm not entirely sure I understand her, especially the part about 'first aid training' which doesn't sound like it translates properly, but Vypr is nodding.

"What do you think?" he asks me.

"I'll do anything to get out of here, you know that," I admit.

"Except let Orvos near you." Robin laughs, and the sound makes my soul sing.

I look up at my Vypr. He nods his approval.
"Get Orvos. It's time to go home." I grin.

Robin

Ayar gives me one of his slight unhinged smiles. If I thought I'd spent plenty of time Gryn watching, enough to get to know these males, I was wrong. Over the last three days, Ayar has run Orvos ragged. He won't stay on his ledge, crawling between them if he thinks the medic isn't watching, because his injury clearly makes it too painful for him to walk.

But of course, he still has to use the sanitary facilities, so someone has to help him, and when Vypr isn't around (and that's when Ayar behaves), it's Orvos doing the deed.

Yesterday things came to a head. After helping him, Orvos shoved one of his sedative sponges under Ayar's nose, and the big warrior went down, eyes closing, wings flailing, unconsciousness claiming him.

For about five minutes.

When he came around, just before he started roaring about ripping Orvos's head off, the look on his face ate my heart up.

He looked totally betrayed, like a lost child, abandoned by his parents.

He looked like he had never been loved.

I know it's not true. The way Vypr is with him, they are so clearly in love. Most of the time, Ayar grumps at him, folding his arms and refusing to eat anything Vypr brings because he wants to leave. Leaving poor Vypr exasperated and worried. Then, when he goes, Ayar gobbles down the treats like a warrior possessed.

Since the incident with the sedative, Orvos has been treated with high suspicion, growls and threats of supreme violence. So the smashed bottle of tranquilizer seems to be the last straw all round and somehow, to keep the peace, I've found myself volunteering my assistance.

The last thing I want is to end up helping Orvos in his duties in any way. I want out of the surgery probably even more than Ayar does. I'm just not prepared to start smashing stuff up. Unlike Mr. No Filter.

Ayar does what he wants when he wants.

His manic, full on attitude, all piss and vinegar, should terrify me. But for some reason, it doesn't.

I've probably caught cabin fever...

"Stand back," Ayar growls when Orvos appears, followed by a meek looking Vypr who's obviously had to do some groveling on Ayar's behalf, not that Ayar cares. "The female will do what you tell her."

The female?

I walk around his ledge so I'm on the side where his injury is and, with an evil smile, I rip the plaster off him.

To give him his due, Ayar only hisses at the sudden removal of the sticky patch from his skin.

"Ouch," he says with a glare.

"My name is Robin. Use it," I growl back at him.

He narrows his eyes at me, and I return his stare.

"What do you want me to do now?" I ask Orvos.

"Get some cleanser and give the wound a clean. Tell me if it is anything other than red or if there is any smell at all."

I head to the back of the room, collecting the supplies, items I know only too well from my enforced stay, and then I head back to the alien stand-off between Orvos and Ayar, both staring daggers at each other.

"This might be a little cold," I say as I pour on some of the pungent liquid onto a clean piece of gauze-like material.

Ayar wrinkles his nose. "Don't like it."

"You like being tranqued even less," Vypr says. "Let Robin do her job," he adds in a warning tone.

Ayar stares daggers at him too, then he shivers as I slowly wipe over the wound. I've not seen much in the way of this sort of injury in the past. My job meant I occasionally had to offer assistance to someone with a sprained ankle or a busted head, given I spent a lot of time hanging around in bars when following up leads for a story. But Ayar's injury seems to be healing nicely; the edges of the wound have been stapled together with something plastic. It's a little red but there's no sickly sour smell of infection. Given how bad it was a few days ago, I'm impressed at the level of healing.

"You're doing fine," I say to Ayar, who's watching me intently, propped up on his elbows, wings spilling their feathers onto the floor on either side of his bed.

My movements skirt the waistband of his pants, and someone growls low. It's difficult to know who, then Ayar shivers again and, work done, I lift my hands away.

"Wound's clean. Now what?" I call out to Orvos.

He leans over as far as he dares towards Ayar. "No sign of infection?"

"No, clean as a whistle," I reply to a frown from all three males. "I mean it's nice and clean."

"Shame the same can't be said for Ayar," Orvos grumbles.

"Huh," Ayar snorts at him. "I bathe."

It's Vypr's turn to snort, and a smile flickers over his face, lighting it up. If I thought he was handsome before, when he was all serious and worried, the smile takes his gorgeousness to new heights.

Nope. Stop it, Robin. Not only is your heart out of bounds, but you've had more than your share of difficult men. He spoilt you for anyone else, and what's more, he told you he would.

These males are off limits, even if they were on the market. But Vypr and Ayar are mated, and that's the end of it. I carefully and slowly breathe in before letting out the breath to center myself, to quell my pounding heart, which flutters in my chest like a bird attempting to take flight.

Ayar's dark eyes are on me.

"Robin?" He says my name as if it means something to him. "Orvos says you can cover me up."

I blink, not entirely sure what he means, given I've obviously missed something while I've been trying to get my heart rate back under control.

"Oh, yes." I grab the unused dressing. "Let's get you ready to leave, shall we?"

I'm rewarded by a pair of smiles, one relieved, one happy. Vypr hums something which sounds tuneless, but it calms Ayar as I stick the dressing back over the wound.

"Right." Orvos stares at us all. "He can go. Ayar is discharged. I'll send you up some cleanser and fresh dressings, but I don't want him back in here again unless something is hanging off." The medic turns on his heel and stomps off to his desk, where he sits heavily and ignores us.

"Thank you, Robin," Vypr says.

There's nothing from Ayar. He's already out of the door; it flaps slightly in his wake.

"For an injured warrior, he can sure move fast, can't he?" I'm unable to hide my smile at Ayar's almost instant disappearance.

Vypr sighs. "He is grateful for your help."

"I'm grateful for the entertainment value he's brought to my existence." I venture a glance at Orvos. Ayar might have gotten out of here, but there's still no sign of my discharge.

"You are not a prisoner," Vypr says, seriously. "You can leave when you want."

"Apparently not," I reply. "Females are important." I intone in my best impression of Orvos. "I can't leave until he says. So I'm stuck unless I start throwing things." Vypr looks over at the door, and I'm aware I'm keeping him from Ayar. "You'd better go after him. Who knows what trouble he's getting himself into?" I laugh.

Vypr gives me a wry smile. "Take care, little Robin." He gives my hand a brief squeeze, and then he's gone too, feathers rustling.

I look over at the brooding Orvos.

"Looks like it's just you and me then," I mutter to myself as I return to my bed. "Until the end of bloody time," I add, bitterly.

Vypr

Unbelievably, as I round the corner into the central shaft of the lair, Ayar is squaring up to a couple of young mercs.

"What the vrex are you doing?" I grab his wing and haul him back. "Vrex off!" I fire at the pair, and they slink away.

"They looked at me."

"By the goddess, Ayar, what do you expect? You're one of the elite, and you've got a huge bandage. Of course they're going to look."

He huffs angrily. "Are we going back to the eyrie?" he asks.

"Yes, but don't think for a second you're flying anywhere!" Before he can do or say anything, I've scooped him off his feet and, wings beating hard, I'm in the air. "Don't struggle," I say in his ear.

Ayar stills immediately. He's not as limp as he was when I brought him to the surgery, thank Nisis. I'm not sure I could stand it if he was, but he's warm in my arms, and his musky scent fills my nostrils.

I circle the eyrie and drop down onto the roof.

"Are we not going back to the barracks?" Ayar asks as I put him on his feet.

He's still quite pale, partially from his enforced stay in the surgery, although I find myself thinking he's not as pale as Robin. She's been inside the lair for a long time, from what she told me, quietly distracting me from my worrying over an unconscious Ayar.

"No, I got permission from Strykr to take over a small barrack room, just the two of us, until you're properly healed."

Ayar grins.

"I convinced him that you'd be more of an annoyance to the rest of the unit if you were ledge-bound than they will be to you."

He grins even more.

I take him by the hand and lead my mate into the eyrie. We circle down past the area where Strykr has his nest with Kat and into the rear of the eyrie, where I spotted the single quarters with a small sanitary area down the corridor a few months ago.

Ayar makes slow progress. His earlier burst of energy has exhausted him, and by the time we reach our new quarters, he's dragging his feet, wings drooping. I wrap my arm around his shoulders and open the door to our new home, for the time being anyway.

"Vypr," Ayar croons, an arm snaking around my waist.

"I got fresh furs." I rub the back of my neck. "I didn't know what else you'd like."

"I like our nest." Ayar turns to face me. "And I love you." He wraps his arms around me, nuzzling at the crook of my neck, lips and fangs tracing over my skin.

The lonely nights without him come piling back on me, and my body reacts to him, to my poor injured warrior. Ayar rubs at my hard lengths through my pants.

"We don't have to do this if you're not up to it," I murmur in his ear.

"I've been without you too long. I need you," he says.

"Vrex!" My cocks jump, swelling even more, straining to be free, to be inside him. Ayar has released the mag catch on my pants and is stroking me from balls to tips. My hips jerk at him.

"Go and lay down," I tell him. "I want to see you in our nest."

He withdraws from me reluctantly, but not so reluctantly he risks me dealing with him in the way he knows I will, regardless of his injury. Feathers rattling ever so slightly, he stalks across the small room to the bed I've prepared, wider than our ledges. He coos his approval and looks over his shoulder at me, through his great wings, before he kicks off his boots and lowers his pants.

Ayar might be covered in scars, his most recent wound adding to the tale of him etched over his body, but he's beautiful, powerful, and delicious to me as he bares the globes of his ass, before turning to face me, his enormous cocks standing proudly. Unlike me, his nodes and ridges are highly pronounced and perfect for pleasure, but he won't be pleasuring me, not today. My need is too great.

"Stroke yourself for me, mate," I growl, shedding my clothes. "Let me see you."

Ayar collapses backwards onto the furs as he grasps his lengths, just like I told him. His huge, clawed hand still not making his obscenely large cocks look any smaller, he groans as he pumps them. I stalk over to him, staring down as he enjoys himself.

"Does that feel good?"

Ayar mumbles something, his hand moving faster. Precum beads on the tips of both members as he separates them out.

"Stop."

He opens his eyes, full of lust, hands slowing as I lower myself over him. My cocks bob against his abdomen, slick with my pre cum. They rub over his, and he groans out loud at our touch.

"Vypr!" I know what he wants. His hand grasps for my cocks.

"No. You're going to take me, all of me," I growl, pinning his wings against the furs as I seat myself between his legs, glaring down at him. "Because I've been without you for too long."

Ayar shudders as I run my hand over his huge cocks, grasping mine at the same time and pumping us both as he makes a strangled sound of delight. Once my fingers are slick with our pre-cum, I caress his balls, down to his anus, swirling my digits around his pucker, delving inside, making him slick for me as my mate flaps his wings in ecstasy.

Once he's ready, I push the tip of my main cock at his glorious tight hole and slip an arm under one of his thighs before thrusting hard, until I'm buried in him.

"Vrex," I moan as his hands delve into my feathers, working at the skin underneath with the points of his claws.

I begin to move, slowly at first, making sure he isn't in pain, but of course my Ayar is loving every single second of being mated, his eyes not leaving me for a second, though he whines at me.

"What is it, my mate?" I increase my thrusts, setting up a delicious, dark rhythm which pleasures me. "What do you want? What are you daring to ask me for?"

"Vypr, I..."

I circle my hips. His eyes roll in his head, his request forgotten immediately as I lean into him just a little more, his cocks slick between us, my body caressing them, even as I hold him still in order to go deeper.

"What is it, my mate?" I croon. "Do you need to come? Do you want me to let you come?"

"Please!" His word is a thread of desire, of need and of his lust. "Vypr," he moans, "let me come. I want to come."

"You have to wait," I reply as he bucks his hips at me.

I fist his cocks while I pound into him, reveling in the silky feeling of his skin and each delicious bump and ridge. I'm incredibly close, my orgasm rising the more I watch my mate writhing under me.

"I can't..." He howls, "I can't hold! Vypr!"

Ayar stills for an instant, then his body spasms, cocks fountaining their creamy contents all over his stomach and chest as I roar my climax, filling him completely.

Claiming him entirely.

Making sure he is mine.

Ayar

My body is burning, furs cloying under me. It's dark, very dark, and I'm soaked with sweat. I'm not sure where I am for a while, blinking to myself, wondering if my eyes are open.

The dream.

A dream. It's been so long since closing my eyes meant anything other than the horrors I had been subjected to in the machine. The pain, the hallucinations, more pain, the voices. Wanting me to do terrible things.

The pain still haunts me, the headaches which plague me and the times I'm not sure things are real, or just in my head.

Only this time, I know it was a dream. It was a dream of her. A female.

The female.

Robin.

"Ayar?" Vypr stirs sleepily next to me, feathers rustling as he shifts, already knowing I'm awake. "You're very hot."

I snigger, because I'm a youngling at heart, but also because I don't feel hot. If anything, I feel cold.

A hand is on my forehead, nice and cool. Vypr shifts

rapidly and uncovers the small bundle of bioluminescent plants, which light the room. Our nest. He always promised me one, but I didn't think I'd have to end up stabbed by a table for it to happen.

"You're burning up," he says, urgently. "How's your wound?"

"Sore." I notice it now. It aches. "I need Robin." I say, emphatically.

Vypr doesn't give me what I want; he never gives me what I want, only what I need, and I need her.

"The human female? Why?" Vypr asks.

"I don't know." I drop my gaze from his face, the face I normally could look at until the end of time. The face I watch when he's sleeping, and I can't sleep. The face I take strength from every time I see it. "I had a dream." I shake my head, wanting to be able to articulate what happened, what the dream was about. To be able to talk like I used to.

Before the machine.

"It's okay, Ayar. You're not well. I'll go see Orvos, get you something for your fever." He tucks my errant hair behind my ear and runs a hand down the edge of my wing in a way he knows I love.

Because Vypr knows what I love.

"I'm not going back there." I shrink away from him, knowing I'm no match for the big warrior in my current condition but prepared to run all the same. "But, my dream... bring me Robin, please?" I beg, studying his eyes, his face, the planes of his cheekbones, the dark shadows under his eyes from the sleepless nights he's spent waiting for me.

He gazes back, confused. "You have nightmares," is all he can say.

"I know, but this was a dream. Robin...I...you..." I'm stumbling over my explanation. I press the heels of my hands into my eye sockets, the points of my claws pressing into the skin of my forehead. The sharp pricks of pain penetrate the mind fog which always dogs me. "I can't explain. I'm sorry, Vypr, but it's important, somehow."

My hands are withdrawn from my eyes, and his handsome face peers into mine, concerned.

"The nightmares are better because of you, my Vypr." I'm still struggling, the words forming in my mind but not coming out through my tongue. "And my dream, it was all of us. Together."

The residual feeling of sweet and light sits in my head. It's clear, unlike so much of my memories. And for once, there's no pain. Only...pleasure. I stare at Vypr, willing him to see the dream, to feel what I feel.

"I'll speak to Orvos," Vypr says. He's not denying me Robin, the little human, all pale skin and soft, perfect calmness. A female I know he noticed too, when Jay had first returned, and we visited him and his mate in the surgery. "But you have to stay here until I get back. Promise."

He runs a hand through my feathers. Vypr knows I'm prone to wandering sometimes. Except, I ache, all over. I don't want to go anywhere.

"I promise."

I get another ruffle of feathers for my agreement, and Vypr unfolds himself from the furs, pulling on his pants and boots.

"I'll be back soon." In a rush of feathers, he has his hand cupped around the back of my neck, forehead against mine, his eyes closed, and I am becalmed by his love.

I just wish he knew how much I loved him, too.

And I wish I knew how Robin fits into all of this.

Robin

Okay, I'll admit it. It's been pretty damn quiet since Ayar left. I hadn't quite grasped how much the big, bonkers warrior had wormed his way into my life in the few days he spent in the surgery.

When he wasn't finding ways of playing havoc in order not to do something he disliked, he was thinking up ways of being able to do things he did like. All of which from an almost prone position.

He did like me. He liked it when I sat with him, when I sent Vypr out to get some food. He would stare at me for a while, then flop a massive, clawed hand in my lap, exhorting me without saying a word, to massage it.

Turns out the three week-long undercover investigation at a spa, which meant I had to take a massage course in order to fit in, and where I learned a tiny bit of massage therapy from a very kind therapist, had its uses after all. If, for no other reason, to keep a huge alien warrior with zero ability to control himself happy and quiet.

Basically, having Ayar and Vypr in the surgery was as much fun as I've had since I had been abducted by aliens. Not that any of it was fun. Waking up on the Drahon ship, terrified, then being pushed into the cell with Diana, Jen, and the monstrous Gryn, Huntr, wasn't much fun. Neither was being blown up and finding myself at the mercy of hundreds of male warriors.

But spending even such a short time with two aliens has filled me with an insatiable desire to get out of the surgery. My natural curiosity, for so long channeled into my work, kept crushed under the weight of him, I'm beginning to feel it again. The reason I ended up as a journalist in the first place.

Can I even...can I possibly believe I'm free of him?

I get off my bed and begin the slow walk up the surgery. Orvos said if I can walk it the entire length normally without being out of breath, I can go. I've been bed bound for so long, I know I need to build up my stamina, so I've started making slow progress up and down the room when it's quiet and there are no mercs present.

I'm just turning to come back when I see Vypr watching me from the doorway. He leans against the wall, arms folded over his impressive chest, wings neat against his back. His dark eyes glitter with something I can't quite fathom. I lose my balance a little under his gaze and stumble forward.

And then I'm in his arms, my hand clutching at his huge bicep as he holds me upright.

"Thanks," I breathe out.

He smells utterly amazing. Whereas Ayar was all musk and the hint of a bonfire, Vypr is spicy delicious.

What am I thinking? He and Ayar are mates, the Gryn equivalent of a relationship. Neither of them is interested in me, and even if they were...

"You're getting better then?" Vypr rumbles with a half-smile.

"Orvos says if I can walk the length of the surgery, he'll let me out," I say.

"You really want out?" Vypr asks, his handsome face all serious as he releases me and I sink onto a nearby bed, attempting not to pant.

"I'm so grateful for everything Orvos has done, but I'm bored out of my mind. I need to know more about where I am. The suspense is killing me," I reply.

"The suspense?" Vypr looks confused.

"Of being on a new planet, seeing new things, meeting new people...aliens." My mouth runs away with me.

How come I didn't chatter like this when he was here with Ayar? Instead, we kept conversation to a minimum, but now I'm gabbling like a stupid teenager. Vypr relaxes, his face softening.

"You are a curious one, aren't you?"

"Is Ayar okay?" I suddenly realize he's here alone and, given Ayar's behavior when I saw him last, Vypr can only be back if something's wrong.

"Okay or not, he's not coming back here," Orvos calls out as he appears from the back room.

I choke back a laugh. Like Ayar is ever going to come back here under his own steam.

"He has a fever. Nothing bad, but he needs a tonic," Vypr replies practically. "And he has requested Robin." His dark eyes turn on me, but this time, they're unreadable. "From what she tells me, the pair of them could use the company until they are healed."

Wait. What?

Vypr

Little Robin. The female is small, pretty, with her big blue eyes, pale like the sky above Ustokos's interminable clouds. Her hair looks silky smooth, similar to the feathers under Ayar's wings, next to his skin. She is undeniably attractive. I can see why Ayar might *see* her. But why do I have to give him everything he wants, all the time?

We are more than mates, we are a team. A third being? I can't see how it would work, even if the being he wants is wrapped up in a package of luscious curves and a scent...

By Nisis, Robin smells delicious, almost edible. Why didn't I notice it before?

Ayar, again. My mate, as usual, took all of my attention. Except, I scented her before, when we were visiting the surgery to see Jay's mate. Only I dismissed the pang my heart felt because I have Ayar.

My Ayar, who needs a tonic to bring his fever under control and who will absolutely not take it without some serious cajoling.

And this is where Robin comes in, so I can't deny my reasons for getting her to come with me, back to our nest, are not entirely to help her. She was so good with my mate, so kind, so patient. If anyone can get him to take the tonic, she will.

"I don't know." The words tumble out of her mouth as she looks between Orvos and me. At once ready to leave and, at the same time, there's something behind her eyes, a wall she's trying not to break down.

It's a look I know all too well. One I see every morning I wake up.

"Ayar would really like you to come, and I'm sure you're ready to see the rest of Ustokos, or even a small corner of it," I say, dropping my arms by my side and drooping my wings back to appear less threatening.

That something about Robin? It's something to do with males. I'm not sure how I know, but I do. If I want her help with my reluctant mate, I'm going to have to work hard.

Orvos folds his arms. "I'm not entirely sure you're ready to be discharged. You still have some pain, and you're still struggling to walk the distance I prescribed."

Robin's eyes flash with spirit at his words. "I am much better. I can do the walk. Look." She shoves herself into a standing position with a flourish and proceeds to saunter down the long surgery, between the rows of ledges, her hips swinging deliciously. At the end, she twirls around and comes back. "There!" she replies.

Her chest is heaving, and I can't help my eyes being drawn to it. Round globes shudder delightfully as she does her best to keep her breathing under control. I can't deny I like females, even if Ayar is my mate. I certainly spent time with the Mochi females before him, as well as enjoying the occasional merc if he was willing. But Robin is nothing like the furry feline females. She is unique.

And Ayar is my mate. He needs help, and I don't have time to either charm this female or deal with Orvos's gak.

"The female is certainly well enough to spend time with Ayar. He remains injured too," I say, pointedly. "They can look after each other," I add.

Orvos's snort of derision tells me exactly what he thinks of that suggestion. He looks Robin up and down.

"If you want to go with Vypr, I won't stop you. But if you get any discomfort, have any further trouble with your breathing, I expect him to bring you right back here," he says, and then he looks at me. "If I discharge Robin, she is in your care. I fully expect you to protect her at all times. Both you and Ayar. Especially Ayar. She is not a plaything for him."

Robin makes a choking sound.

"Ayar does not have *playthings*," I snarl. "Neither do I. We are the elite, sworn to protect Ustokos and all its inhabitants," I fire at him. "Robin will be more than safe with us."

I'm not sure where the eruption of anger is coming from, but I feel it rising inside me, just like it used to before I found my Ayar. The problem is, without him, I'm not sure I can stop it.

"Hey!" Robin's voice penetrates the anger. "I am here, you know. I can speak for myself." What's penetrating my emotions is her own anger. She vibrates slightly on her feet as if she wants to hit something. "If Orvos is prepared to let me out of here, and I hope to god that's what he's saying, then I don't mind helping Ayar."

She folds her arms over her chest, drawing my attention to her breasts again and stopping any ire I might have in its tracks.

Which is a first.

Orvos takes a step back from the annoyed female, eyeing her carefully. "If that is what you want, Robin, I will discharge you."

I wonder for a second if she is going to fall, her body relaxes so suddenly.

"Let me get a tonic for Ayar, and you can go." He turns with a flurry of feathers and bustles into the back room, where I hear the clinking of bottles.

Robin stares at me, unblinking. I rub the back of my neck, feeling somewhat unsure what to do next. "Uh, do you want to get your belongings?"

"You're looking at them." She doesn't move and doesn't unfold her arms. The earlier relaxation gone, her posture is stiff again.

She's wearing something which can only be described as a sack. Pale blue in color, it's not even tied at the waist, and the front hangs low, baggily over her clearly delicious breasts. On her feet are something I can't even describe, but they are not sturdy boots, and boots are an essential for Ustokos. A planet which is being rebuilt is not a place for poor performing footwear.

"You have nothing else?" The words are out of my mouth, filled with incredulity, before I remember myself.

My old commander's mate, Bianca, had plenty of clothing, always. I didn't pay too much attention—it wasn't exactly the safest thing to do around a mated Gryn, but I'm not sure I saw her in the same outfit twice. Plus, all the other humans have much more comfortable things to wear. The Mochi regularly bring clothing to the lair, both for Gryn and, I'm sure, for humans too.

That Robin has been left wearing the sack has to be an oversight. One I resolve to remedy immediately.

Robin

I clutch the flask of tonic Orvos gave me for Ayar and follow Vypr out of the surgery. His huge, dark wings swing from side to side as he walks, feathers rustling. My heart pounds in my chest, part excitement but mostly terror.

The surgery has been a refuge from everything which has happened to me in the last few months, and the knowledge I'm leaving starts to hit home as I come out of the short corridor where I'm faced with a huge central space which seems to be full of flying males.

Noisy flying males, who holler and screech as they circle the airspace. It makes me want to go back to the surgery, the darkness of my fear overriding my usual interest in anything new.

"Robin?" A soft, deep voice, made of velvet and the night, reaches my ears, and I meet the burnt umber of Vypr's eyes. "Everything okay?"

He says it like he really cares. I've fallen for something similar, words he said, words dripping like honey in my ear. Words which were meaningless when he told me I had to service him or I'd lose everything.

He was my boss. He thought he was my lover. He was my blackmailer, my loan shark, and my jailer all rolled into one. He trapped me, stifled me, and made me go on the lonely stake-out in the docklands where I was abducted. By lizards. It doesn't matter how far away I am from him, I still hear his voice, feel his hands on me.

I still feel dirty and worthless. Because of him.

So an entire building filled with males? Not going to get over it quickly.

I moderate my breathing, concentrating on taking in and letting out a single breath at a time until my heart stills. I can do this.

He won't define me.

"I've just been in the surgery a long time." I smile brightly and falsely at Vypr, keeping my tone light. "And I was too unwell when they brought me here to see any of this." I wave my hand at the open space in front of us. "So it's all new."

"The mercs can take some getting used to." Vypr turns from me to follow the progress of two males who spin in the air, firing out limbs at each other. "The eyrie is mostly warriors, no younglings. I won't say it's quieter, but it's different." He looks back at me. "We can take things slow. Whatever you want."

Whatever I want?

There's a phrase I haven't heard in a very, very long time. I want to believe Vypr, but maybe not yet. I study my shoes, unable to tell him anything. Even though, for some reason, I want to tell him everything.

"First things, first." He wraps an arm around my waist. "We need to get you properly clothed. If I'm to keep my promise to Orvos, I can't have you running around the eyrie half-dressed."

His eyes flare as my stomach does a flip at his phrase 'half-dressed.' This is bonkers. He and Ayar are an item, and Gryn mate for life. He doesn't want me, and I'm not going to fall at the feet of the first male who says something nice.

That would be terminally stupid, and I'm over stupid. I have a chance to start again on a new planet. It's a chance I should grab with both hands, whatever the planet has in store for me.

With incredible ease, Vypr lifts me off my feet, unfurling a huge set of shining wings. Before I can let out even a squeak of surprise, we're in the air. For such an enormous, feathered predator, he's light and lithe as he turns slowly, descending in a careful arc down the shaft. I expected to be going up, and out, so this direction is intriguing. Vypr folds his wings, and we shoot through a crumbling wide doorway and out into another huge room.

It has a large opening in one wall. It's outside, and I can see daylight. Up in the sky, two ghostly moons hang, one enormous and one a little smaller.

Vypr gently lowers me to my feet, and I hang onto him, mesmerized by the sight of the celestial orbs, at once familiar and completely alien.

"Little Robin?" His voice wraps around me, warm and inviting.

Get a grip, Robin.

"Robin is fine," I say frostily. Vypr backs up a single pace.

"This way." He bows very slightly, feathers pooling behind him, and he indicates I should go left.

The cavernous place is full of crates, some in space age materials, some made out of what looks like wood. On the far side, I can see (and smell) creatures which look like cattle.

"Maraha." Vypr follows my gaze. "The Mochi raise them, we trade for them. We've got a lot of hungry warriors and mercs to feed."

"The Mochi?"

"Over there." I follow Vypr's outstretched hand, and my breath catches.

"Cat people!" I whisper, and then realize how silly it sounds.

"One of the other organic species on Ustokos," Vypr explains, thankfully ignoring my comment. "I'm sure you'll see the others in time."

My head spins. There are more than just hawk people and cat people?

We approach a set of cubes, all piled on top of each other, almost as if they're creating a wall.

"Jesic?" Vypr calls out.

"Yes?" The response is more of a purr than a word.

Before I can say or do anything, I'm ushered around the back of the cases, and I'm standing in front of a cat lady.

She has golden fur covering her entire body, or at least the parts I can see and which are not covered in richly embroidered fabric. She's wearing a halter top and a pair of harem trousers. Her face is incredibly cat like. Whiskers sprout from her top lip. Ears sit atop her head, swiveling to catch the sounds going on around us. I'm aware I'm staring, and I have my mouth open because I can't help myself.

"Ah, a new human." She smiles at me, a cat smile which is full of warmth as she looks me up and down. "One who needs clothing as soon as possible. Who's left her in this state? You?" she says accusingly at Vypr.

"I've not been well." I jump in before Vypr can say anything. "I was injured when the Gryn rescued me, and I've been stuck in the surgery ever since."

Jesic huffs, unimpressed. She gives Vypr the side eye. "You can go, Gryn. I'll tell you when we are done." She waves a clawed paw at him.

He looks between Jesic and me. "I'll be right outside," he says and stalks around the containers.

"Now," Jesic takes the flask from me and puts it down on a table which is covered in folded clothing, "let's get you dressed to impress."

Ayar

Another shiver runs over me. I probably should go in the warm healing pool, but it would mean getting wet and possibly bathing, which is not something I do voluntarily. Instead, I pull another fur over my damp skin and hope Vypr comes back soon.

With Robin.

The more I think about the dream, the muddier it gets, and all I'm left with is the vague feeling about her and Vypr. A good, warm feeling which settles in my stomach, and, despite my fever, I like it.

My heart is a mystery to me. I lost the ability to connect to anything because of the machine. Vypr makes me happy. He fills the pit inside me which was despair. I don't want to do anything to upset him or drive him away. Without Vypr, my life would be nothing.

And yet, the female, the human female, stands in my mind's eye, hands on her hips, smile quirking her lips, staring straight at me, challenging, needing, wanting.

Both of us.

Another shudder wracks my body, and for half a second, I

worry my fevered mind has made all of it up. Except I saw how Vypr reacted to her in the surgery. He accepted her help; his eyes followed her around the room.

He sought her out when he wanted me looked after.

There is something about Robin and my nature, all instant gratification and the fight, it makes me ache to find out. I can't help myself. It's as if I've forgotten how to wait and the only being who can make me is my Vypr.

"There he is." Vypr stalks into our nest, wings held out. He looks glorious, the very picture of health. In his arms are several packages and no sign of a tonic, which pleases me. I'd rather just ride out the fever, despite my stomach burning at me.

"Jesus! He looks terrible!" A pretty face peers around Vypr's wings.

"Robin." I push myself up but fall back again as the pair approach the bed.

Vypr drops the packages and runs his hand over my forehead. "I wish you'd said how bad you were feeling," he grumbles.

"No surgery," I snort at them, although I'm not sure I could stop Vypr from taking me.

"I've only just gotten out. I'm not going back." Robin grins at me. "Anyway, Orvos sent this for you." She holds up a flask.

I press my lips together, hard, and growl a deep 'NO' sound. All that happens is Robin begins to laugh. Her scent perfumes the air. She smells of warm feathers and Vypr because he would have had to carry her wingless form here.

"The tonic is brilliant. The only thing Orvos didn't have to force me to take," she says, unscrewing the top. "It doesn't make you sleepy, just makes you feel good, really good." She winks at me and then takes a long swallow of the liquid.

Her throat bobs and something inside me squirms. Not

only do I want the tonic, but I want to touch her skin, where it moves. Next to me, Vypr shifts, and his scent changes. His eyes flit between Robin and me.

"Are you going to drink the tonic?" he asks, his voice challenging.

After seeing Robin enjoy it, my instinct is taking over.

"Want," I growl out.

"Oh, do you?" Robin teases, holding the flask just out of my reach.

I growl again, and she laughs harder but brings the flask up to my lips and slides her hand behind my head, helping me to drink.

The tonic is cool, slightly sweet with the hint of a buzz as it slides over my tongue. But what's even better is the proximity to Robin, her chest, encased in a soft maraha hide top of deep red molded to her form. I inhale her scent.

"Are you smelling me, Ayar?" she asks, her mouth quirked into a half smile.

"Yes. You smell good," I reply, and I'm rewarded with more tonic.

In fact, I get quite a lot of tonic, and I feel so much better. Vypr has stayed beside me the whole time, and now he leans forward and brushes at my hair.

"Are you up for a bath? Clean you up a bit?" he asks.

He cleaned me up after we mated, his hands causing me to stiffen again, and the same hands giving me more relief. I shouldn't want a bath, but like Robin said, I feel good, and I feel like I'll do anything he asks.

"Yeah," I say, dreamily. "Can Robin come?"

"Er...maybe not," Robin replies. "Robin has to sort out her new wardrobe."

"You are staying, aren't you?" I manage to push myself up onto my elbows.

"Robin is staying. She'll be in the room next to ours."

Vypr slips an arm around my waist and lifts me into a sitting position. The rooms spins slightly, like I've been drinking var beer. It's a good kind of spin.

He goes to lift me up. "I'm not wearing any pants," I hiss at him.

Robin gets to her feet rapidly and grabs at the packages, heaving them into her arms with a wince. "I'll find my way," she says, hurriedly.

"No, wait!" Vypr calls after her. "I don't want you to injure yourself."

He gazes into my face. "You look pretty vrexed. Stay here and don't move. I need to help Robin."

I give him a soggy smile and watch as he chases after her.

I don't plan, but if I did, this could not have gone better.

Vypr

I promised Orvos Robin would be safe and protected, yet she's just run off with the two heavy packages containing all the clothing she got from Jesic.

"Wait!" I call out again, catching up with her and plucking the bundles from her arms.

From the look of pain on her face, picking them up and carrying them was something she knows she shouldn't have done.

"I'm sorry," she apologizes, and I'm confused.

"Why? I'm here to look after you, like I told Orvos. You helped with Ayar. You got him to drink the tonic, and you have my eternal gratitude, but you need to get better, too."

A pair of stunning blue eyes look up at me. Behind their beauty, there is pain. Not physical pain—it's the pain I sometimes see written in Ayar's eyes. Perhaps that's why he wants her around. Maybe he wants someone who understands his pain more than I ever can.

"You're just in here," I say, more gruffly than I intended, shoving at the door into the little barrack room. "There's a sanitary facility behind the wall. You'll need to share bathing with me and Ayar..."

Robin looks up at me, eyes wide. "Maybe we can come to some sort of rota arrangement," she says in a low voice. "Is anyone else joining me?" she asks, looking at the two ledges.

"No, this is your room. You won't be sharing with any other males...or females," I add hastily.

You won't be sharing with any other males, ever.

The anger bubbles up inside me at the mere thought of Robin near another male.

No, my mate is Ayar. He's all I need, and I'm all he needs.

"You can go anywhere you like in the eyrie, but I'd recommend you let me know if you want to go outside."

"Oh yeah? Why?" Robin has her hands on her hips, and I see the bristle she gave Orvos earlier.

"The terrain is a little rough. You're still healing," I reply, attempting to keep my voice even.

I want to get away from her, from whatever it is she's doing to me. Intentionally or unintentionally. My heart already belongs to another. I won't be parted from Ayar, no matter what.

He'll be healed in another few turns, maybe a week, and then Robin can go live with the other humans. Ayar doesn't like them much because getting too close to another Gryn's mate, which he has done in the past, can result in a beating he doesn't enjoy.

"Okay, I guess you're right." Robin takes her hands from her hips and circles the small barrack room, peering into the sanitary area and coming back out.

I put her packages down and try not to notice the form fitting outfit Jesic put her in. Black maraha hide pants and a deep red top which sets off her golden hair.

"I'm going to see to Ayar and then maybe we can eat

together, if you want?" I say, regretting my earlier gruffness given how small the female looks in the room.

"Okay." She sits on the bed. "I'll see you later."

With that, it appears I am dismissed.

AYAR IS DOZING WHEN I RETURN, A SMILE ON HIS face and a string of drool from his mouth. He also feels much cooler as I help him up.

"The tonic was good stuff, then?"

"Robin's good stuff, don't you think?"

My mate might be a drooling mess today, but he's always been able to be sharp, even from the depths of a vat of var beer. A flask of tonic is clearly no different.

"You like her. Not just because of the dream?" I couch my question carefully.

I want an answer, an honest answer, not that Ayar has much capacity for lying, or is very good at it when he tries.

"You like her too. I can tell." He yawns and is, impressively for him, avoiding my question.

I help him through to the healing pool, sliding him into the water and making sure his wings are propped up on the sides before I strip off and join him. He nestles against me, the tonic making him happily limp in my arms.

If only he knew how much I loved him, how my soul is bonded to his. It's always been difficult to tell how much he understands. We knew nothing about the machine which held him captive, and Ayar hasn't been able to enlighten me much as to what it did, only that it caused him spectacular pain, robbed him of who he was before we found him, and made him hopelessly angry.

I understand his anger. Which is why I understand Ayar. My own rage is a deep well I have to control at all costs. It's an anger born of everything I've witnessed, all the wrongs Proto, the sentient AI which once ran this planet, did to us as a species. Of what it did to Ayar.

"I think Robin is for us." Ayar gently scoops up some water and lets it run down my chest, his claws fully retracted for a change. "I think she's ours and we get to keep her."

"Don't you want to be my mate?" The question is out of my mouth before I can stop it, snapping into reality with a force I didn't mean.

"I am your mate," Ayar says, sleepy and unconcerned by my tone. "I want to mate Robin too. I want you to mate her. I want younglings." His head hits my chest as he gets closer.

I sit in the water in silence. Ayar likes and dislikes things. He has wants and needs which are basic and easy to fulfill. But in all the time we've been together, he's never been clear about his emotions.

And he has never told me he wanted younglings.

Robin

A creature howls at me through the darkness. Its maw open wide, full of teeth. It gets closer and closer until I can see it's a hybrid of him and something without a name. I back away, slowly at first, until I'm running and running. Panting and sweating, I jerk awake.

I'm on Ustokos. A gentle light glows from the small bioluminescent plants the Gryn use to light much of their buildings. My bed is a heap of soft furs. I breathe a sigh of relief. *I've just been abducted to an alien planet, it's all okay.*

Except the howling hasn't stopped.

It carries on, a thin reedy sound filled with terror. I can't stand it. Whatever creature is making the noise needs to be found.

Slipping out of my bed, I push the door to my room open, and the noise gets louder, less of terror and more anger. It's coming from Vypr and Ayar's rooms.

Now I hesitate. Whatever's happening in there is none of my business. They have each other, and I should respect their privacy.

Only, I'm supposed to be here for Ayar. What if Vypr isn't

in there? What if Ayar is suffering? All the 'what ifs' pile in on me, crowding out my common sense until I find myself sliding the door open and peering in.

Vypr hunches beside Ayar on their large bed of furs. Ayar whines, his eyes closed, his body twisted. As I watch, he lets out another long howl, but it's not physical pain he feels. The noise he makes only ever comes from a soul in torment.

"Is everything okay?" I ask, quietly. *Typical British understatement.*

Vypr's head comes up. His dark eyes turn to me, and they're filled with pain.

"He gets like this. Nightmares. That's all. He'll be better in the morning," Vypr says. His wings droop behind him, the very definition of defeat.

He runs a hand over Ayar's forehead, whispering to him. Ayar tosses from side to side, his eyes half open. He murmurs something I can't hear, but Vypr stiffens.

"He wants you."

"Me?" I stand in the doorway unmoving. "I don't think I'm the right person..."

"He wants you," Vypr says through gritted teeth.

The memory of the howling looms large. I'm supposed to be here to help Vypr with Ayar, despite everything in the huge warrior's body language suggesting he'd rather I wasn't here.

"Didn't you hear what I said? He wants you," Vypr repeats, not looking at me.

Ayar shudders on the bed, and I feel compelled to walk over. As I reach the pair of males, Vypr stands, enormous wings flaring, his fresh rain scent filling my senses.

"I'll leave you to it," he rumbles, more growl than words.

"No," I say, boldly. "Stay." I sit next to Ayar and take his hand in mine, rubbing it gently until his liquid dark eyes open and his sad gaze meets mine.

Such beautiful eyes.

I'm aware of rustling behind me as Vypr moves closer.

"Hi, Ayar," I say. "I'm here. Will you let me try something?" I ask him.

His brow furrows.

"He might not recognize you straight away," Vypr says in my ear. "Just keep talking."

He sounds strangely hopeful, such a difference from the surly Gryn he was a moment ago when his worry for Ayar overtook anything, even the quiet, kind male who took me to get a whole new wardrobe.

"I'd like to touch your face and head. Will you let me do that?" I run my hand up Ayar's arm in a smooth, strong stroke.

Ayar nods, very slowly, eyes still guarded, brow still furrowed.

I look up at Vypr, seeking his approval to touch Ayar too. He gives me a curt nod.

I don't make any sudden moves, not in this room filled with predatory males. Sudden moves can be dangerous in highly charged situations. Instead, I rub Ayar's hand a little more, then move my hands until I'm cupping his chin, moving my fingers over the pressure points on his face, massaging slowly up to his forehead, where I smooth out his frown and continue up into his hair.

He might look dishevelled, but his hair is clean and silky. It makes me want to find out what his feathers feel like. I let my hands work over his scalp. It's covered in dips and scars, like the rest of Ayar. A feathered warrior who wears everything on show and yet is an entirely closed book. Under my touch, I feel him relax. As if something is draining from him.

Next to me, Vypr sinks down onto the bed. He takes Ayar's hand and begins his tuneless humming. Ayar battles sleep for a while longer, but finally, his eyelids droop, and he makes a soft snoring sound.

I shake out my hands. A slight cramp has entered the fingers and my broken wrist aches.

"How often does this happen?" I whisper to Vypr, who gazes down at his mate with such love, my heart squeezes in my chest.

"Too often. I've never seen him calm this quickly." His dark eyes meet mine. "Thank you."

"I'm just here doing what you got me released for," I reply, unable to fathom what is going on between us all.

"You're here because Ayar wanted you." Vypr looks back at his sleeping mate. One wing is askew. He gently folds it up, tucking the feathers under him carefully.

"What about you?" The words almost stick in my throat, grumbling out and sounding peevish. "Don't you want me here?"

"I want whatever Ayar wants," Vypr says, not looking up. "He's all I care about."

I guess I know exactly where I sit in the grand scheme of things.

I don't want, or need, a relationship with another human male, let alone an alien one.

So why am I so bothered that Ayar wants me and Vypr doesn't?

Vypr

I should have treated Robin better. Ayar has never settled after an episode in the way he has tonight. Sleeping like a youngling after she touched his hands, face, and head.

Why wasn't I raging at her? Why did I let her close to him?

Because Ayar asked me to. And instead of rage, I only felt calm watching them together. I only wanted to join them, to become three.

Once he fell asleep, and the spell was broken, I became a vrexing idiot. Instead of her staying with us, something I feel in the pit of my stomach she should have done, she scurried back to her room, leaving us alone.

I have a pair of eyes on me.

"Where's Robin?" Ayar asks.

"She's in her room." I try to sound upbeat. "She had a late night with you."

My mate stretches his wings out luxuriously, continuing until it pulls at his abdomen and he hisses with pain at his wound. "I feel good," he says, in direct defiance of how his body has just betrayed him. "Was I bad last night?"

"You were, but Robin helped."

Ayar grins at me, eyes lazy under half-closed lids, and I see the furs are raised with his arousal. "You should have let her stay."

"Is this what you want, really?" I ask him, rubbing over the skin on his chest. "You want Robin?"

"I want you and Robin," Ayar says, hooking one arm behind his head and shoving his hand under the furs, clearly stroking himself. "It might sound greedy, but that's what I want." He shudders, hips bucking at his touch.

"It is greedy. You are a greedy male who has a job to do." I kneel on the bed and peel away my pants, exposing both of my hard shafts to him. "And I want a good job, so stop touching yourself and deal with me."

I get another gorgeous, lazy smile before he sits carefully, the fur slipping away from his middle. His cocks stand proud, dripping his pre-cum copiously. He rolls onto his hands and knees and, with a practiced move he knows I love, he takes hold of both my cocks and sucks them deep into his throat.

"Vrex!" I steady myself by grasping his head at the sudden but delicious touch, my eyes closing involuntarily as he takes my cocks deeper. "Good warrior," I croon as he works his tongue over me.

Ayar has always been a master with his mouth, doing things to me I didn't even think were possible, things which have me seeing all the stars of Ustokos.

He adds a second hand, working both shafts, giving them equal attention as I hold the shoulder of his wings.

"You're too good at sucking my cocks, dirty mate," I admonish him. "Suck me harder."

With a deep hum, he increases his efforts, and he's going to tip me over the edge. I'm sorely tempted to let him, knowing just how much pleasure Ayar derives from milking me of my seed, even if he doesn't escape lightly when he does suck me to completion.

I put my hand back on his head, holding him onto my cocks, and he grasps my balls in a move designed to make me explode, to make me give him my load. My eyes close as I thrust into his mouth, hard, needing to come, needing him.

From the other side of room, there's an almost inaudible gasp. My eyes fly open, and Robin stands, like she did last night, staring at us both. Ayar's seen her too. His eyes are fixed on her, but he doesn't stop with his tongue and hands. If anything, he works me harder, eliciting a groan from my lips.

"Shit!" Robin swears in her own language, seemingly not wanting to witness the best cock sucking ever but unable to move.

It's then it reaches me.

Her scent. The sweetest ambrosia. Arousal.

I have no options left to me.

I extend my hand out to her. "Come, little female. Join us."

Robin

I can't quite believe what I walked in on, or in fact that I chose to walk in to Ayar and Vypr's room at all. But from the gasps and groans, I was initially worried Ayar was unwell again.

Could I have been more wrong? Instead, I find the pair of them naked and Vypr enjoying Ayar's attentions.

Both males are glorious when naked. Muscles which go on forever, each defined area simple perfection. They glisten slightly with sweat from their exertions. Wings are held high. Ayar laps his way over Vypr's enormous...cocks?

These aliens have two cocks!

Two cocks.

And not only are they double, but in both male's case, each member is, frankly, enormous. 'How is it going to fit?' enormous. 'Hung like a donkey' enormous.

Ayar palms his cocks, his dark eyes glittering even as he continues to lap at Vypr. His other hand massages at the male's balls, making him let out a groan of enjoyment.

I should leave. I cannot be seeing this.

I can't move.

Their scent, musky rain, spice, and hot leather, has me pinned to the spot. The longer I stare, the harder it is to not stare. To not enjoy the magnificent sight of the two males. After everything I've been through, this sight of two alpha predators taking pleasure from each other can't possibly be turning me on, can it?

"Come, little human. Join us." Vypr extends a clawed hand. To me.

He wants me. Ayar releases his cocks with a soft 'pop.' "Let us pleasure you, little Robin," he says, before going back to his sucking.

Vypr's hips snap at him, and I see a grin at the corner of Ayar's mouth, his busy mouth. A mouth I could imagine on mine or on any other part of my anatomy.

Neither male's eyes leave me for a second.

Do I want this?

Every single inch of me wants it, wants them with a craving I've never felt before in my entire life. These males have invaded my broken soul, and I've no idea how.

Without my bidding, my foot slides forward, and I'm moving across the room towards Vypr. He pushes Ayar's head away from his cocks, and slowly, the big, scarred male levers himself upright, until he's kneeling next to Vypr.

Four cocks jut out at me.

Four.

Up close, I see the deep ridges which run up the center of both the top and bottom cock. Ayar's is studded with nodes, symmetrically placed all over both of his. Vypr's are sparser, but both males are magnificent. But I don't know what to do, and I suddenly feel very hot.

"Too many clothes," Ayar murmurs. He reaches out and, taking hold of my arm, pulls me to him, slipping both hands under my top. He pulls it over my head and tosses it away.

"These too." Vypr has moved behind me, hands around

my waist. He drags my trousers down, then carefully removes first one boot, then the other before spiriting my pants to the other side of the room.

Now only the short corset top and a pair of fetching gray knickers stand between me and these two huge males. Vypr nuzzles at my neck, his clawed fingers exploring the edges of the corset before he pulls it free with a sudden jerk, and I gasp out loud.

"Still too many clothes," he growls in my ear and with a slight ripping sound, I feel a breeze on my bare bum as my knickers follow my pants. "Now you are perfect for us."

Hands are everywhere as the two males explore my body. Fingers tweak nipples, invade between my legs, tongues lap at my skin as these sensual predators get a sense of their prey. At the same time, cocks press against my bare skin, Ayar's slippery with pre-cum, Vypr's slippery with Ayar's earlier attention.

I feel like I'm drowning in males. Their scent, their hands, their touch. I'm gasping for breath. It rasps in my throat. It hitches when a claw flicks over a hard nipple. My thighs are drenched.

"Robin," Ayar murmurs, his voice thick with desire.

His lips trail over my collarbone, and I put my arms around his neck. He lifts his head, and dark eyes drill into mine. I lean in and press a kiss to his sculpted lips. For a second, he freezes and opens his mouth a little. I take full advantage and run my tongue over them. Something sparks, like static, but before I can move, there is a clawed hand tangled in my hair and Ayar's tongue in my mouth as we explore each other. I taste him and Vypr, a heady mix of sweetness and salt.

"What was that?" He pulls away from me, eyes wide. He looks at Vypr over my shoulder. The huge male is cupping my buttocks in one big hand, and the other is rolling one of my breasts.

"What was what?" I can't string much of a sentence together with all the new sensations, especially as Vypr has just brushed over my anus in a very, very slow movement.

"With your mouth." Ayar breathes in my face.

"A kiss?"

Vypr's fingers slip between my legs, and he gently invades my hot, slick pussy as I lean back on him.

"Humans kiss," Vypr says knowledgeably, licking over the shell of my ear. "I've seen the seniors kiss their mates. It is lip touching."

"And tongues." Ayar says enthusiastically.

"Tongues?"

I'm lifted off the ground and spun to face Vypr. His eyes flash, and I reach for his impossibly handsome face. The face of a male I thought didn't want me. He leans in, eyes closing, and our lips meet. This time, a crackle of electricity flows through me and for a second, I can't move. But I need to taste Vypr properly, and my tongue probes at his lips.

As if in surprise, he parts them and allows me in. My tongue does a sweep of his mouth, and he cups my face in his huge hands, pulling me to him so he can return my kiss, his tongue demanding my attention, his cocks hard against my belly.

I'm panting again as he releases me from a kiss to end all kisses, one which turned my vision black.

"Tongues." He grins over my shoulder at Ayar. "Now, pretty Robin, what should I do with you?" He runs a knuckle down my cheek.

Behind me, Ayar presses his cock between my butt cheeks, snuffling in my hair.

"Do I give you to Ayar?" Vypr cocks his head to one side, gazing at me, dark eyes even darker with lust. "He wants to breed you. Or do I taste you for myself first?"

"Vypr!" Ayar whines.

"You don't get to choose, dirty mate," Vypr snarls at him. "Robin is my little morsel. I'll tell you when you can be good and when you can be bad with her." His hand is around the back of my neck, the pins of his claws pressing into my skin.

"And what about you?" I say, breathlessly. "Who tells Vypr what to do?"

"No one tells me what to do. I'm always bad, sweet female. And always obeyed." He smashes his lips to mine in a bruising kiss.

Ayar

I inhale Robin's scent deeply as she uses her human kiss on Vypr. I want to taste her again, but I want Vypr to bond with her more.

I know more than ever she's important. I still can't quite work out how or why. My head's still foggy as to what she is to us. But what I do know is she was there when the nightmare gripped me, the one where I'm back in the machine, when I thought I would never get out.

Her soft voice, perfect smell, and clever hands pulled me out of it, into Vypr's comforting presence. With both of them next to me, my sleep was peaceful.

But right now, I want her. I want to be inside her, mate with her, and fill her with my youngling. I want to watch as Vypr takes her sweet cunt, dripping with my seed. My wants are visceral, feral, and I growl over the smooth skin on her shoulder, nipping at it with my teeth, my hands cupping her delicious breasts. My cocks prodding at her back. She is a little thing I will enjoy devouring.

"Do you need this scrap of a female, Ayar?" Vypr asks me

once he releases her mouth. "Because she needs Gryn cocks, and I want to see you mate her until she begs for more, while I mate you harder."

I shudder, my cocks jerking harder against Robin's silky skin. Vypr's growled order nearly has me fountaining my seed everywhere.

"Robin, my Robin," I murmur into her fragrant hair. "How do you want me to take you, mate you? My cocks ache to be inside you, sweet Robin. Let me in."

Her whole body shakes under my touch. I slip my hand between her thighs. She's soaking, her juices running down her legs. I explore higher, higher, and find she's swollen as she drips, her body bucking against me as I run a claw through her folds, a cry escaping her lips.

Vypr kisses her and spins her round to face me. Her face is flushed, beautiful, blue eyes boring into mine, and her mouth is open, inviting. I enclose her with my wings as I take her head in my hands and drop my lips to hers. My tongue enjoys her sweet mouth, but I know what I want to enjoy more.

"Let me taste you, Robin," I moan over her, pushing her back onto the furs and lapping my way down her front, pausing to lavish attention on her gorgeous breasts until I reach the source of all her delicate, intoxicating scent, her soaking pussy.

"Are you going to fill that pretty cunt, Ayar?" Vypr fists his cocks. "Or will you suck me while I taste?"

I whine. The overwhelming need to breed this tiny female is all encompassing. But I need to obey my Vypr, too. Pre cum spurts from my shafts, covering Robin's belly.

She moans, and I can't hold any longer. I want to taste. I want to suck and lick, but I have to be sheathed in her. I tremble, and a pair of bright blue eyes hold mine.

"Ayar," she whispers, lips brushing over my jawline.

"Let me mate you," I breathe, knowing I want all of her, every single delicious inch, but right now, I can only think of my cocks plundering her.

I nudge between her hot thighs, and she spreads for me so beautifully I shake even harder. A clawed hand grasps my buttock and, as I glance over my shoulder, I see Vypr. He dips his head to lick over my shoulder and his cocks press into the cleft of my ass.

I thrust forward, my main cock breaching her tight pussy, as she flutters around me. My secondary cock presses up against her little pucker, gently easing in and out.

Her eyes are wide. "I've never..." she murmurs. "Not in there."

"Gryn are made to pleasure," I say. "This is my pleasure for you." I press just a little harder, wanting her enjoyment to be even greater than my own.

My secondary cock is slick with pre-cum and natural lubrication, so it slides into her easily as her chest heaves.

"Oh! So full!" she exclaims as I seat myself.

Vypr presses up behind me. "That's good, Ayar. Take this little morsel and fill her," he growls in my ear.

His cocks are rods of the hardest metal pressed against my back as he grinds against me. He wants to take me. I can almost taste it, but he's holding back so I can enjoy Robin.

I lift back, withdrawing nearly all the way out of her and then thrust back, circling my hips as she mewls under me.

"Is this what you wanted, sweet female?" Vypr asks her from over my shoulder. "To be mated by a male with both of his cocks? Are you good enough for him to spill his seed in you?"

She can't speak and neither can I, the beautiful, incredible pleasure of being enclosed in her hot channels, while Vypr pumps his cocks and caresses my wings means I'm coming whether I want to or not. Pleasure blinding me, Robin's pussy sucking at my main cock as she writhes under me, the warm heat of Vypr's climax covering my thighs and butt cheeks.

Robin

I'm gasping for air, my lungs burning at me through the orgasm I've just experienced. It was nothing like any brief climax I've had before.

Nothing.

This shook the very marrow of my bones. I felt it in every part of my body, and I've never felt like that before.

Sex hasn't been a pleasure for me for a long time. It's been a necessity.

Ayar cages me, wings drooping over us, his breathing ragged. I'm soaked, in my own juices, the enormous amount of cum he just pumped into me, which is leaking everywhere, and Vypr's spend, which covers us both. The scent of males and sex hang in the air.

What have I just done?

A wing is nudged aside, and Vypr's handsome face appears. He nudges up closer until Ayar shifts to one side, his cocks pulling out of me and leaving me empty. Soft feathers cover me, warm bodies surround me.

Did I really just try anal for the first time with an alien?

My head spins as we lie in breathless silence. I've just had sex with Ayar, unprotected sex. I already know it's possible to get knocked up by these males, given Kat is probably only a month from giving birth to Strykr's baby.

I've literally only just met Ayar and Vypr. They can't possibly want a child with me. I can't possibly want a child with them.

And I've just fucked Ayar as if nothing mattered. My gasping becomes more acute. Panic rises within me. On Earth, I was on the pill, not that he knew, but I had to, only because there was no way I'd end up any more dependent on him than I already was.

But the pill is a distant memory. I've fallen straight into the trap. If Ayar knocks me up, I'm at the mercy of these males, too. I never thought. I never think things through.

I am an idiot.

"Are you okay, Robin?" Vypr rumbles next to me, his voice a deep chocolate velvet.

"I have to go." I scramble upright. "I have to..." I'm already on my feet, not even stopping for my clothes. I race across the room and out of the door, back to my own quarters, where I curl up on the bed and shake.

My boss, Magnus Finson, did this to me. Even the thought of his name sends ice speeding through my veins. He's the last thing in the universe I should be thinking of, and yet he's the only person who fills my mind. His handsome face twisted with anger. Anger which was always directed at me.

After a while, I get up, use the sanitary facility, marvel at how the human body can accommodate large items, and pull on a shift which Jesic gave me for sleeping in. I let my mind go blank, trying to just be, for a short while, before I try to make sense of it all. If any sense can be made.

"Robin?" I look up to see my two males, both, thankfully, wearing pants. Vypr holds my clothes, and Ayar has a tray in one hand. "Can we come in?"

They both look very worried. Ayar in particular has a look of abject woe, his wings drooping behind him and, together with his bandage, he presents as a pathetic figure. I pull the furs around me and nod, my voice temporarily gone. Both of them troop in. Vypr places my clothes on the unused bed opposite me, and Ayar stands, clearly unsure what to do next.

"We brought you something to eat," Vypr says.

"I didn't hurt you, did I?" Ayar blurts out. "That's not why you ran is it? Because sometimes I don't know my own strength. Sometimes I get things wrong, and I don't mean to. I would never hurt you, Robin. Never." He shakes his head so hard, he nearly spins, and Vypr grabs the tray.

My heart, the organ I thought could never be moved again, jumps in my chest. Fluttering like a butterfly caught against a window. The enormous, feathered warrior is terrified our lovemaking might have been painful, when it was the best I've ever experienced. Instead, my stupid brain, which told me to run, has hurt him.

"I'm fine, Ayar. You didn't hurt me, not at all. In fact, what you did was wonderful. The best ever." I'm on my feet, my arms wrapped around him. "I know you would never hurt me."

Ayar snuffles into my hair, his big, clawed hands curled around me. I tilt my head back to look up at him, and tears streak his scarred cheeks.

"Oh, Ayar, my darling." I touch him gently on the scarred side of his face before lifting myself onto tiptoes to press a kiss to his lips. "Don't cry. It's not you, not at all, it's me." I luxuriate in his gorgeous warmth even as my heart breaks for him.

It breaks because I didn't think for an instant how running from them both might look.

"As long as you are okay," Vypr says. "That's what matters."

"I guess I was overwhelmed, and when I am, I run. I should have talked to you," I say, my voice muffled in Ayar.

"I'm no good at talking, my Robin. But I know running doesn't help either," Ayar says, his voice rumbling through me.

"Can you ever forgive me?" I look up at the huge male, taking one of his hands in mine, stroking his skin.

"Only if you tell us why you ran," Vypr says.

"I know humans can get pregnant by the Gryn. I'm not sure I'm ready for that."

"Oh, little Robin." Vypr chuckles with a laugh as rich as chocolate. "I know Ayar wants to breed you, but the Gryn are honorable males. He would only do so with your permission."

"But...what we did?"

"A Gryn can only fill a female's belly if he uses both cocks in her sweet pussy at the same time," Vypr says.

Ayar runs his hand through my hair, feeling the strands of it.

"We will never, ever do anything you don't want us to do, beautiful," he says, dark eyes raking over me. "I want to take everything you have, as long as it's given willingly."

I don't mean to cry. I don't mean to burden these sweet males with any more of my crap, but the tears flow. Tears of regret I should have cried years ago, tears of guilt that I hurt Ayar and Vypr with my behavior.

"I'm sorry. It's just I had a hard time with a male once," I sob out into Ayar's arms.

"Who hurt you?" Vypr growls, the tray dropped on the empty bed. He bristles violently. "If any merc has laid a finger on you, I'll rip his wings off and feed them to him."

"And I'll shred the rest of him," Ayar joins in, tears forgotten. Both males are almost shivering with repressed anger.

He holds me tightly. I'm warm and safe in his embrace, his scent musky compared to the fruity deep scent of Vypr, who stands at my back, his presence comforting in a way I've never known. Two predators, ensuring their female is protected and cared for.

What's happened in my past shouldn't have any bearing on my future. Or at least it's what I tell myself over and over.

Only it does. Every damn day I wake up. Even on an alien planet, millions of light years from Earth. Until I unburden myself, it will always be part of me.

"No Gryn has hurt me. It was a human man on Earth, Magnus Finson," I begin. "He was my employer initially. He took over the agency I worked for, from a boss I loved. He seemed friendly and nice. Then my car broke down, and he offered me a loan to get it fixed." I fix my eyes on Ayar's feathers as I run my fingers though the silky fluff. It means I can distance myself from what I'm going to say next. "But when I wanted to repay him, he said he didn't want my money. He wanted me. He'd wipe out the whole loan if I..." I swallow hard, tears blurring my vision. "Let him mate with me. I thought it was a one off, but he..." I try to work out a way to explain the blackmail Magnus put me through, the video he'd taken, the threats to post it on the internet, all of which are alien concepts to Ayar and Vypr. "After that, he basically did what he wanted."

Vypr moves closer, his heat infusing into my back, arms wrapping around my waist. Ayar increases his grip. They are not repelled by my story, entirely the opposite.

"You are ours now," Ayar murmurs. "No one else can have you, and my offer to shred him if he ever comes here still stands." His hand snakes into my hair. He's rubbing the strands together between his fingers as he inhales. "I love your hair, sweet Robin. It's so smooth, so..." He's lost for words.

"Ayar likes to touch things," Vypr says. He's still pressed behind me, and I can't see his face, but a big, clawed hand reaches around and ruffles Ayar's hair. "It helps with his headaches and pain. Doesn't it, my big warrior?"

Ayar croons into my hair, a soft sound entirely at odds with his fearsome predatory appearance. He is happy.

And somehow, despite having told two almost complete strangers (save for the glorious sex) what a loser I was, I am happy, too.

Vypr

Ayar and I hold Robin for a long time. I can't believe any male would have treated her in the way she describes. Clearly, human males lack honor. Ayar is particularly peaceful in her presence. When he thought he had done something wrong, he was beside himself.

My emotions are in turmoil. What we all just did together was something I did not foresee. My heart belongs to Ayar and it always will. He is the reason Ustokos turns. But Robin...

I can't deny my heart beat twice as fast when I thought she might have rejected us. But do we have room for another? Can a Gryn have two *eregri*s—two fated mates?

As for Ayar's desire for younglings, maybe I should be thinking of our future, rather than living in the day to day. If he wants a youngling, why shouldn't he have one?

I'm drawn to Robin as much as he is, only I don't wear it on my sleeve. I can't deny I want to hold her in my arms, breathe in her scent, and mate her thoroughly for days on end. And yet I'm already a mated male.

My emotions churn as we hold each other in comfortable union.

"Strykr has a meeting arranged this morning with the unit to discuss the next mission," I eventually say, breaking our sweet silence. "You'll be sitting this one out," I say to Ayar.

"Good, I hate meetings," he grumbles.

"And the mission too."

"No!" he says sharply. "I always go."

"With your injury? Not likely. You'll be staying to keep Robin safe."

As soon as the words are out of my mouth, a spike of ice runs up my spine. I want to stay with them both, and I certainly don't actually want to leave Ayar on his own, even if he has Robin. But I already know I will be going on the mission. If I want to keep this nest, I'll need to step up.

Ayar hisses his displeasure. Releasing Robin, he stalks from the room.

"He likes his job," Robin says quietly. "It's not good to keep him from it."

Suddenly, I want to yell at her that she knows nothing about Ayar.

"He told me when we were in the surgery together," she continues, and I feel my anger dissipate. "He likes it when you make explosions. It makes him feel, how did he put it? 'Squashy inside'." She says, her fingers on her lips. "He loves you so much." She smiles, but there is a sadness to her eyes.

A sadness which slams me like a laser bolt. Robin cares. She cares about Ayar. She cares that he loves me, and I know it. It cracks my walls.

I will not have my female sad.

I catch her chin with my hand and tilt her face up to mine. "Ayar said it and now I'm saying it, too. You are mine. Mine and ours. You are not to look or think of another male again, especially not *him.*" I spit out the final word, to make it known to her just what I think of the human. "Because you have us, and we are honorable Gryn warriors, who will protect you with our lives."

"I appreciate that, Vypr." She puts her hand over mine.

Why do I feel there's a 'but' to her sentence? Whatever this is between all of us, we'll need to work it out, but after my meeting with Strykr.

"I need to go." I look at the tray we brought in. "Maybe take the food back to Ayar? I think he wanted it more than you, anyway." I run a finger through her hair, the color of Usokos's first sun. "When I'm back, we'll talk."

She nods, putting her tiny hand on my chest. It's so warm, I'm almost tempted to take her back to Ayar and make sure she's mated again before I leave. But duty calls and, instead, I place my lips on her forehead and release her.

Out in the central atrium, I'm joined by Syn.

"Meeting?" he calls out.

"Yeah." I fold my wings and drop towards the ground.

Syn is not my favorite unit member or Gryn warrior. He has a problem with Ayar I can't fathom, but it means he either teases him or needles him until he gets a reaction. And he'll always get a reaction because Ayar can't help himself.

Today he seems in a friendly mood. "Do you think this latest mission will allow us to go off world?" he asks as we land, and I make my way down into the bowels of the eyrie to where the unit has its headquarters, away from the rest of the warriors assigned to the eyrie and who are slowly filling the place.

"Because we did such a good job last time?" I raise my eyebrows at him, referencing the mission to the space station in orbit around Ustokos, the one Ayar blew a hole in.

"We've proved ourselves capable since then," Syn replies, not taking the opportunity to denigrate Ayar.

He must want something.

"After we lost one of our three spaceships to an enemy which doesn't know how to fight," I point out.

"That's why we need to get off world," Syn says excitedly. "Take the fight to the Drahon."

"Hmmm." I stroll into the meeting room where Strykr, Mylo, Jay, and Huntr are already waiting.

Mylo has, as always, found himself something to eat, happily stuffing in what looks like one of the good pies, created by the human mate of Myk, the lair's weapons master.

Strykr, my Guv, waits patiently, sitting at the small table we've appropriated from somewhere. It might not be as awe-inspiring as the one crafted from bot parts by Myk, the one the seniors use in the lair for their high level szent meetings, but it suits our unit. Cobbled together on a wing and a prayer to the Goddess.

Jay has his arms folded. He smiles warmly at me as I enter. He's always been one of the best of us, and I'm pleased he's happily mated.

At the far side of the room, Huntr paces. He was held by the Drahon. We don't know for how long or where he was before they took him. He won't tell us and from the little Strykr has told me, even Ryak, the lair's security master, hasn't been able to get any information from him.

All I know is he knows the Drahon, their tech, and can fight. That makes him valuable to the team, and clearly Strykr feels the same way.

His pacing is getting on my nerves though.

"Do we have a mission, Guv?" I ask as I seat myself at the table.

"How's Ayar?" he asks.

"Healing."

"Good, because we're going to need everyone, especially Ayar," Strykr says. Syn snorts. So much for whatever he wanted from me. Strykr ignores him. "How long until he's healed enough to go into space?"

"I'll have to ask Orvos. He was only discharged from the surgery yesterday. But it's Ayar. It won't be long."

"Orvos will say anything to get him out of his feathers, no doubt." Mylo grins at me.

"And back in mine." I give him a friendly kick under the table. "Although you're welcome to visit any time."

"No fear!" Mylo recoils in a good-natured fashion. "Ayar? Injured? It'd be like dealing with a female Mochi and cubs. Dangerous and messy." He leans back in his chair. "Anyway, I heard you had help." He gives me a dirty wink. "Female help."

"One of the human females from the Drahon ship. She agreed to help care for Ayar once Orvos let him out," I explain to Strykr.

This wasn't exactly how I wanted to introduce my new living arrangements to my Guv, but gossip in the eyrie is worse than in the lair.

"As long as she agreed, and it's helping Ayar heal faster," Strykr replies, cocking his head to one side as he looks straight at me. "Females are a precious commodity."

I struggle to hold back my anger. Like I would think of Robin in any other way!

"They are...she is..." Under the table, I curl my hands into fists, claws pricking at my palms.

"What's the mission, Guv?" Jay asks, diverting attention from the unfolding potential faceoff between me and several members of the team.

Since he mated, he's become even more valuable to us, not only as our sniper but as the male who can ease tensions, almost before we even know they exist ourselves.

Strykr stares at me for another few seconds. The Guv is a

formidable fighter. Not one I would willingly go one to one with, unless perhaps I had Ayar by my side. Even then, the odds would still be in his favor.

But I'd kill him for looking at my mates. I know it. The volcano of rage inside me is already rising.

"Ryak has intelligence that the Drahon dropped off a shipment of weapons with the Kijg. We don't want either the Kijg or, more importantly, any Drahon left on Ustokos to have those weapons. Our mission is to liberate them without the Kijg finding out."

There are a few snorts of excited laughter around the room.

"We weren't there, and no one is to know we were. It's a serious mission and an indication of just how much faith the seniors are placing in our unit," Strykr continues. "I know you all won't let me down."

"When do we leave?" Huntr hasn't stopped his feral pacing. "If there are any Drahon, I need to deal with them."

I give Strykr a long look. When we were tasked with retrieving Jay and the ship the Drahon stole back from us, we captured a few Drahon, alive, until Huntr had gotten to them.

"This is a find and retrieve mission, Huntr," Strykr says, not even looking around. "You don't get to kill any Drahon this time." He looks around at all of us. "We'll be leaving in three turns. Be ready. Dismissed."

I rise from the table. Mylo slings his arm around Jay's shoulders, leading him away with some talk of laser rifles. The big warrior is our combat expert. He's the only one of us who can get the Guv out of breath in the training pit. Laser rifles are his interest, even if he'll never be as good a shot as Jay.

Huntr immediately stalks out of the room, and he's followed swiftly by Syn. I feel the pull of my mates and turn to follow them when Strykr calls out my name.

"I need to speak with you, about Ayar," he says quietly. "Come with me." He gestures to the small back room where he has his office.

"What is it, Guv?" I ask as we step through the door, and he takes a seat behind a desk he dwarfs.

"Close the door."

Now I know this can't be good, but I do as he asks.

"Ayar's incident in the eyrie food hall hasn't gone unnoticed by the seniors." Strykr runs his hand over his face. "Ryak intervened, but Fyn's not happy. He doesn't like the idea of any merc having the level of access we do anyway, and with Ayar's antics, it's put the entire unit's existence in jeopardy."

"Ayar doesn't mean to vrex things up. You know that, Guv," I plead. "He's an excellent warrior, and there's no one better with all the laser weapons, you know it."

"That's the only reason he's still on the team, Vypr," Strykr says. "But his lack of control could get us all killed, or worse, captured by the Drahon. He's got to learn to curb his urges and act like more of a team player or..."

"Or what, Guv?" My stomach turns over.

"Or he'll be off the unit. He'll go back under Fyn's control."

"Vrex." I half mutter the swearword under my breath.

"Vrex, indeed." Strykr fixes me with a serious gaze. "I don't like this any more than you, Vypr, but Fyn's not going to be turned, and the Prime is backing him."

Like the seniors haven't had their moments! Fyn, our Prime's second in command, in particular. Rumor has it he had to be healed by some early version of a medi-chair in order to be able to function as he does now. And the fact he has a short temper and even shorter patience means I wonder how bad he was before he was healed.

"I'll speak to Ayar. He'll be fine, Guv," I lie.

"That's what I want to hear." Strykr relaxes. "I'd rather have Ayar at my back any turn. I want him as part of our unit as much as you do, Vypr."

Robin

I carry the tray back into the larger room next to mine. The bed of furs where I was fucked senseless remains rumpled from our activities. My pussy and bottom burn with the reminders of what we did.

What I did.

I shake my head slightly. I've never been so bold before and not only that, but with *two* alien males.

It must be something in the water.

"Ayar?" I call out, shifting the tray to my other hand.

A rustle of feathers has me spinning on the spot. In the corner of the room, my big, scarred warrior is hunched over.

"Shit! Are you okay?" I put the tray on the floor, and I'm swiftly across the room, expecting to see his wound reopened or something equally as worrying.

He lifts his head, eyes slightly glazed, then a smile spreads over his face. Not the slightly insane one I've seen him use, but something much warmer, full of recognition and pleasure.

"Robin!" he says, happily. He reaches out an arm and snags my waist, pulling me sharply into his side, and he inhales deeply.

I'm enclosed by a cloud of musky sweet feathers. He's so big, even though I'm standing and he is seated, I'm still not taller than him. In front of my wounded warrior is a large collection of brightly colored polished stones. They are arranged in order of size and color.

"Are these yours?" I ask softly.

"Vypr finds them for me, and I clean them up," Ayar says, his claws tripping lightly over the stones' neat rows. "I like doing it. Makes me feel calm."

The sudden rush of emotion takes me by surprise, and I find myself with my arm around Ayar, my hand delving into his feathers as he carefully rearranges the stones.

"You're more than meets the eye, aren't you?" I say, quietly. "Both of you."

I still haven't had the chance to process what happened earlier between the three of us. My heart beats harder because it wants this to be something, but my head…it's still unsure.

"I'm going to have a bath and change." I find myself pressing a kiss to the side of Ayar's head. "You have something to eat, and when Vypr gets back, we'll talk."

Ayar coos a happy sound, shuffling his wings. He turns his dark eyes on me, so deep I could fall in and swim among the pinpricks of light which dance there.

"Maybe we can mate again?" he asks hopefully.

Against all the odds, and the burning sensation between my legs, I feel a flood of moisture and a pang of lust.

"Maybe." I give him a squeeze and duck out from under his warm wing, immediately feeling its loss.

I walk away, but I'm aware Ayar's eyes don't leave me. He doesn't go back to his stones. Why does his lack of motion make my heart pound in my chest?

I'm back in my room, gathering up the towel Jesic gave me and one of the strange soap-like bars which smell surprisingly fragrant for a planet full of males, when there's a knock on the door.

"I told you, Ayar, I'll be back once I've had my bath." I laugh as I open the door.

To see two very interested female faces looking at me.

"Goodness, you've gotten comfortable quickly," Diana says, stalking past into my room.

Jen drops her head, her long, dark hair hiding her face, but I'm sure I see her eyes are red as she hurries past me, following Diana.

"Nice, nice," Diana says, spinning around. "Just for you?"

"For the moment. I'm looking after Ayar, and he's sort of looking after me, while we both heal. After that, I guess I'm coming to stay with you." I grin.

"Scratch that!" Diana laughs. "I'm coming to stay with you! This place is bigger than ours, and there's two extra bunks."

"If you don't mind being in close proximity to two Gryn warriors, I guess we could sort something out," I say, carefully.

Diana and Jen are my friends. We went through a lot together at the hands of the Drahon, and I'm not about to abandon them.

"I'm joking, hun. You know you're welcome to come to our little abode once your time is up. That was always the plan." She wraps her arms around me for a gentle hug. "I'm just pleased to see you out of the surgery."

"Orvos told us you'd come here," Jen says, sounding a bit peeved.

"It's not like Robin could have texted, Jen," Diana says.

"Suppose." Jen sits down on my bed.

"Ignore her. She's having problems with the monster in the cupboard."

"Huntr?" I query. "But he's free, just like us."

Diana lets out a frustrated noise but says nothing.

"It doesn't matter." Jen waves her hand, attempting to look dismissive, but instead, she looks distraught. "Just be careful how you get involved with these warriors." She leans forward. "I've heard Ayar is a bit...you know...bonkers."

"What do you mean?" Diana asks, loudly.

"I mean he's dangerous to be around. He's known to get into fights, blow things up, and generally cause havoc everywhere he goes," Jen fires out. "I don't want you getting hurt again," she says quietly.

"So I should keep my distance from Mr. Mad, Bad, and Dangerous?" I can't help the smile which quirks my lips at the corners. Mainly because I've suddenly got a flashback to being railed senseless by Ayar. "What about Vypr?"

Jen seems at a loss, and I can see what's happening here. Whatever is bothering her, she's trying to project it onto me. I've spent so many hours training to read people, to understand their motives, what drives them in order to be able to get the answers I want, I can read her like a book.

And she's hurting so bad.

"I...I don't know," Jen stutters out.

I sit down next to her, putting my arm around her shoulders.

"Both Vypr and Ayar have only been kind to me. Ayar's been injured, and he's a teddy bear when you get to know him. You don't need to worry about me, honestly, Jen."

To Diana's surprise, but not mine, Jen bursts into tears and slams her head into my shoulder.

Ayar

I didn't mean to follow Robin, but I couldn't help myself. The problem was the other females get to her first, so I shrink back into the doorway of our nest.

One of the females smells strongly of a male Gryn. I wrinkle my nose. Vypr understands how sensitive I am to scent, it can drive me to distraction, make my temper short and my ability to control myself disappear. He likes to make sure I smell of him.

Robin answers the door using my name, and I almost step out into the corridor when something stops me. Three females together, one smelling of another Gryn? Deep down, I know it's not something I should participate in.

But once they're inside and the door closes, I can't help but creep along towards Robin's barrack room. I should just go and eat like she told me to, but part of me wants to see if I can bathe with her. Another, deeper part of me which I don't recognize, wants to protect her, even from these harmless females.

I reach the door and hesitate. Perhaps I should go back to

my nest, eat my food, and have a rest. My wound is aching at me, and a nap would do me good.

But I don't want to nap. I want Robin safe in my arms, and I want my Vypr.

Female voices carry through the door and out into the corridor. Raised voices which make my wings flare. At least the females don't include Strykr's mate and her little bot. I've gotten used to it, just, but the smell of it chills my blood every time I'm near it.

Because of the machine.

I snort out a breath, shaking my head to rid it of the memories which rise within. I need Robin, and I need her now. I lift my hand to knock.

"So I should keep my distance from Mr. Mad, Bad, and Dangerous?" Robin's voice rings out, and I pause. "What about Vypr?"

I take in a breath. Does Robin mean me and Vypr? Is she talking about another male? There's silence until another female voice says something I don't quite hear.

And then, from behind the door, there are sounds of a female in distress.

I promised my Robin I would protect her, from anything and anyone.

No one hurts my Robin.

The door doesn't stand a chance. I wrench it off its hinges and heave it to one side before I leap into the room, wings held high, claws out, ready for anything.

I'm met with three pairs of shocked eyes. Robin has her arms around the female who smells of another male. This one has eyes which are red and her face wet.

"Ayar? What. The. Fuck?" Robin says, and her eyes widen further. "Shit!" She fires out what I assume is a swearword in her language. "What have you done to yourself?"

I don't understand what she's asking about for a second,

until I feel a searing pain in my abdomen. Looking down, the white plaster stuck to me is now red.

"Oh, vrex." I put my hand on it, and it comes away scarlet. "Vypr's going to be vrexing livid."

I stare at her for a second. The other two females have their mouths open. I know I need to get away, and I turn, heading back to my nest to work out what I'm going to do. I was supposed to be resting. I was supposed to look after Robin, and all I've done is vrex things up.

Back in my nest, I collapse on the bed. My stomach aches and burns. I think Vypr brought some medical supplies with him when he came back with Robin, but I don't know where they are. I roll onto my back with a groan. Why am I such a vrexing disaster? Why couldn't I just have left Robin alone?

"What on earth did you think you were doing?" Robin's voice penetrates my haze of pain and regret.

Sure, steady hands are working over my stomach, and I open my eyes to see her pretty, concerned face staring down at me.

"I thought you were hurting, my Robin. I came to help you."

"Sweetheart, you could have just knocked."

ROBIN

I CAREFULLY UNPEEL THE SOAKING PLASTER FROM Ayar's stomach, half expecting to see an enormous gaping wound. Instead, the injury looks similar to how it was when I examined it for him in the surgery, save for a tiny part of the plastic stitching which has popped open.

"I can't go back," Ayar whispers, attempting to lift his head to look at what he's done to himself. "I can't let him put me in the machine again." His voice is rasping and desperate.

And yet his body is limp, as if he's lost any power he might have. He mumbles to himself about the machine, staring at the ceiling, one wing thumping pathetically against the furs.

I get on with cleaning him up and gently push the plastic staple back into place, before covering the whole area with a clean plaster.

"Ayar...Ayar!" I call softly to him. When he doesn't respond, only babbles, I catch his cheek with my hand and turn him to face me. "You're fine. I've patched you up, look." I slide my hand around the back of his big head and lift it so he can see his stomach.

His breath hitches. A viciously clawed hand hovers over the white patch.

"I'm healed again? Not by Orvos?" he says, voice raw. "No surgery?"

"I think Orvos did a good job the first time around. Maybe he knew you'd bust your stitches at some point. There was no damage done. You're good." I run my hand over his forehead.

His eyelids flutter at me, but his eyes remain open, staring.

"We can't tell Vypr. He'll kill me."

"You can't tell Vypr what?" Vypr's voice booms out from behind me.

I turn to see the big, dark warrior stood in the doorway. Ayar scrabbles at my hand, eyes pleading.

"What happened to your door, Robin?"

"I don't think we can keep it a secret," I say to Ayar, taking hold of one of his huge hands and rubbing the spots he likes best. "Ayar was protecting me from being hurt. The door got in his way."

"Vrex the goddess!" Vypr stomps across the room and sits down heavily on the bed next to us. "You weren't in danger, were you?" he asks, warm brown eyes full of concern.

"No, it was a misunderstanding." I look down at Ayar who studies us both from his prone position.

"Could today not have been without incident? Does anyone else know about this?" Vypr runs a hand through his hair and places it on Ayar's thigh.

"No," I reply. "Well, two of the other humans, Diana and Jen. They were here, but I doubt they'll say anything to anyone." I try to sound confident but remember what Jen said about Ayar.

"Within the eyrie or the lair, if there were witnesses, everyone will know soon enough," Vypr says, standing and beginning to pace.

"Does it matter?" I ask. I didn't take Vypr for a male who cared about gossip.

"Yeah." Ayar snorts. "It doesn't matter. I was only protecting Robin, and I didn't hurt myself much."

Vypr is immediately back on the bed, hovering over Ayar with concern. "Where?" He looks at me, eyes full of pain.

"It's absolutely fine." I run my hand through his wing feathers. "Ayar just slightly reopened his wound. I've dealt with it."

Vypr spots the pile of bloody plaster and cleaning cloths next to the bed, and his mouth hardens.

"I couldn't bear it if anything happened to you, mate." He nuzzles at Ayar's nose and, tentatively, places a kiss on his mouth.

I feel like I should turn my head away at this display of intimacy because it seems so personal. But I can't. I want to watch. I want to be part of it.

I want to be part of it.

"My *eregri*," Vypr murmurs to Ayar. "What would I do without you?"

Ayar hums with pleasure. His vicious claws retracted, he has his hands in Vypr's feathers and kisses him back. I get a funny sense of pride I introduced these males to a new thing.

It's then I'm grabbed and unceremoniously sandwiched between them both. "Hey! Mind the ribs!" I laugh as kisses are dropped over every inch of my exposed skin.

I don't know when it happened, but my heart has opened to Vypr and Ayar in a way I never expected. And in a way I think I like.

I had thought any chance of being happy with any man was long gone. Maybe I was wrong.

Vypr

It's impossible to stay mad at Ayar. Just seeing my mates together, how Robin has settled him after she fixed him up. His scent is absolutely delicious, and it's all I can do not to eat him up.

I should tell him what Strykr said, but I can't bring myself to say anything, especially when he snags Robin to join us, and I get the opportunity to taste her too.

In fact, tasting her has given me an idea.

"Robin and I are going to get food from the food hall." I lever myself away from our warm scrum of bodies. Ayar flails, attempting to follow me, but I put a hand on his chest. "You're staying here and not getting into any more trouble."

"I am trouble." Ayar grins at me, tucking his arm behind his head.

"Agreed." Robin slips off the bed. "Come on then, I want to see the eyrie," she says to me.

I'd almost forgotten she's spent most of her time in the lair surgery until now, and I mentally kick myself I didn't give her a tour earlier. Instead we were too busy doing other things which I don't regret for a second.

Ayar whines.

"You will stay here and wait patiently. It's about time you learned the meaning of the word."

He groans but stays put, still grinning wildly.

I hold out my hand to Robin, and she takes it with a shy smile. My heart, my treacherous heart which was only ever meant for one mate, flips in my chest. I can't possibly want her the way I want Ayar, can I?

We make our way out of the nesting area to the main atrium.

"Can we walk?" she asks me. "It's not that I don't like flying, but my bones are sore, and I don't want to be jiggled too much."

I raise my eyebrows.

"Yet," she adds, with a naughty glint in her eye. It looks like she's beginning to understand our dynamic.

"The food hall is only three floors down, so no need to fly if you don't want to."

We begin our descent, walking slowly down the ramp which circles the atrium. A lip at about waist height for me blocks some of Robin's view, but she stays close to it, staring over with eyes wide at the falling plants which have started to grow here. They make the air fresh, and I like them. Perhaps I will get some for our nest if Robin likes them too.

As we reach the food hall level, more mercs appear, landing heavily as they fly up from the ground far below us.

"It can get busy in there. Stay in front of me," I tell Robin and we enter the scrum which is the midday meal.

Robin sticks close as mercs jostle with wings to get to the food. It would probably have made sense to leave getting our meal until later, but I need to talk to Robin before I tackle Ayar.

I grab us two cups of cala, and Robin picks up a platter. I surround her with my wings as she selects meat, pies, and some of the bread rolls, now a favorite among both the lair and eyrie. I feel oddly possessive of this tiny female who relies on me to keep her safe.

The female who needs to understand how well a male, or males, can treat her. Not like the piece of human scum who sought to control her and hurt her on Earth. I feel my feathers bristling at the mere thought of her being touched or even being looked at by another male.

"Let's sit over here for a while." I steer her through the crowd to a table near the back which is mercifully only being used by a single merc.

He takes one look at me and picks up his platter, stalking off in a riot of feathers in an attempt to save face.

"You didn't need to look at him like that, Vypr," Robin admonishes me as she slides onto the bench with a wince, and I sit opposite her, putting down the cups of cala.

"Only Ayar and I get close to you," I growl unapologetically. "While you are healing," I add as an afterthought when she narrows her eyes at me.

Tiny but fierce.

She stares around at the hubbub of males, wing bumping, small scraps breaking out over nothing at all, all with a calm serenity on her face. She is unfazed by the life of the Gryn laid bare here.

"I never thought I'd miss things being busy." She shrugs as she sips her cala. "Or that I'd enjoy watching an entire crowd of males."

I hear someone growl and realize it's me.

"I didn't mean it like that." She laughs, a sound so delicious I wish I could consume her. "My job was all about observation. I was good at it."

Robin's out of her seat and sat next to me, snuggled up against my side as I wrap a wing around her. She holds her cup in two hands.

"Look at those two males over there, next to the food." She nods towards a couple of young mercs, relatively new to the eyrie. "They're going to squabble over a piece of meat, and then the taller one will let the other one have it."

I frown at her. "You can't possibly know that." I go back to watching the mercs.

Sure enough, they both reach for the same piece of maraha. The older of the two, and the taller, slams his wing into the younger. He squeaks but doesn't let go. They stare at each other for a short while, and then the older one releases the piece of food, smiles, and picks up another piece of his own.

"How...how did you know?"

"It's all about reading body language. I thought it would be different because we're different species, but I watched what was going on when I was in the surgery and started to pick up on what the Gryn do."

I shake my head in amazement. "You are something very special."

Robin drops her head, looking down at her cup. "I'm not, really."

"You are. For a start, you're incredible with Ayar. He's never been so calm."

"He ripped a door off its hinges." She looks up at me, the hint of a smile on her face.

"Before you, he'd have gone through the wall." I chuckle, although it is true.

"He needs to face what happened to him. There's another Ayar inside. I've seen him, one which has control. One who isn't so angry and terrified."

"I don't know if it's possible for him to do that, not anymore. The machine he mentions, it was truly terrible." I sigh. "And there's another complication."

"What?"

"Our seniors are not impressed with his little stunt which caused his recent injury. If there are any further incidents, he'll be out of the unit and back in the lair," I say, quietly.

If I thought it would help telling Robin, saying it out loud makes the whole situation seem impossible. Ayar needs to be well enough for the next mission, which he won't be if he keeps destroying the eyrie.

"How long have we got?" Robin asks, sitting up and looking me straight in the eye, her entire body vibrating with energy.

"Three turns."

Robin

Somehow, I've gone from being the human female in the corner to being the woman who saves a warrior.

A warrior who is presently spread eagled — literally — on the bed, snoring his head off.

Vypr stops dead as we enter and see Ayar's body.

"He sleeps," he says in a half whisper. "He actually sleeps." He turns to look at me.

"I don't want to come between you," I reply, quietly, not wanting to wake Ayar. "He is your mate, and I know he wanted me here. If you don't, I understand."

I'm saying something I don't believe in because I'm not sure I'm ready for whatever this is between us. It's intense, like Vypr, and chaos, like Ayar.

And I'm only just getting to grips with being abducted, smashed, and my long stay in the surgery. Do I want chaotic intensity?

"I want you here, Robin." Vypr turns me to face him. "And not just for Ayar. I don't know what this is, but somehow, he's never wrong about these things." He looks over at the rumbling male.

Ayar is an impressive starfish shape.

The chaos.

"He can be so...Ayar...all destruction and violence." Vypr drops his chin to his chest. "And then he can tell me how I'm feeling, and he's completely right. Almost like you and those mercs." He smiles at me. "Stay with us, Robin."

The intensity.

"I..." I search for the right words.

Words which will tell him how I feel.

Except I don't know how I feel.

"Stay with us, Robin," a sleepy voice calls out across the room.

Now I have two pairs of dark eyes trained on me, both wanting different things. Ayar just needs me. Vypr is more complex. He needs me too, for Ayar and for their future. He might need me in another way, but I don't think he's sure yet.

Ayar blinks at me, long and languid. He's the definition of relaxed. My stomach dips. I'm not sure I can imagine not seeing his eyes.

Or his impressive abs.

Or Vypr's handsome face...and equally impressive abs.

Way to go, Robin, thinking with your clit!

"I'm not going anywhere, Ayar." I smile at him and take the platter from Vypr. "We brought you something to eat, and it's time you ate."

I walk over to the bed as he heaves himself eagerly into a sitting position with a slight groan, one arm over his wound. My instincts tell me this male might, just might, be putting some of this on.

Is Ayar playing for my sympathy?

I put the tray down. He reaches for some of the food and winces, scrunching up his face impressively. Vypr thumps down next to us, grabs a large hunk of meat and hands it to Ayar with a sympathetic smile.

These two are literally their own worst enemies. Vypr because he indulges Ayar, and Ayar because he lets him. It's not doing them any favors.

Sometimes I wish I'd had as much clarity about Magnus as I do about everyone else and their relationships. Even aliens can be 'read.' It seems I can fix anyone except myself.

Because one part of me wants to believe Ayar and Vypr want me, for who I am. That they will behave honorably towards me, that I can feel safe with them.

Why is there a voice inside me shouting about time? Will time make any difference? My main concern has to be that I am the interloper here.

Right now, Ayar is lounging over Vypr, his head resting on Vypr's abdomen as he's fed morsels of meat from the larger chunk. They look so completely comfortable with each other, it causes my heart to stutter in my chest.

Ayar wants what he wants, but Vypr is different. He isn't sure what is going on between us, and I don't blame him. The last thing I want to do is tear them apart.

For me, any relationship has to be on my terms too. If I want a relationship at all, because, like Ayar, when I close my eyes, I still see my tormentor.

Demanding, shouting, cajoling. Hand raised. He didn't care for me, and I knew it.

He made me think so little of myself, I was prepared to let him treat me like dirt.

And I'm not sure I can go back to being that person. The one who pretended on the outside everything was fine, that she wasn't scared shitless and had it all together.

"I'm going to take the bath I was trying to have earlier when I was interrupted," I announce.

Still running away, Robin, just not so far.

"Can we bring your things in here?" Ayar asks, smiling widely.

"Do I have much choice? You ruined my door." I laugh at him.

Vypr raises his head from Ayar, a broad smile on his face. "We'll bring your things in here," he says, easily.

Ayar's eyes dance. He reaches out, and before I can move away, I'm snagged and pulled in next to him and Vypr.

"Hey!" I call out, wriggling but not making too much of an effort to get away because I'm trapped in a feather bed which smells completely delicious, all fresh, like a cat who's just finished grooming. "We need to talk about boundaries."

"All I want is for you to stay, Robin," Ayar says, with a serious look on his face. "Boundaries are not needed."

"I...will stay." I hesitate over whether I should use 'want.' I look up at Vypr. "I'll stay and help, like I said I would."

"Good," Vypr says. "Because this one needs a lot of helping." He rubs a huge, clawed hand over the uninjured part of Ayar's torso, and the male squirms happily.

"Then it's settled. Robin is moving in with us!" he says.

"And we have training this afternoon. You can sit out the combat training, but we have some weapons detail you can manage," Vypr says to him.

Ayar lets out a theatrical groan, eyes closed, hand over his abs.

"You're on you own with him until I get back from my bath." I giggle, and when Ayar opens one eye, I give him a wink, and his eyes twinkle because he's amused me.

There is so much more to Ayar than meets the eye.

Perhaps this won't be such a bad arrangement after all.

Ayar

When I woke to find my two favorite creatures in our nest, my heart did a funny thing. It did a little jump and my head stopped aching.

Without the ache, I could feel them both. Vypr, so serious and stoic. He wants the planet to be right, for us and for the Gryn. He wants much for everyone except himself. Robin is different, harder to read.

I know what I want. I want my mates, and I want her belly to swell with my youngling. And then Vypr sits next to me, and I'm lost in his scent and the food he has brought.

My head is happy, maybe clearer than it has been in a while, full of thoughts of mating, of being mated, of being a father and of the perfectly roasted maraha my Vypr has for me.

The only other thing I need is my Robin, and once she's in my arms, I am happy. Really happy.

And, as if a light has switched on, one of the artificial ones we get in the underground lairs, bright, beautiful, and *her*.

Robin likes me. I am important to her, but she's worried she can't help me control myself. She's worried Vypr might reject her if I have more problems. I don't like her being worried. Not one bit.

"I'm in control, aren't I?" I ask Vypr once Robin has left our nest to collect her things and head to the bath.

I lever myself up and get off the bed once I see her walk past the open door to our nest on her way to the healing pool.

"Where are you going?" Vypr queries.

"To bathe with Robin," I reply.

"No," he says, firmly, and my wing is grabbed, pulling me back to the bed. "Robin wants to bathe alone."

"She doesn't," I say, unhappily shaking my feathers at him.

"The thing you were saying about control? You don't have any." Vypr raises his eyebrows at me.

"I do. I didn't eat all of the maraha, even though I wanted to." I attempt to spin away, but he has my wing held firmly.

"How come I can't get you to take a bath, but you'll follow Robin without protest?" Vypr releases my wing but runs his hands through my feathers in a way he knows I can't resist.

"I wasn't going to go alone." I grin at him.

"See, no control at all." Vypr unfolds himself from the bed and wraps arms and wings around me, his head nuzzling into my neck as I melt onto him. "Is mating all you think about?"

"Not all. I think about you and Robin. I think about maraha and explosions."

Vypr snorts into my skin. "At the same time."

"Not at the same time, you vrexer." I snarl-laugh, pushing him away. "Do we really have to train today?"

"There's a mission you need to be on in three turns. We get to liberate some Drahon weapons from the Kijg."

"I'm there." I feel every feather on my wings begin to prick. "Absolutely, I'm there."

"Then you need to learn some control and do some serious healing." Vypr raises a clawed finger as I begin to protest. "That means light training, weapons detail, and a regular bath."

"And mating?"

Vypr shakes his wings. "You'll mate when I say. You'll mate when you show me what a good warrior you are," he intones.

And just like that, every single feather on my body flutters, wings shaking violently as they twirl themselves back into position. My abdomen spikes briefly with pain, and then it's gone in the bliss which follows the feather frenzy.

"Ayar, did you just rouse?" Vypr stares at me, like I've grown another head.

"Is that...was that...?" I stammer out.

Rousing is for happy males who don't have horrors in their minds. Rousing is what a Gryn does before he goes into battle because fighting is what we're born to do.

I think I've roused once during my time after the machine. I never rouse.

Except today, apparently, I do.

He wraps his arms around me.

"My brave warrior," he murmurs. Deep from within him, I feel something I've not felt for a long time.

Hope.

Vypr

Seeing Ayar rouse is incredible. As far as I'm aware, he's only ever roused once before. I rouse all the time. I struggle to stop myself some days.

But then my brain isn't fried like Ayar's.

And before, we hadn't met Robin. My stomach knots and unknots. For so long, my life has been about making Ayar happy and safe. Or at least as safe as Ayar can ever be. He is my mate, my *eregri*. My fate.

Something I had known from the moment we'd seen him on the machine. Like a laser bolt searing through me. In his own way, Ayar knew it too, allowing me to carry him to safety, letting me stay by his side until the day he slammed Orvos into the wall and threatened to disembowel him.

The day he was released into my care.

And now, with Robin in our arms, he's changed, and in a good way. Admittedly, we still need to work on his impulse control, given the state of the door to Robin's room. But if I didn't know better, I'd almost say he did it on purpose, so she had to stay with us.

But he doesn't have the capacity to be so sneaky, does he?

I watch him as he sits down on the bed, tucking back into the tray of food with gusto. It appears, despite his protestations, the thought of training appeals to him.

I should tell him about my conversation with Strykr. He would have been party to it had he been uninjured. However, I'm pretty sure I can imagine his response to being told he's at risk of being off the unit, and it wouldn't be pretty.

It would probably be self-destructive. But with Robin around, is it possible he could learn to control himself?

As I watch him polish off the remainder of the food, I wonder how he would react, if I should risk the resulting Ayar explosion. But then he lifts his head, wipes his mouth with the back of his hand, and smiles up at me.

A genuine smile, not his usual manic grin. As he smiles, he shifts to look behind me, and I turn to see Robin stood in the doorway, her hair wet, dark against her head, wearing only a towel.

Vrex! My cocks react immediately. She's so close to being unwrapped. So close I could mate her.

So close Ayar could mate her, fill her belly with a youngling, and make us parents.

"Ayar, come with me, and we'll get Robin's things, move them into the nest." I turn back to him, attempting to shift my cocks into a more comfortable position.

His eyes widen, and he palms his crotch. I shake my head slowly at him.

"Training first," I murmur, and he growls low, feral at me.

I return his growl, grabbing his wing and pulling him to me. He stares at me, then lowers his eyes a fraction.

"Yes, Vypr."

Having moved Robin's few belongings into our nest, Ayar helps to arrange them to their mutual satisfaction. I can't help but enjoy watching my huge, scarred warrior gently and carefully folding her clothes, doing his level best to keep his claws retracted. From the way he holds his wings, he's enjoying himself, and what's more, he is beautifully calm.

"Training," I say, and he straightens.

"Robin comes," he replies.

"What?"

"If I'm training, Robin comes with us." He folds his arms over his chest, emphasizing the large plaster on his abdomen.

Such a stubborn warrior.

"Have you asked Robin if she wants to come to training?" Robin says, her eyes twinkling with mirth at my Ayar.

"Oh, er..." Suddenly, my fearsome warrior dips his head, his hair in his eyes. "Robin?" He's hesitant, not quite able to look her in the eye. "Do you want to come?" His hopefulness sends a frisson of love through my heart.

Robin looks over at me, a smile curling her sweet mouth. I nod my agreement. She steps closer to him, one hand on his broad, scarred chest. "I'd love to."

He nearly explodes with joy. I seize the moment. In two steps, I have Robin in my arms and Ayar on my heels. In a couple more paces, we're out in the air, circling the atrium.

"Is this okay?" I murmur in her ear.

"Is it okay? This is amazing!" Robin replies with a laugh which warms my soul. "I've always wanted to fly like this!"

Ayar hears it too, and the big warrior swirls around us in a riot of feathers before letting out a whoop like a youngling and diving down towards the ground. I increase my grip on my Robin and follow him as she shrieks with delight, arms around my neck and the scent of her, heady and intoxicating, in my nostrils. I land with a thump.

"I'd hold you forever," I murmur in her ear. "And fly with you anywhere."

"Vypr?" She puts her hand on my cheek, bright eyes boring into mine. "Do you mean that?"

I clear my throat, suddenly aware of Ayar's gaze on me too. "Of course."

Because…I do. I want Robin and Ayar in my life.

"Training," Ayar says, but there's a smile on his face which is slightly annoying.

It's as if he planned this. But Ayar doesn't plan.

"Training," I growl at the pair of them as I lower Robin to the ground. "Nothing else until training is complete."

From the grins on both their faces, this is going to be an interesting, and short, training session.

Ayar

Huntr and Syn are in the training area. I scent them before I see them. They smell bitter to me, not unpleasant, but they are males who have their own problems, and right now, I have mates to protect.

Plus, apparently, I'm not supposed to be fighting while I'm healing, which means I don't get to go in the pit. I have energy to expend, and I know how I want to expend it.

"Stop growling," Vypr says in my ear. "Go see Jay and Mylo in the range. Take Robin with you."

I hadn't even realized I was growling, but I stop immediately. I love my weapons and nothing will be more fun than showing them to Robin, especially with Jay. He's my favorite. Eagerly, I grab Robin's hand and head through, past the pits which stink of males, and farther into the depths of the eyrie until we reach the range.

It's nice and dark in here, save for a table lit by artificial downlight where two of my fellow warriors stand, poring over the weapons. Jay and Mylo look up as we approach, and I see they have a rifle and a laser cannon in pieces.

"Ayar!" Jay exclaims, smiling broadly. "How are you, brother?" He eyes my plaster. He was the only one of the unit not present when I had my accident.

"Could still take you, you vrexer," I growl.

"What Ayar means is he's on the mend," Robin says from my side.

Jay and Mylo grin at her and my feathers prick.

"Hi, Jay," she adds, and I'm rattling them now. "How's Lauren?"

She knows Jay's mate. Jay is a mated male. Jay is not a threat.

"She's fine, doing well. We didn't know you were out of the surgery," Jay says as I slow my shaking wings.

"Orvos finally let me out, but only because I promised to look after this one." Robin puts a hand on my arm, and it's everything I can do not to press a human kiss on her pretty face. Something tells me to follow her lead and be calm.

"You're looking after Ayar?" Mylo asks. "Good luck with that." He laughs. "He's likely to destroy, explode, or otherwise cause mayhem, probably the next turn or so."

"Vrexer," I mutter. "Just because I like a good explosion doesn't mean I cause them all."

"I'm Mylo. The combat master and handsome Gryn of the unit." He extends his hand to Robin in the greeting we were taught by the Guv's mate, Kat.

I growl.

Mylo is an unmated mate. Mylo is a threat.

Robin takes his hand, shakes it, and Mylo's eyes flicker to me. With everything I have, I hold on to my desire to remove his hand from his body. He releases her instantly, his wing feathers tightening.

The sturdy combat master has taught me a trick or two in fighting. He can easily have me on my back as much as I can floor him. Any other time, I'd have him in the pit. Except I have Robin with me, and I have this vrexing plaster on my stomach, reminding me of my own stupidity.

I can't protect my mates if I'm injured.

"What are you doing, Jay?" I rasp, getting myself back under enough control I can speak. I reach out and pull Robin close to me, inhaling her scent to calm myself.

"This rifle and this cannon are misfiring. Mylo and I are trying to work out why," Jay says.

"Let me look. I'm restricted to vrexing weapons duty anyway," I say.

"Are these actual laser guns?" Robin peers at the parts on the tables. "Proper, real life lasers?"

Jay laughs as I look at her quizzically. "Humans don't have laser guns, Lauren told me," he says. "You have them in moovies." He struggles with the word I don't recognize.

I look over the parts. It's pretty obvious what the problem is, and with a few small adjustments, I put the weapons back together and carry them over to the range, firing first the rifle multiple times and then the cannon. There are no misfires.

Jay snatches up the rifle, and after shifting the sight, he repeats my experiment with a perfect volley of pinpoint accuracy.

Show off.

"Ayar, you genius!" Mylo claps me on my shoulder, and I cringe a little at his touch because I've never been one for touching or wing bumps. "We've been trying to work out a fix for the last half a turn."

"Can I have a go?" Robin asks, making Mylo remove his hand. I turn to see not only Robin but my Vypr stood in the doorway to the range.

Their presence is a balm to any fractured nerves I might have by being here.

"Sure," I say to her and beckon her forward. I pick up the lighter laser rifle and hand it to her. "Jay should have set the sights." I check over my shoulder, and he nods with an indulgent smile I ignore. "The targets move around, but you can just aim at the one in the middle. It never moves."

I shift my position until I'm behind her and gently nudge her forward into position. She lifts the rifle to her shoulder, presumably because she saw me doing the same. I take hold of her arm and hand, wrapping her in a slightly deadly embrace.

"To fire, press your finger on the pad underneath." I find myself whispering gently into her ear, my hands curling around hers on the rifle. Huge, scarred and clawed over her soft, small, pink ones.

Robin's scent fills my every sense. Knowing Vypr is behind us, watching, makes it even better. I don't even attempt to hide my arousal from her, pressing my hard cocks against her delicious bottom. I want her to know how I feel. I want Vypr to know too.

She stills for half a second, or maybe less. I'm too drunk on her to know exactly, and then she presses the trigger. Moving the rifle precisely, easily, she hits all the targets and the middle one. The range flashes orange to show she scored a complete cycle.

Jay makes a low whistling sound.

"Beginner's luck!" Mylo scoffs.

Robin presses herself back into me, grinding slightly over my cocks, which very nearly go off in my pants at the aroma of her arousal.

"I'm not a beginner," she says quietly. "I have weapons training. Human weapons, but point and shoot appears to be the same, whatever the ordinance."

I hear the smile in her voice, and my pride at her radiates through me. My Robin is full of fun secrets. She likes weapons, she likes me, and she likes Vypr.

She wants to stay with us, and I need to make sure she does.

"Well done, Robin," he says, coming up behind me. One hand runs through my feathers, and my cocks grow even harder. I'm unable to stop a low, rumbling groan emanating from somewhere at the bottom of my belly.

"Ayar's fixed these weapons up," Jay says, happily, taking the rifle from Robin. "Are you coming on the next mission?" he asks me.

I look over my shoulder at Vypr.

"Ayar has some healing to do, but you know the Guv wants him on this one," Vypr says.

He thinks I don't know when he's keeping things from me, but I do. It's in the subtle twitches of his mouth and the sparks in his eyes. I've known there was a secret since he came back from the meeting this morning and now it's out.

He's worried I won't be well enough to go on the mission. Which will not be the case. I always go on the mission.

"I'll be fine." I fluff up my feathers. Making my wings seem as big as possible, I stalk past my comrades and out into the central training arena.

Huntr is still in the pit, his chest heaving with repressed anger. He wants the fight. It pours from him. He welcomes all pain because he's in great pain.

The fight. I love the fight. It makes me feel alive. I extend my wings to get his attention. Huntr sees me, beckons me, and I take a step towards the pit.

"Can you show me around a little?" Robin's voice intrudes on my need to fight.

An arm slips around mine. Vypr stands next to her, his arm already in hers.

"I've been cooped up in the surgery since I got here, and I've hardly seen anything of Ustokos," she adds, entwining her fingers with mine and reminding me of just how hard my cocks were only moments ago.

She's here, with my Vypr, and she wants us to be together.

"Not today," I call out to Huntr. "I'm healing. I'll spar with you soon."

"What do you want to see first?" Vypr asks Robin.

"Surprise me!"

Robin

Heaven knows how Vypr kept tabs on Ayar. The male is absolutely a force entirely of his own. He seemed happy enough with the weapons, getting into close proximity with me and a rifle. It had a very interesting effect on his anatomy.

And on me. If I thought my desire, my delight in having glorious sex with Ayar and Vypr was a one off, I was wrong. My body sang with his touch, not just his hands, but the enormous members which pressed against me, reminding me, from the subtle burn still lingering, how much he'd pleasured me.

At the same time, I felt Vypr's presence again, watching, waiting. Directing.

Ayar stalks out of the range in a huff as Vypr stands beside me.

"We should go after him." I look up at the big, dark warrior. I can't quite read the expression on his face.

"I should tell him what the Guv said," he says, quietly. "I shouldn't keep it from him."

"Then tell him." I look over my shoulder at Jay and Mylo, who are engrossed in the work Ayar did on the weapons. "He deserves to know what's at risk. You can't always be there to save him. He has to learn to make the right choices."

I haven't known either Ayar or Vypr long, but their relationship is complicated, and as much as I have a strange desire, a strange pull, towards both of them, they have history which needs to be addressed.

"I'm sorry if that sounds harsh," I add. "Sometimes, when we love someone, we make the wrong choices, even if we think it's best for them."

Suddenly, in a flurry of feathers, I'm caged against the crumbling wall behind me, a pair of big, dark eyes boring into mine.

Vypr's chest heaves.

"You're the key. Your scent..." He closes his gorgeous eyes and inhales. "I didn't ever expect to find another like Ayar. I don't even begin to understand what this is between us all," Vypr confesses, and then he trails his lips over my cheek until he reaches my lips, brushing there for an instant as lust pulses inside me. "But he needs you."

"And what about you? What do you need?" My voice is a mere rasp.

I don't know what I'm getting into with these two males, but I can't remember if anyone ever needed me. *Really* needed me. Robin.

Sure, Magnus wanted me, used me, abused me. My family wanted me to be able to borrow, beg, and steal for them, to provide free labor. But no one ever needed me.

"I need Ayar to be happy and healthy." Vypr's lips brush the shell of my ear. His hands are in my hair, pinpricks of his claws on my scalp. "And I need you by my side."

His answer isn't everything I wanted, but the way he touches me tells me he hasn't yet decided what he wants.

And I want Ayar to be happy and healthy, too. He has

somehow crept into my heart and made it his home. I can't imagine being without him.

Or Vypr.

But he's still a closed book, and I'm not going to push at him because I've learnt pushing just causes more pain. I have to keep my heart caged, like I am in Vypr's fragrant feathers, until I know I can release it.

With every single passing second, my life is changing, and perhaps things should slow down because racing towards the light is never a good idea. I duck under his feathers to follow the direction Ayar took.

Outside of the darkened range, I see Ayar staring down into a shallow depression where another warrior bristles. As I walk towards him, Vypr at my back, I see the warrior beckon Ayar as he opens his wings.

"Vrex it! He's going to fight Huntr," Vypr hisses and takes a step in front of me.

Without thinking, I put out my arm and slip it through his, falling in beside him and making it to Ayar who is just about to drop into the depression.

"Can you show me around a little?" I ask him, with a glance at Vypr. "I've been cooped up in the surgery since I got here, and I've hardly seen anything of Ustokos." I hold my breath as I slide my hand down the corded muscles of Ayar's arm and take his hand.

Maybe it isn't enough, but I don't want him hurt again. Not in a way which will ensure my own safety, like I always was with Magnus, walking on glass. I want Ayar to remain unharmed for himself and for Vypr, who remains tense beside me.

Ayar turns his scarred face towards me, and his wings lower.

"Not today," he says to the other warrior. "I'm healing. I'll spar with you soon."

The big scarred warrior turns his entire attention on me.

"What do you want to see first?" Vypr asks.

I contemplate my options. I'm on a brand new planet and, with these two males, my options are infinite.

"Surprise me!" I say and find myself scooped off my feet yet again, this time by Ayar.

He buries his head in my hair, inhaling deeply, and strides out of the underground part of the eyrie until we're back in the atrium, in the air and firing out of an exit into the clouded sky outside. He beats hard to gain height, and I'm crying out in delight as he spins around the outside of the eyrie.

"Do you like flying, my Robin?" he murmurs in my ear.

"You've no idea!" My heart is in my throat, delighting in his proximity, adrenaline pumping at being in the air with him and Vypr, who keeps easy pace with us, his presence reassuring as I'm dangling hundreds of feet up in the sky.

I'm laughing now, as we swoop down low, skimming over the ruins of the city. My curiosity is piqued, not just by these two males but by what I see below me. A city destroyed and a species on the rise.

"Robin!" I spin on the spot when I hear Diana's voice as Vypr lands with me in his arms.

Both Ayar and Vypr took it in turns to fly me around over the former city of Kos, one of the major cities of the Gryn civilization, when there was one. Ayar took the lion's share of flying with me. At my request, he even slung me underneath him, so I could spread my arms wide and stare down at the ground as we swooped and swirled, dove, and climbed.

Vypr was not amused. Apparently, he thinks flying like that, with me, is dangerous. I disagreed.

Finally, my rumbling stomach had us all returning to the eyrie in search of food.

"I'll meet you at the food hall," I say to the two males as I take a few paces towards Diana. Ayar emits a low growl. "Ayar, it's Diana. You met her when you wrenched the door from its hinges."

His dark look lifts slightly. "Was she the one in distress?" he asks.

"No, that was Jen."

"Oh." Ayar nods sagely, clearly unable to distinguish Diana from Jen even though despite my clarification.

"I'll be fine with Diana. Go and get some food and make sure you save some for me."

Ayar still hesitates, his wings raised as he contemplates the other woman. Vypr curls a hand around his arm, and he turns to look at him. "Come," Vypr says, his eyes raking over Ayar, his voice the deepest of midnights.

As Ayar follows him, I'm very tempted to follow, too. It's hard to resist a voice so delicious I could almost spread it on toast and eat it.

"How are you doing?" Diana asks once Vypr and Ayar have departed, however unwillingly.

"I'm doing much better now I'm out of the surgery."

"I meant with those two." She lowers her voice.

I'm not entirely sure what to say. I stopped having friends when Magnus got to me. I can't remember the last time I had a heart-to-heart with a friend, and yet Diana and I have been through so much together. If I can't talk to her, who can I talk to?

"I love spending time with them." I sink down onto a nearby crumbling ledge, some way from the open hole in the eyrie wall where we landed. Diana sits beside me, her face a picture of concern, like it was when I first opened my eyes in the surgery. "Whatever Jen said about Ayar, he's a mixed up male who's been through so much. You can't judge him by what he says and does or what he looks like."

"I would never do that," Diana says, immediately. "I think we were more concerned for you. Jen and I know how frightened you were when you first arrived."

I sigh. She's right. The thought of being surrounded by males was awful at first. All I had was a head full of him, my tormentor, Magnus. He had made my life such a misery if I mentioned any other men. But then he just made my life a misery, period.

"I was, but…I trust them, Ayar and Vypr. I don't…I can't explain it. I just do. They make me feel…" I hesitate.

"Look, sweetheart." Diana takes my closed hand in hers, her skin warm against mine, and the gesture is so lovely, tears prick my eyelids. "We're not going home. We're stuck here on this planet. Even if the Gryn had the capability to take us back to Earth, they're not going to waste the resources, however honorable they claim to be."

"I'm not bothered about going home," I say quickly. Too quickly perhaps? But it's my instant reaction.

I don't want to go back to Earth.

"Good. Then you need to make the best of what we have here, whatever that is. Just be careful." Her eyes are full of pain. "Please be careful. There are so few of us here, I can't imagine what it would be like to lose any more humans." She lets out a harsh laugh which is more of a sob.

"You've not heard about Freya?" It's my turn to take her hand in mine, holding her tightly.

Diana shakes her head, her mouth set in a hard line. "It's as if she vanished into thin air."

"If she was with you, she's got to be somewhere the Gryn can find her."

"I'm working on it," Diana says, her eyes taking on a mysterious quality.

"Are you?"

"Don't come all Miss Marple with me, *Agatha*." Diana laughs. She loves the idea of my investigative profession. "Anyway, it looks like you're wanted." She nods over my shoulder, and I turn to see Ayar stood at the far end of the corridor, hands by his sides, wings high. He looks pensive. "Guess he can't eat without you."

I smile and shake my head. "He is an honorable male, just one who likes blowing things up."

Diana's eyes widen as it's my turn to laugh. I give her hand one last squeeze and get to my feet.

"I'm on my way, Ayar," I call out. "Don't worry about me, Diana. I think I'm going to be fine."

Vypr

We didn't make it to the food hall before Ayar wanted to go back for Robin. I don't blame him. I didn't want to leave her alone either, not in the eyrie full of other males, despite the fact she was with another human.

It's instinct for a Gryn to want to protect his mate, and I'm feeling the same pull to Robin as I feel to Ayar. Except Ayar is my *eregri*, my fate. How can Robin possibly fit into what he is to me?

So much of Gryn social history has been lost. Most of us were younglings when we lost our females, and few of us remember much beyond glimpses of mating behavior. Male and female Gryn have always preened each other, spent time together, been together, that I know. But did Gryn ever take more than one mate?

But as soon as I see Ayar walking up the ramp with Robin by his side, his hand in hers, my heart leaps into my throat. The pair of them, together. They are all I ever wanted.

"Ayar thinks I'm hungry." Robin raises her eyebrows at me. "Apparently, that's the reason he came back."

"Are you?" I ask her.

She inclines her head and looks up at us from underneath long lashes, her pretty mouth pouting. "I guess I am, and I wasn't doing any flying." She laughs. "So you two must be starving!"

"I am." Ayar sweeps an arm around her and one around me. "Let's eat!"

He was never a male to hold back. Ayar lives large with everything he has, mating and eating included. I find myself wishing we were up in our nest as he piles the table with food he likes. I want to take Robin onto my lap, have him by my side as we consume our meal, but despite the food hall being quiet, it's not something I'm going to do. That sort of intimacy is for a nest.

"Are you sure you've eaten enough?" Ayar asks Robin for the thousandth time.

"Ayar, if I have any more, I'm going to burst!" Robin pats her little rounded stomach, and my cocks leap into overdrive at the action. "You literally cannot put another morsel inside me."

Immediately, her cheeks begin to go pink as she looks over at me. I'm not entirely sure what the coloration means, but her gorgeous face looks even more delectable. Our female requires mating.

"We need to return to the nest," I announce, although it will mean I have to stand up, and given my level of arousal, I'm sure Robin will know exactly why we need to go.

A scent fills the air. Ayar lifts his head. Robin wants to be mated. By both of us. Ayar stands, his glorious cocks clearly outlined through his maraha hide pants.

I have to mate them both.

"Now," I growl.

Instantly, Ayar has Robin in his arms, striding across the food hall. He's in the air in seconds, and I'm so close behind, I'm almost on top of them.

I land and stride ahead into our nest. My cocks are so hard, I'm stripping off my boots and pants as soon as I enter. Behind me, Ayar kisses Robin and lowers her down his chest to the floor. She stands, hand on his chest, eyes half lidded with desire.

"Are you ready to mate my Ayar, Robin?" I rasp. "Are you ready to breed with him? Take everything his cocks can give you?"

She shudders in his arms, and Ayar moans gently. I see his cocks pushing painfully at the maraha hide of his pants. The pair of them seem almost paralyzed with desire. So I walk over and run my hand through Ayar's wing feathers. He vibrates with lust.

"Take off your coverings," I tell Robin, who breathes out, long and low, before she lifts her top over her head and reveals the strange thing covering her beautiful breasts. A single claw deals with it, and it drops away, showing her off to Ayar.

He still hasn't moved, mesmerized by my removal of Robin's clothing. I gently stroke down his chest, over his abdomen. His breath hitches as I touch his plaster, and his eyes clear slightly. "You are to be careful, my *eregri*," I warn him as I reach his waistband, slowly unclipping his mag catch and pulling his pants down to reveal his glorious cocks.

Ayar makes a strangled sound as I stroke him, one cock in each hand. He sways on his feet, a groan escaping his lips at my touch.

"Still clothed?" I ask Robin, who cannot take her eyes off where I'm touching Ayar, my own cocks pressing against his hip, my pre-cum dripping onto him. "We need you naked."

Almost in a trance, Robin removes her footwear and shoves down her pants. She's finally revealed to us. Her feminine body, all curves, her sweet little pussy, which I am dying to taste, guarded by a slight wisp of fluff. Her aroma, all ripe, perfect, and ready hits Ayar and me at the same time, and we release identical groans of delight.

"What are you going to do with this little morsel of a female, Ayar?" I murmur in his ear, pumping his cocks. "I think you're going to eat her. But first, you have to show her how it's done."

His dark eyes are torn away from the trembling female in front of us. They meet mine. He's desperate for relief, and he knows he cannot have it. Not yet.

With a low rumble, he drops to his knees, grasps my cocks, and sucks them down his beautiful throat as I roar my approval.

Robin

I didn't intend finding myself naked with two equally as bare Gryn warriors so soon, but their scent is quite simply too intoxicating to think straight. Their feathers, as they shift, release a smell reminiscent of warm baking, but both Ayar and Vypr together, their spicy musky scent, I could drown in it, and perhaps I can.

Vypr growls at Ayar and he drops to his knees. My core pulses in response to the growl and to the action. My thighs are slippery with my need as I watch him take hold of both Vypr's cocks and wrap his mouth around them.

Ayar sucks Vypr in deep, cheeks hollowing as he works the big warrior. Vypr stares down at him, one hand on Ayar's wing and the other on his head.

"Touch yourself," he orders me. "Show me us what you like, and we will make you scream our names." He groans as Ayar takes him deeper, one hand working his cocks, and the other caressing his full balls.

I let my hand drift down my abdomen and over my mound, slipping a single finger between my folds. I feel incredibly self-conscious. And incredibly turned on.

"Too slow, little Robin," Vypr growls, and I feel a rush of moisture at the rumble which vibrates through me. "I need to see you. Part your legs."

"Oh god!" I groan, throwing my head back, my entire body shaking as I make my stance wider and delve inside myself, my thumb rubbing at my clit.

"Vrex the goddess!" Ayar lifts his head from where he's working at Vypr's cocks to see me, fingers deep inside, slick with my juices.

"You're going to mate this wanton female, Ayar. You're going to fill her with your seed until she grows round with your youngling, and I mate you hard," Vypr rasps. "Do you want to be mated and bred, little Robin?"

"I don't..." I find myself on my back on the bed, with Ayar staring down at me, his dark eyes even darker than usual.

"I will only mate you if you want me," he says, his words barely understandable as they catch in his chest. "But I want you, I want to be in you. I want us all to be together," he breathes.

I reach up and touch his face, brushing his long hair out of his eyes, his beautiful eyes, as I see Vypr through his wings, held out, hovering, the long feathers shaking slightly.

"I want you. Both of you."

Ayar closes his eyes and inhales deeply.

"She will be tight, my mate," Vypr says. "Maybe too tight for your cocks. You need to prepare her."

At his order, Ayar drops down over my body. Taking a single nipple in his mouth, he sucks the tight peak, causing sweet agony to fire through me as he hums with delight.

"Lower, my mate. She needs your attention lower," Vypr growls. He pumps his cocks, which drip copiously with pre-cum.

Ayar releases my nipple reluctantly but trails his lips down my stomach until he reaches my pussy. In a swift movement, he parts my thighs and drops his head between my legs, running a rough tongue deep between my folds and up to my clit.

Unable to help myself, my hips fire up at him, and I squeak with delight.

"Vypr, she has a special place," he rumbles, the vibrations this time going straight to my 'special place.'

"Do you want me to touch your special place?" Vypr asks, his voice suddenly soft.

Ayar stutters over my clit as Vypr grasps the shoulders of both of his wings and gets in close, his clawed hands sliding down the feathers, making a sound like silk over silk until they disappear and instead, Ayar moans over me.

"Good warrior," Vypr growls. "Now make sure Robin is ready to receive your cocks."

Ayar laps through my folds once again until his tongue reaches my clit, and he circles it, slowly, testing my reactions, his eyes never leaving mine as he splays a huge onyx clawed hand over my stomach. Lips purse and he's sucking with a fervor I've never had from any human man. He delights in me, breaking off only when I scream his name and my entire body convulses with an orgasm to end all orgasms.

But he's not done. A thick tongue laps up everything, and he groans with delight.

"Robin, you taste like ambrosia," he murmurs, sliding in two thick fingers, eyes widening as I pulse over him.

"Is her sweet cunt soaking for you, Ayar? Is Robin ready to receive you? Because it's time you were mated, my gorgeous warrior." Vypr shudders behind him.

"She is delicious, my Vypr. I want to mate her. I want to fill her so much." Ayar lifts himself over me.

"Take me, Ayar," I murmur, only just able to speak.

He slides his arms under my thighs and lifts me up. All I

can see is endless abs, huge wings, and dark eyes. Something absolutely huge probes at my entrance.

"By the goddess, you are tight." Ayar throws his head back and his hips fire towards me.

With all the lubrication he drew out of me, the huge heads of his cocks breach me, and he slides in with the most tremendous, delicious stretch. I feel every single ridge, every single node, my breath stuttering with the perfection, the sting and the closeness of Ayar. I'm grasping at his shoulders, his wings, and I press my lips to his as he closes his eyes in pleasure.

"So full!" I whisper, because my voice has all but deserted me in the face of my two glorious warriors.

"Look at Robin taking both your cocks," Vypr murmurs, his dark eyes staring at where Ayar and I are joined. "Look at how you're filling her."

"Vypr..." Ayar pulls out and thrusts back in, causing both of us to pant and me to moan, because even such a swift action sends pleasure curling through me.

"I'm going to mate you, Ayar, while you mate our gorgeous Robin. Are you ready?"

Before I can take in what he's saying, he's positioned himself behind Ayar, and I feel his muscular body tense, then relax. He lets out a long, long breath.

I touch his face, and I see his pupils, dark inside the deep liquid of his eyes.

"Slowly," Vypr says, his teeth gritted, and he starts to move behind Ayar, who circles his hips, making me moan.

"I can't do slow." Ayar gazes down at me. "Our female needs this hard and fast."

I can't do anything but moan his name and reach up so I can grab Vypr's hand, which sits on his shoulder. Ayar withdraws from me and thumps back, making me see the stars above. Stars I don't recognize, not anymore, but it doesn't matter because I have these two males, two aliens, two mates who only want to be in this moment, with each other and with me.

This time, when my climax hits, I think I might pass out, each and every nerve firing as convulsions take me, my core pulsing as if I've never come before. Above me, Ayar and Vypr roar in unison as they orgasm, Ayar filling me with hot cum and a new, burning, spiking stretch as I'm suddenly fuller than ever.

He drops down over me, skin damp, and I brush my lips over his, kissing my alien angel, who wants to be bad but in fact is the sweetest male anyone could meet. Vypr crashes down next to us, and I turn to kiss him. His sensual lips give beautifully, returning my kiss with a deep passion before he pulls away, grabs Ayar, and kisses him too.

I am unbound by the perfectness of Vypr and Ayar.

Ayar

I'm surrounded by all the scents I love. My Vypr, my Robin, mating. Beneath me, the little female lies, her chest heaving, her gorgeous breasts undulating. Vypr drops next to us, kissing first her, then me. I'm overwhelmed by calmness, reveling in filling Robin to the absolute brim with seed from both my cocks and to the intense pleasure of mating and being mated.

I don't want to crush her, and although my cocks are still hard, I try to withdraw.

I can't.

Beside me, Vypr chuckles.

"You are locked, my mate." He brushes his hand over my hair and into my wings, looking down at Robin. "Your secondary cock has swollen inside this gorgeous, ripe, little female, to keep your seed inside her.

"Locked?" Robin's eyes are wide. "For how long?"

"Not long, sweet Robin. Long enough to ensure your belly is filled," Vypr tells her, running a knuckle down her cheek.

She looks between the two of us.

"I guess this is really happening, isn't it?" she says, her voice quiet. "I'm really with you both."

I look at Vypr. I knew from the moment I awakened in the surgery Robin would be part of our lives, but I know now, only because my mind is strangely clear, Vypr has been reluctant.

"We want you, Robin, if you want us," Vypr says, and my heart jumps up, up into my throat, as if it wants to see for itself the beauty unfolding here and now. "We are honorable males. We would not make you do anything you didn't want to do."

I stare down at the delicate creature under me, filled with my seed. My Robin. I want to protect her until the end of my days.

"You are ours, Robin. And we are yours," I murmur, rubbing the silky strands of her hair through my fingers. Its texture is fascinating, delicious, calming. "Let us keep you safe. Let us pleasure you and fill you with young."

She puts one hand on my cheek, and the other, she runs through Vypr's feathers.

"I got hurt when I was on Earth. It's made things difficult for me with males, with trust. I want to be with you, I do."

"Then we take it one day at a time, *eregri*," Vypr says. This time, my heart almost skips a beat when he calls her our fated mate. "And see what time brings."

ROBIN IS NESTLED BETWEEN VYPR AND ME. SHE sleeps soundly, the hint of a smile on her sweet, pretty face. I can't quite stop myself from touching her hair, her skin, just her, even while she is asleep.

"Is everything okay?" Vypr asks me, his fingers tripping through my feathers, covering our mate. "You seem quiet."

So often, I struggle with words and emotions, but mating has brought me clarity. Except it's not the sort of clarity I welcome.

"What if..." My words catch in my throat because if I say them out loud, I make my fears real.

Vypr shifts, not enough to disturb the sleeping Robin, but enough so he can stare into my eyes. "Go on."

"What if, after everything Proto did to me...I can't have younglings?" I say in a rush, forcing all the emotion out, trying to get it away from me to stave off the inevitable headache.

"You really want a youngling, don't you, my mate?" Vypr's voice is soft. The voice he uses to calm me and to pleasure me. He traces a path down the ridge of my wing.

"I've never thought about it before." Vypr's concern spears through me. "If we'd not met Robin, I never would have considered it." I look down at our mate. "But with her, it's what I want." I reach out and take his chin, running my thumb over his skin. "Say you want to mate her, too. Say you want to fill her womb like I do. Then we know we'll have a youngling, our youngling." The words tumble out, easily, not jumbled.

"Providing it's what Robin wants, I'll mate her too, my warrior." Vypr takes hold of my hand, running his rough thumb over my gnarled hands, up to my claws. "You know I'd do anything for you."

I seize his hand in mine. "And I would die for you, my mate. It will always be you and Robin. You are my beating heart."

Vypr's eyes widen. "Is that how you feel, Ayar?" he breathes.

"My *eregri*," I reply, as I touch my lips to his.

I've wanted so many things since the day I was freed from the nightmare. Mostly to be safe or free of pain. I liked and disliked. But now, since my mating with Vypr and Robin, a nuance is creeping back into my soul.

Not only can I feel more, but I know what I want.

And it's to be with them, always.

Vypr

Ayar rumbles a snore beside me. Lying on his back, arms, legs, and wings spread wide, he is thoroughly mated.

I'd like to join him in sleep, but I can't help thinking about his desire for a youngling. And his fears Proto might have robbed him of the chance to fill Robin with his young.

I don't want to take it from him, and whatever Ayar wants, Ayar always gets.

A smaller form shifts, and there are a pair of bright blue eyes fixed on mine. Robin watches. She watches because it's what she does.

"Go to sleep, little mate," I whisper at her.

All she does is shift closer to me, her cool body against mine. Humans are not as warm as Gryn, and I want to make sure she's warm, so I lift her up onto my stomach and fold a wing over her.

Now I have a soft, warm, tiny human draped over me. One who has all the scent of Ayar, all the scent of me, and something entirely unique to her. Something irresistible. Someone who needs to be filled.

"Is his seed still dripping from you?" I rasp. "Let me check." I run my hand over her back, her plump buttock and down, skirting over her sweet pucker until I find her pussy. It's slick, wet, and open because Ayar is a huge male.

Robin's breath stutters as I dip in a finger.

"I think you need more mating, sweet Robin. I think you want to be filled by me as well as by Ayar, and I want to be sheathed in you while you're full of his seed."

"Yes, Vypr," she murmurs.

"You're a needy little thing, aren't you?" I push her down my abdomen where my cocks are already waiting for her. It's no surprise when they slide straight in, she's been so well prepared. "Ayar wants to fill your belly, but I need to make sure you grow round with a youngling, for him."

I thrust up, lifting her from my chest, fondling her gorgeous breasts, and it's my turn for breathing to become difficult.

Being inside Robin is something else entirely. She's tight but slippery at the same time. I'm sheathed in her. She fits me like nothing else. Nothing else I've ever experienced. She is new and beautiful as she rises over me, taking me deep inside her.

I risk a glance at Ayar, expecting him to still be asleep, but a pair of dark eyes are following our every move. He's willing me to do this, to mate her. To fill her.

"Vypr!" Robin groans my name as my hips flip up at her.

I normally have every level of control, but with Ayar watching and the heat of Robin surrounding me, I can't hold. I can't stop and, as she suddenly starts pulsing over me, I find myself filling her, my secondary cock swelling inside her until we are stuck, fast.

My breath is ragged with my release as Robin topples onto me, her sweetness filling my every sense. Our mating was vrexing perfection.

Beside me, Ayar chuckles, and a hand rakes through my wing.

Ayar didn't even protest when, on waking, we left a fully mated Robin in the furs and I took him for a bath. Not a single complaint, and he even got into the water first.

The three of us being mated obviously agrees with him. And I can't deny, mating last night was something else entirely. Something perfect. Being able to touch Robin's soft skin, drink in her delectable fragrance as Ayar plundered her little body. The taste of her on my tongue. The enjoyment of her long, sensual kisses, all of which I also love seeing her lavish on Ayar.

If I thought I would be happy with one contented mate, I was wrong. I am the happiest I've ever been with two contented mates.

One of which is merrily splashing his way around the healing pool like a youngling. Something I've never seen him do. Which means, of course, I have to jump in with him.

"Come here!" I growl, and Ayar laughs, swishing through the water to get away from me, until I grab a wing and tow him back. "You're in a good mood," I murmur in his ear as I clutch his back to my chest and seat myself on an underwater shelf.

Picking up a cleansing bar, I work it over the skin on his shoulders, keeping a close watch on where I touch his scarring because he's sensitive.

"I am in a good mood, aren't I?" Ayar says, rumbling with enjoyment at my touch. "I even like my bath this morning."

I spin him in the water, and he straddles my lap. He bites his lower lip as I work my way over his abdomen, avoiding his plaster, and down to his cocks, both of which are ready and erect for me. He grunts and shoves them into my hands as I ensure they are fully cleansed.

"I was thinking Robin might like to see more of Ustokos today," he says, his breath hitching slightly as I cup him, squeezing gently.

"She might. I was thinking you performed well in training and when we flew yesterday. If we have a trial run today and you're okay, we should be good for the mission," I tell him, giving his cocks a couple of extra strokes before spinning him around again, with a smack on his glorious ass. "What do you think?"

"I think there's a trading post out there with our names on it!" Ayar says, enthusiastically.

He actually wants to go out and not damage things. Possibly even spend time around other organics, even though he normally hates crowds. If this continues, I won't ever have to tell him about the risk to his position in the unit. It won't even matter because he will be able to continue being the best warrior I know he can be.

"Then, as long as Robin wants to go, we'll go," I say, his happiness coursing through me like an invisible thread of joy.

"ROBIN!" Ayar lifts himself out of the pool in a single beat when he spots our sweet female standing in the doorway to the pool. She's wrapped a very small fur around herself and is yawning widely.

"Hey! You're all wet!" she says as she's swept up in a soggy Ayar hug. "And what's this about a *trading post*?"

She kisses him on his cheek, and the naked warrior beams, his cocks still fully erect from my earlier attentions.

"It's how the species on Ustokos trade, sometimes for coin, sometimes in exchange for other goods. They all gather at trading posts in various parts of the old cities," I explain to her, rising out of the pool and heading over to her, water sluicing off my wings and body. "We used to provide protection against Proto. Now we act to assist the others and to deal with the odd dispute which may arise."

Robin reaches out for me as I get up close, her hand caressing my wing.

"Sounds interesting," she says, her voice husky with sleep, and I enclose her and Ayar in my wings.

"We thought you might want to go see some more of Ustokos," Ayar adds with a grin a mile wide. "With us, I mean," he says, as if it needs clarifying.

Robin smiles and somehow it lights up my heart to have both of my mates happy at the same time.

Both mates.

The thought resonates around my head. Is it possible to have two mates? Can my heart be big enough for them both? My big, scarred Ayar nuzzles at Robin's hair, and he already has one hand between her legs. The aroma of her arousal is unmistakable.

"I don't think we'll get anywhere at this rate," she moans as I strip away the fur covering her body. My lips on hers, a thick finger slipping between her folds.

She hisses out a short breath and Ayar tips her into his arms, looking at me balefully. "Robin is sore."

"Vrex! Are you?" I ask, removing my hand immediately.

"A little. You are big males. *BIG* males." Her eyes wander down to where our erections jut out towards her. "I enjoyed last night, but I might need a little while to recover?" she asks, one finger on her cheek as she colors a deeper pink.

"You need to be bathed, sweet Robin," Ayar rumbles. "Bathed and fed."

He gives me another long look, both typically Ayar and yet with an undertone of need I understand only too well. He wants to help another. He wants to make sure our mate is happy.

It looks like I'm going to be a very busy Gryn.

Robin

Ayar makes sure I'm thoroughly bathed in a way which is at once intensely sexy and at the same time completely chaste. I wouldn't have thought it was possible, but the scarred warrior managed it. His arousal oh-so-obvious the entire time. While both Ayar and Vypr are big all over, Ayar's cocks are something else entirely. Huge, ridged, and studded with nodes that can reach all the right spots.

It's as if he was made for sex.

As for Vypr, he only has to growl, and I'm soaking.

How on Earth did it come to this?

Because you're not on Earth anymore, Robin, I remind myself. Like Diana said, even with the pain in her eyes at the thought of never seeing her sister again. Maybe we have to roll with it.

But that's what I thought all those million miles away on Earth. I thought I could control what happened to me, and I was wrong.

And yet, Ayar and Vypr are different, not just because they are aliens, but because they are so much more passionate, so much more alive.

They also want me pregnant. Obviously, I know Gryn can get humans pregnant. I've seen the big bump on Kat, and I'm pretty certain Lauren's expanding, too. Plus, Orvos mentioned other humans and their children when I was in the surgery.

I was on the pill when I was on Earth, not that Magnus knew. I kept it a secret from him because the last thing I ever wanted was to get pregnant and be tied to him for the rest of my life. But, as Ayar makes sure I'm dried, the thought of having his child is intriguing.

And not terrifying.

The only thing I'm scared of is my own feelings. My stomach squirms, and Ayar's dark eyes are trained on me as he wraps the fur around my naked body.

"Little Robin," he rumbles, and I lift myself on tiptoes to kiss him, my hands delving in his soft, slightly damp wing feathers.

Because the last thing I want to do is hurt this sweet male. He's scarred enough.

Oh shit! I already care about them!

Ayar lifts every single feather and shakes them out, almost like a dog shaking his fur. Once he's done, a look of beatific delight spreads across his face.

"Come, my *eregri*. Vypr will have food for us." He takes my hand and leads me back into the main room.

"SIT IN HERE," VYPR TELLS ME, HOLDING OUT THE leather strap which is wrapped around Ayar's shoulders. "It's the easiest way for us to carry you," he adds as I inspect it.

Both Ayar and Vypr wear low slung belts with a laser pistol strapped on one side and a short dagger on the other. It appears Ustokos is a planet not without its issues if they have to go armed.

I quite liked being carried by Ayar, but I can see how the sling might be more comfortable. I shove my bum into it, and Ayar stifles a groan.

"Really?" Vypr asks with a shake of his head.

"She feels soft," he says and gently runs his hand through Vypr's feathers.

"Concentrate." Vypr smiles at him. "You have precious cargo."

"I've never been called that before." I look at both males, attempting to keep my face straight.

"'Precious' or 'cargo'?" Ayar asks. Vypr gives him a sudden sharp look as Ayar grins.

"Either, although I'm more keen on being called 'precious'."

"Then you will be precious," Vypr says. "Are you comfortable, *precious*?" he asks as I settle myself into the sling.

"Very much," I reply, snuggling against Ayar's musky, scented skin. "Onwards, Jeeves," I order.

Ayar springs into the air, his huge wings beating down hard as he gains height. I insisted to Vypr he was the one to carry me, so I could be sure he wasn't over-exerting himself. Vypr agreed, but his reluctance stemmed from the distance we were flying.

"Make sure you land if your wound bothers you," Vypr calls out as Ayar sets his wings, and we shoot through the clouds which, it appears, persist on Ustokos, and suddenly we're out in a clear blue sky.

A huge sun burns close, with another, a smaller ball of flame, in the distance. Big moons hang low and ghostly. If I wanted a timely reminder I was on another planet, I just had one shoved in my face, and that's not the acres of bare chest of my flying alien I'm clinging to.

"We're passing the outskirts of the city," Ayar says, or at

least I think he's speaking to me. His words almost seem to be inside my head.

He's lost height now, and we're skimming over ruined buildings which might once have been alien but are nothing more than half a wall or two. They slip past us and instead I see we are flying above a sort of plain. Long grass waves in a wind I can't feel because I'm already battling against the air created by our passage.

"How far to the trading post?" I ask, yelling over the noise.

"Not far, little precious." Vypr is flying in close formation and together my two warriors put on a spurt of speed, meaning we're moving at a tremendous pace. "Look ahead."

I squint my eyes as I see some less damaged buildings up ahead, surrounded by tiny things, almost like ants. As we get closer, the buildings resolve into the beginnings of another town or city. The buildings, like the eyrie, are occupied, and in a large, open area, stalls are set up, covered with flapping, multi-colored fabrics.

"Roof," Vypr calls out to Ayar, and the pair of them swing up to land on the crumbling walls of the highest building, joining four other Gryn warriors, all of whom rise from their crouched positions at our arrival.

"What do you want, Vypr? This is our patrol area." One of them steps forward, peering over Vypr's shoulder at Ayar and me. "And what's he doing here? I thought he was injured?"

"The trading posts are not out of bounds to the unit, and we are not here for a patrol, merely recon for a mission which has nothing to do with you," Vypr says evenly, as the other Gryn step forward, closer to me and Ayar.

My scarred warrior gently lowers me to the ground, out of the sling.

"Look, Kakar, he has a female!" the warrior closest to us says. "The vrexing unit nutter has a female!" He spits.

"How on Ustokos does that vrexer end up with a human female?" The leader of the patrol glares at us all.

"It has nothing to do with you, Kakar." Vypr's voice remains cold and detached, but I see his fist curling. "You stick to your patrol and leave us to unit business."

"And trust him to behave himself? Find another trading post to cause chaos in." Kakar snarls, his eyes not leaving Ayar.

Ayar stares off into the distance, ignoring him, one hand resting lightly on my shoulder. From Vypr's stance, he's not happy but prepared to back off.

Then one of the other warriors takes a step towards me. Immediately, the air is full of feathers and dust. There is the crunching of bone on bone and several loud groans.

Two of the warriors are on their backs. Vypr has his boot on one of them and holds another by his wings, clasped at the shoulder as the male struggles but is unable to get free.

Ayar has his hand nonchalantly around Kakar's throat, claws pressing into the skin as he holds the male at arm's length.

"No one touches Robin," Vypr snarls, his voice strangled with anger. "Understand?"

In an almost involuntary action, Ayar squeezes at Kakar's throat, and the male squeaks out, "Yes!"

Vypr smiles widely and releases the warrior he's holding, who scrambles away. "Good. Then go about your business, and I'll make sure Fyn gets an excellent report." He nods at Ayar.

Ayar doesn't move. His eyes are not on the remainder of the Gryn. The two fallen warriors are crawling away and the third is shaking his wings. He hasn't released Kakar and the Gryn is starting to turn purple.

"Ayar?" Vypr queries.

"Get him off me," Kakar chokes out.

"Not my job." Vypr looks at his claws.

"Ayar?" I say, and he slowly turns his head to me. I smile and his eyes, which were darker than ever, clear.

He lets go of Kakar as if he's a piece of trash he's dropping into a garbage can.

Which results in a lot of theatrical coughing. Ayar looks down at him and shakes his head.

"Come, my precious Robin. I want to show you Ustokos," he says, eyes now firmly on me. He holds out his hand, and I'm twirled against his hard abs.

I look at the four large warriors, all of whom have found something far more interesting than me, putting as much distance between Ayar and Vypr as they can on the roof.

For the first time in a very long time, I feel something.

I feel empowered.

With Ayar and Vypr, I can do anything, because they want me to be safe.

And free.

Ayar

Robin's fresh scent is in my nostrils as we descend down the side of the building and into the area of the trading post. Vypr lands with a thump next to me, and he slings his arm around my shoulder.

"I am proud of you, my mate," he murmurs in my ear.

Robin leans against my chest. "Me too," she says.

I bask in their adoration, even though I'm not sure why I deserve it. No one threatens my mates and gets away with it.

Instead, I shake out my wing feathers happily. The sight of the large Kijg I saw from the roof walking down the same path we are now on still lingers. There was something not right about the cold-blooded creature. Something I can't quite put my finger on.

But Robin curls her hand into mine, and I forget about the Kijg for the time being, instead concentrating on being out. Out on Ustokos, not on a mission, but with my mates by my side. I'm actually...

Enjoying myself?

Vypr has his arm around my shoulders, and as we step into

the market, the other species part for us. Gryn are formidable warriors. We will not be challenged.

Initially, Robin is quiet, until Vypr moves to walk beside her, and she settles, peering around at everything with interest.

"What are they?" She stares at a Kijg. He stares right back until I growl.

"They are Kijg," Vypr tells her. "You met Jesic. She's a Mochi." He points out a couple of the furred felines.

"Are there any other species on Ustokos?" Robin asks as she approaches a stall selling preserved maraha goods.

My stomach rumbles at the sight of the meat. Despite the good breakfast we fed Robin earlier, I'm hungry after our flight and the most recent fight. Not that it was much of a fight. I've no idea what Fyn is teaching his mercs these days, but their hand-to-hand combat is poor.

Or at least, no match for Vypr and me.

"There are the Zio, but they don't venture far from their forests," I hear Vypr saying to Robin as I salivate next to the stall.

It's then I see the Kijg again. Possibly the same Kijg. It's hard to tell, other than this one is larger than most Kijg.

Plus he smells different.

He smells like a Drahon.

"Ayar!" Vypr whispers. "You're growling!"

"The Drahon are here," I respond, as quietly as I can, given I want to kill the scaly bastids on sight.

"Vrex!" Vypr pulls me away from the stall and over to one side.

Robin is wandering a little ahead of us. I notice the way she holds herself. Not frightened but wary. She's interested and making sure she knows her surroundings.

"If there's Drahon here, then the Guv's intel was right. There has to be either the weapons dump or a ship nearby," Vypr says in a low voice.

"If there was a ship, surely we would have seen it or the patrol would have reported it?"

Vypr raises his eyebrows at me, feathers pricked.

"Okay so maybe that patrol wouldn't have seen it. I think we would," I say with a shrug.

"Either way, we need to follow the Drahon, find out where he's going. Then we can go back for the unit." Vypr rubs his chin.

"If there's time." I watch as Robin turns back to us, smiling as she spots a stall selling clothing. She points in the direction she's going, and I nod at her.

"We don't have the fire power if there's more than half a dozen Drahon. Plus we have Robin with us." Vypr folds his arms. He's also watching the progress of our mate.

I contemplate our options. Vypr is correct. We only have two laser pistols between us. The Drahon are pathetic fighters, and their only defense against two Gryn will be if they have numbers and weapons. Less than six and we're laughing.

But it still leaves us with the problem of Robin. She can't be in any danger, not ever.

"I think it's time we found somewhere to have a party," Vypr announces, rather loudly. I give him a quizzical look. "Roll with it, my mate. I'll explain shortly." He grins at me.

Excitement flares through me, but for once it's not accompanied by the stomach churn which makes me want to kill anything in sight. Instead, I'm focused on one thing. Keeping my mates safe. Whatever happens with the Drahon, it comes second to my real job—protecting them.

Vypr

My strong warrior narrows his eyes at my suggestion of a party. He knows I normally try to avoid letting him near anything alcoholic, as his thin restraint is stretched to the snapping point with beer in the mix.

And especially given his recent accident.

But the Drahon are interested in the Gryn and not in a good way. Admittedly, it means I'm going to be holding myself out as bait, but it won't be the first time I've done something similar when we were battling Proto. I'm not about to let such a little thing get in the way of Ayar proving himself to the seniors.

Because this mission before the mission, especially if we get some Drahon prisoners along with weapons, would be the ideal way to show my mate is a capable and fully functioning member of the elite unit.

Ayar eyes me with concern as I sling my arm around his shoulder again, and we make our way over to where Robin is staring at some Kijg cooking pots.

"What the hell are these for?" She looks at the pots as if they are dangerous.

"Cooking," I reply and look up at the Kijg stall holder. "We're looking for a party. Know where there are any?" I ask with a grin.

"You're part of the patrol, are you not?" the Kijg says, carefully, his little black eyes straying to Robin.

"Nope, not part of the patrol. Just a couple of Gryn looking for a party outside the lair..." I lean in, holding my breath because I've always hated the stink of the Kijg. "We're banned from partying at the moment." I wink at him, which is wasted because the cold blooded reptiles can't wink.

However, it must have worked, as he leans into me, checking around for bystanders. "Third building down from where your patrol resides. You'll find what you want there," he says.

"It looks like a chamber pot," Robin says, loudly, turning the pot over in her hands, frowning. "Are you sure you cook in it?"

"Pot?" Ayar queries, his attention solidly on her. "What is a *chamberpot*?"

Robin beckons him down to her and whispers in his ear. Ayar straightens, takes the pot from her, and puts it carefully back. His lips twitch with the effort of not laughing.

"What?" I ask him, dying to be let in on the joke.

"I'll tell you when you tell me the plan," he says, looking at Robin.

"You'll tell me now," I growl, and he caves.

"Let's just say, if you thought Kijg food tasted like gak, then it's probably what they cook it in," he says, cryptically.

My big, scarred warrior. Suddenly, he's in his element, alongside the tiny human female who, frankly, already looks at home in her new environment. Her eyes are everywhere, soaking everything in. I feel my heart swelling in my chest as I gaze on my two mates. Ayar covers her with a wing, so protective, and I move around them in order to lead the way to the place we've been directed.

The building is in better shape than most which surround the trading post. It's a square block, probably Gryn made, although our territorial boundaries have changed immeasurably from when this place had been built. If it was built by the ancients, it will follow a similar pattern to Gryn lairs, which is good for our plan.

"Are we really partying?" Ayar asks from behind me. He sounds almost disappointed, which is unusual for him.

I turn to face him. "You love a party, don't you, Ayar?" I ask loudly, clapping him on the shoulder before leaning in. "This is going to be the only way we get the information we need. We're not actually partying."

"Oh." What flits across his face is a mixture of confusion, interest, and excitement.

"Spying?" Robin suggests hopefully, beside him.

"You are to stay close to us at all times. Do not leave our sight, not even for a second," I intone.

Robin gives me a huge grin. "Not for a second, Vypr. Promise."

Why do I suddenly feel like she's going to be even more trouble than my Ayar?

I step beside her, and along with Ayar, we walk up the short staircase leading to the main door of the building. I keep our pace deliberately slow so we can be seen entering.

"Where's the party?" I ask a Mochi male, who stumbles forward into the light from the doorway. He waves an inebriated paw behind him, mumbling about a room.

"Hope they have var beer!" Ayar says.

"No vrexing var beer. We're doing recon."

"This is me doing recon."

"I think Ayar was just getting into the part," a small female voice pipes up.

She is definitely going to be more trouble than Ayar.

Ahead, I see a group of Mochi males and a pair of Kijg standing near a door. Shaking out my feathers, I tuck Robin behind us and approach them.

Not a single male acknowledges our presence, merely moving aside to allow entry farther into the building. The doorway opens into a decrepit central atrium, as I expected. On the far side, there is a rudimentary bar, several barrels of Mochi beer, and a handful of bottles which most likely contain spirits.

"On the house." The Mochi bartender slaps two large tankards down in front of us as we approach. "For your service," he adds.

The male, a striped Mochi-ka has a scarred muzzle and one eye is a milky color. I'd recognize the scars anywhere.

"Joykill?" I ask, sipping at my beer and watching Ayar carefully.

He has pulled Robin into his feathers so she is partially concealed from any prying eyes. He lifts the tankard and sniffs the contents, making a sour face. When he sees me looking at him, he pretends to take a drink.

I hear a snort of laughter from our female and attempt to ignore it.

"Foul bots. We are well rid of Proto," the bartender grumbles.

"Some might not think so," I say.

The Mochi grimaces. "Then they are fools. Deluded fools."

Ayar takes this opportunity to cough into his drink, presumably because he doesn't like it, given he's never been keen on the Mochi beer, despite putting a considerable amount away whenever he was given the opportunity.

"Prefer your Gryn brew, do you?" The bar keeper looks

over at Ayar, and his green eyes widen when he spots Robin. I'm immediately on edge.

"Better than this gak," Ayar says, in a not unfriendly tone.

"You look like a Gryn who appreciates something finer." The Mochi smiles, exposing his double canines in a display which could be considered aggressive but is just what these felines do when relaxed. "Take a seat, and I'll bring you something you won't be able to resist." He motions across the atrium to an area which is empty of patrons and contains a couple of tables and benches.

I'm just about to say something, but Ayar is already swaggering off, wings swaying. Robin looks up at me.

"He's good at this, isn't he?" She grins.

Double trouble.

Robin

Ayar is being an idiot, an adorable idiot. But what's better is how funny Vypr is. I can't help myself but join with Ayar, especially while Vypr won't tell us what he's planning.

"Is there any chance you can take this seriously?" Vypr says in a furious whisper when we reach the tables, and Ayar sits with a flourish.

"I'm supposed to be partying." Ayar puts his tankard down and spreads out his hands, claws extended. "If this was a real party..."

"You'd be in the middle of a fight after your third tankard," Vypr cuts in. "I know you too well, my warrior."

Ayar huffs, picks up his tankard, and sniffs at it. "Not going to drink this stuff," he grumbles. "This is a vrexing pathetic party."

"It's not supposed to be a party!" Vypr flares his wings, exasperated. "We're getting intel. And this Mochi is going to help us."

I nod at Ayar. "Vypr's right. The best place to get any good local information is from your friendly pub owner."

Both males frown at me. "The Mochi," I hiss, jerking my head back towards the bar.

Realization dawns, and I'm treated to two utterly handsome faces smiling at me. My core pulses. How did I end up here, doing the job I used to love, with a pair of gorgeous aliens who do devastating things to my knickers?

Is it possible being abducted was the best thing which could have happened to me?

"Look, I used to do this sort of thing back on Earth. I can help you, if you'll let me," I say to Vypr.

"I want Robin to help us," Ayar says, and I give his wing a little stroke.

Vypr bristles, so I give his wing a stroke too.

"I'm not sure." He looks pensive. "It's not safe for us, let alone you, if the Drahon are here."

"I'm pretty sure I can handle myself if I need to. And I've firsthand experience of the Drahon too," I point out. Not that my limited self-defense classes helped much against the Drahon and their stun sticks, but I'm not going to tell Vypr.

"Let's see what the Mochi has to say and take it from there," Ayar counters.

Vypr contemplates him for a few seconds, then gives him a curt nod.

"He's coming," I whisper loudly as the big cat man, striped like a tiger, ambles towards us. He has a tray in one paw and a bottle in the other.

"Vrex," Vypr mutters. "Lynk."

"Lynk?" Ayar brightens.

"We're not partying."

"Maybe just a little?"

"No."

"Oh, dear god." I roll my eyes. "Ayar, there's being in character and there's *being in character*. Pick one!"

My sweet, scarred male grins at me. He digs the tips of his

claws into the tabletop. I get both a glint of the wild male he was in the surgery and also something else. A calculating, clever male who knows exactly what he's doing.

"Fellow warriors." The barkeeper puts down the tray with a flourish. On it are strips of meat, cooked rare.

Ayar licks his lips. I'm pretty sure he's a bottomless pit given how much he eats and how much he tries to get me to eat.

A bottle and four glasses are also placed down.

"I presume your female will also have a taste?" the big furry cat asks.

"Yes, the *female* will," I say, and he gives me an impressively toothy grin.

"I've heard human females are a force to be reckoned with."

"Bit like Mochi females. Are you mated, friend?" Vypr asks conversationally.

"For many cycles. I have many cubs," he says proudly.

"We're hoping to have a youngling." Ayar pulls me tight to him, proprietorially. "Providing, of course, we can ensure our young are safe."

For the first time, the Mochi looks uncomfortable. He pours out a clear liquid into the glasses, and Ayar snags two, handing one to me.

The first whiff of alcohol almost has me retching. The beer my males were served earlier didn't have much of a scent, but this spirit is very strong. I like to think I can handle my booze, but I already know I can't put this stuff anywhere near my lips or I will be losing my breakfast.

Fortunately, the cat man isn't looking at me. Ayar has already drunk his and holds out his glass for a refill, much to Vypr's obvious annoyance.

I'm guessing my warriors haven't done much in the way of

subtle investigation. I suspect they're more of a blunt instrument.

"Yes, the Gryn did Ustokos a great favor in disposing of Proto. But what's going to fill the space left by it?" Cat man shakes his head. "Further conflict is coming."

"Not if our seniors have anything to say about it. We don't want our planet to be divided any more than the Mochi do. All we want to do is live peacefully."

"Can warriors like the Gryn be peaceful?" The barkeeper tosses back his glass of spirits as I dump mine on the floor, and when he looks back, I smile at him.

Ayar holds out his glass for a third refill. Vypr growls.

"The Gryn can be peaceful, providing they're not threatened," I say.

For the first time, the Mochi really looks at me.

"I heard the Gryn rescued humans from Proto. What happened to your females was despicable." He snarls. "No species should lose their mates."

"No species should lose anyone, male or female," Ayar says, his voice low and his eyes dark. "Peace is what Ustokos needs now, not war. It needs time to heal, to rebuild. It doesn't need to be plundered and exploited by others not from this planet."

The cat man looks over his shoulder at his handful of other patrons, who all seem engrossed in their business. Ayar takes the opportunity to snag a couple of slices of meat and shove them into his mouth.

"I agree, friends. You should know, the Kijg at this trading post are not what they pretend to be. Apart from a handful, they do not trade, but instead, there are others, larger Kijg, and they spend much of their time underground."

"Where?" Vypr asks.

"Under the empty trading square. They have an entrance, but I don't know where it is."

Ayar yawns and shoves his glass across the table for yet another refill. Vypr looks daggers at him, but the Mochi smiles and fills up his glass.

"You're welcome to stay as long as you like, friends. I would recommend, if you wish to go exploring, you take the rest of your patrol."

"You are a good warrior." Vypr pats the striped cat man on the shoulder as Ayar wavers unsteadily, having thrown back his fourth shot.

"And the Gryn made Ustokos a safe place for me to bring up my cubs. I'm sure they will continue to be our protectors." The Mochi gets to his feet and picks up the empty tray, ambling slowly back to the bar, his long tail swishing behind him.

"Ayar!" Vypr hisses. "You're not supposed to be partying!"

"I'm not." He adopts a hurt tone. Eyes which were glassy not a second ago are clear.

He opens his wing, angling his body towards me and Vypr, and I see the soaked feathers. I can't help but let out a low chuckle. I wasn't the only one avoiding the drinks.

"Thank the goddess! You and Lynk do *not* mix." Vypr sits back, hands spread on the table in front of him, to either side of his empty glass.

"One of us had to appear as if we were up for a party." Ayar rolls his eyes. "Now that we have all the information we need, I'm in the mood for a fight."

Vypr

I shift on my seat, my pants uncomfortably tight. Ayar wants a fight, and my brave, resourceful Robin has helped us get the information we need.

Both of which have made me as horny as a maraha bull in season. I want to mate the pair of them. We're supposed to be on a mission, albeit one we were not ordered to undertake, but all I can think of is ripping off Robin's clothing and filling her while Ayar watches. I'm becoming as impetuous as my wicked mate, who now stinks of strong alcohol and is gouging great lines in the table with his claws.

My little trouble, she's sitting back, arms folded, watching Ayar with a careful gaze. As he goes to dig deeper, she puts a hand on his wing, and he stops.

"I think we need to consider our next steps before we fight," I say, pleased I have some assistance with my big, chaotic warrior for a change.

Ayar shivers, his wing feathers shaking. "I'd prefer to kill some Drahon, but I'm listening."

"I think we need to get Robin somewhere safe first."

"Agreed."

"You do know I'm here, don't you?" Robin says, and her mouth is pinched.

I believe we've made our precious little trouble mad.

"I was thinking we might be able to leave her with the patrol." I fold my arms as well and look directly at Ayar.

"I'm not leaving her with that bunch of vrexers," he snarls, with a sideways glance at Robin. "We'd be better off leaving her on another building with a laser pistol."

"I. Am. Right. Here," Robin says through gritted teeth. "And I'm only going where you go. I told you, this is what I did for a living back on Earth. You need me."

She glares at us both, daring us to contradict her. She's all fire, all fight. Ayar slides closer to her, and she's half buried in his feathers, fortunately not the side soaked with Lynk.

"Precious, all we want to do is ensure you are protected. We don't want to rush off chasing Drahon without making sure you are safe."

"I'm safe with you," she says, firmly. "And I want to stay with you."

She has her hand on Ayar's chest and gazes at me. Goddess be damned, she's melting my heart.

There's a scraping sound behind us, and I look over to see a small cohort of Kijg entering, and none of them look like they're interested in partying. The exit door is slammed in the unfortunate Mochi barkeeper's face and weapons are drawn.

"We need to go." I grin over at Ayar. "Would you like to suggest a route?"

He has his arms around Robin as he twists, eyes glittering, a smile of complete delight on his lips. "I suggest we split up. Give them multiple targets and you know the Kijg will fail to hit any."

Ayar is charged, and yet he has a focus about him I've only rarely seen. Robin gasps as she's trapped against his chest, and he opens his wings. Across the atrium, the Kijg move. In a single beat, Ayar is in the air and heading up the atrium to the roof. In a few short seconds, there is the crunching of wing meeting plex-glas, and shards rain down on the assembled Kijg, who cover their heads, ducking to keep out of the way of the falling debris.

I pull out my laser pistol and advance on the Kijg, if nothing else, to see what they do. Kijg are no more warriors than their larger counterparts, the Drahon, but this group seem to have their wits about them. From within the bunch, I hear the sizzle of a laser weapon being discharged.

The bolt flies over my head, and I'm wondering if the Kijg just has a terrible aim when there's a rumbling above me and something heavy hits the back of my head. Immediately, I'm in the air, and as I twist, I see the heavy netting hit the ground where I was standing.

This entire place is a huge trap. Another laser bolt zaps past me, singing the edge of a primary feather on my left wing. Above me is the hole left by Ayar and, although I wanted to confuse our erstwhile captors by leaving by a different 'door,' it looks like I'm going out the same way.

But as I rise, a Kijg appears on a ledge above me, and suddenly, I hit an almost invisible obstruction. My left wing flails, trying to keep me in the air, but it gets tangled.

Tangled in an ultra-fine net which is now strung across the atrium. I reach for my dagger, but I'm unbalanced with only one wing, and then I'm spinning, the knife I could have used to free myself falling away as I become more and more trapped in the net. Even when I stop moving, my momentum simply makes things worse until I can't escape, whether I try or not.

As soon as I go limp, the net begins to descend. I shake and roar at my captors, but it makes no difference. I'm caught.

"We got one!" a Kijg exclaims as I hit the floor, hard, winding me. "We got a Gryn." He pokes me with his boot and jumps back as I roar out.

"Yeah, but the other one and the human female got away," a second one grumbles. "The female was worth a good amount of coin if the Gryn had mated her and filled her belly."

"It doesn't matter." A larger Kijg, one I recognize, steps into the light.

"Grid, you'd better let me go. You know the consequences," I growl as I stare up into his smug, but damaged, face.

A face I damaged when we were rescuing Robin and the other humans. A Kijg who was helping the Drahon and who ultimately escaped.

Now I'm cursing myself we didn't look harder for him when we had the chance.

"I absolutely know the consequences. Your Ryak will come for you. Your legion will come for you, and it's the legion we need."

"They will not attempt to rescue one Gryn. We may care for our own, unlike the Kijg, but we don't sacrifice all for the one. If we did, there would be no Gryn left." I glare up at him from my net cage. "You will regret my capture. Of that, you can be sure."

"I wouldn't be sure of anything, Gryn." Grid snarls. "When the Drahon are finished with you, you won't even know your own name." He looks over his shoulder. "Shoot him up and get him out of here. Use the underground. I don't want the patrol seeing anything."

"What about the other Gryn and the human?" the complainer says. "They're worth coin, too."

Another Kijg slams a thin tube into my bicep, and a hiss denotes the narcotic being fed into my system. I buck against my bonds, attempting to get away, but he puts his foot on my abdomen and bares his teeth.

A darkness envelops me, slowly narrowing down my vision, my ability to scent, my hearing.

"If you can find them, we'll take them too," I hear Grid say. Although every atom of my body is crying out to get to my mates, not a single element obeys.

Instead, my eyes close, and I hope beyond hope when I wake, I can make good my escape and get back to my Ayar and my Robin.

Robin

Ayar fires us both through the skylight of the atrium. His head and wings take the brunt of the force needed to get through. I shake out my hair as we spiral upwards and pieces of the plastic glass drop away below us.

He keeps on climbing. "I need to get you out of laser range," he murmurs in my ear. Or are his words in my head? It's hard to tell when the wind is rushing, and my heart is beating out of my chest because of the adrenaline filling my veins.

I risk a look down to see we're a long way above the ground.

"What about Vypr?" I ask.

"He'll be fine. Nothing we've not done before," Ayar says with absolute confidence, clutching me tightly. "Don't worry, little mate." He nuzzles into my wild hair. "We'll be back with him in no time."

He evens out his flight and begins to circle, occasionally looking down. I can almost feel him vibrating with excitement. He's loving this.

We're slowly starting to descend, lazily losing height.

"He'll be done now. Half a dozen Kijg are no match for my Vypr." Ayar laughs.

"Good," I reply. The last thing I wanted to do was abandon him, but Ayar didn't give me much option.

Having spun around in stomach churning circles, Ayar goes in long and low, flipping over the tops of the crumbling and damaged buildings until we reach the one with the bar. Ayar lands on the roof and gently puts me on my feet.

He immediately goes to drop through the damaged skylight, but I put my arm across his abdomen.

"Wait. Something doesn't feel right about this." I look up at him.

Ayar's eyes are full of fire, but at my words, he stops.

"What is it?" he asks.

"I don't know exactly, but we can't charge back in there. Not the same way we got out. Surely, if Vypr was okay, he'd be out here by now?"

"Not necessarily. Not if there is further information to be gathered. We're under orders not to kill any Drahon we find. The seniors need them for interrogation."

I'm not entirely sure I like the idea of interrogation, but, fearsome as they are, the Gryn don't strike me as unnecessarily cruel.

And I'm also feeling somewhat turned on by the thought of Vypr, all muscles and feathers, doing his dominant warrior thing.

Not appropriate.

Next to me, Ayar shakes with repressed need. I think it's only my touch on his skin which is stopping him from diving back into the building.

"How about we find another way in?" I suggest. "That way, we won't interrupt anything Vypr is doing, and if there are any threats, they won't be expecting us."

Ayar gives me a swift nod and takes off. He drops below

the height of the roof, and I rush over to the edge to see where he went. All I see is a flash of feathers as he disappears around the side of the octagonal building, and I spin on the spot, wondering what he's doing.

Suddenly, there's a rush of wind behind me, and I'm enclosed in a pair of strong arms.

"I've found another way in," he says, glee in his voice. "Let's go!" I'm lifted off my feet before I can even reply.

Diving down, there's a large opening in the wall about halfway down. Ayar folds up his wings, and he's hurtling into the dark with me, helpless in his arms.

"Ayar!" I cry out as the light goes and my eyes don't adjust immediately.

More wind, ears filling with the beating of wings, and things come into focus.

Or rather they don't. I'm being cradled against a very muscular chest, albeit one which smells amazing.

"Any chance you can let me go, Ayar?" I say, my voice somewhat muffled.

I'm released, slowly, and find we're back in the central atrium. The bar is pretty smashed up, the bottles which were on the shelving are gone, in broken heaps on the floor. Near where we were sitting is a tangled pile of what looks like a net. I run over to it and start to pull at the heavy ropes, but it rapidly becomes clear there's no one under it, especially a big, feathered Gryn warrior.

I turn back to Ayar. He's staring at something on the floor. It's a dark stain. My legs begin to shake. I walk towards him, and he crouches down, swiping a clawed hand out at the mark. As I reach him, he stares at the red on his fingertips and slowly looks at me.

But I'm not seeing him. Instead, I see something else, and in several short steps, I'm by the ruined bar.

The dagger stands up, tip buried deep in the wood. It's

almost identical to the one Ayar wears on his belt. I pull at it, but it takes two hands to remove it from its resting place.

"That's Vypr's." Ayar's voice is dull next to me, answering my unasked question.

He takes it from me, turning it over in his hands. Then he spins around. Opening up his wings, he bellows Vypr's name.

I try to be detached. Try to put myself back into work mode. I try to work out how the fight played out. To convince myself Vypr got away. That he's just chasing down the other aliens who were spoiling for a fight.

But there's too much going on. Too much I don't understand.

Too much emotion. My heart has slowed almost to a halt as the ice fills my veins.

Vypr is gone.

Ayar hasn't stopped calling his name, increasing in volume from a low roar, to a banshee like shrike. He circles the atrium, slamming furniture aside and ripping into the bar. I stare down at the congealing pool of blood.

We can't possibly have lost Vypr to those lizards or the Drahon. It can't be possible.

I can't have found him and Ayar only to lose them.

I can't have allowed my heart to hope only for it to be crushed again.

Ayar

I left him. Vypr is not here. All that remains is his dagger and blood. My head fills with rage, blinding rage.

I need my Vypr back, now.

For a while, I don't know what I do. All I know is I end up crouched next to the blood, inhaling the metallic scent, my chest heaving and my muscles screaming at me.

A soft voice penetrates the pain in my head.

"Ayar? We have to get back to the eyrie. We have to tell the others about Vypr." It's Robin.

I know she calms me. I know she's my mate, but without Vypr, I'm lost. All I want to do is to get to him, to have him by my side.

"He might still be somewhere here," she says. "He might have gone after them. We can't just wait for him, and we need help."

I look at her, so delicate and slight. I did what Vypr wanted me to do. I protected her, and I will always protect her. Anything he asks of me will always be done. But it means I've not been able to protect him. I don't like my heart being split like this.

"Hey." She takes my face in her hands, gently tracing over my brow. "It's going to be okay. He's going to be okay."

And my head descends into the darkness. She wants to believe what she's saying, but I know she doesn't. Without Vypr, we are limbless.

I need the unit. I need the Guv. I need Vypr.

I need to keep Robin safe.

"We go." I stand and toss her into my arms, beating hard to gain height. We exit the building.

I'd have stayed forever. It was the last place I saw my mate and the place I feel closest to him. But Robin needs protecting, and I will do what Vypr tells me, even though all I want to do is to tear the trading post apart until I find him.

"Ayar, my darling. Let's speak to the others," Robin says in my ear. Her calmness should soothe me. But instead, all I feel is a bubbling terror.

I need Vypr.

The patrol lounges on the roof of the building. The last thing I want to do is speak to other Gryn who are not part of our unit. Except they might have seen something. Something which will tell me where to find him.

I land with a thump, and the patrol gets to its feet as one, so I'm guessing we made an impression earlier. As soon as I release her, Robin darts towards them.

"Have you seen Vypr?" she asks the leader.

He stares down at her, a sneer on his lips. "Probably partying. That's what the unit is known for." He sniffs at me. "And are good at." His face wrinkles as he takes in the scent of Lynk on me.

It's no use. I snap. Next thing I know, I have three Gryn wrenching at my wings as I pin him to the floor, one set of claws buried in his chest, the rest around his throat creating a red necklace of oozing wounds.

He wriggles under me, choking and scrabbling at my forearms, creating gouges I don't even feel. I can't feel the mercs on my back.

"Ayar," Robin whispers. Or does she call my name? I'm not sure. "He's not the enemy."

"I...can't." I look up at her from the mess I've created.

"I know," she replies. "But you must."

The mercs redouble their efforts, and with a final attempt, I'm wrenched off the patrol leader who scuttles away from me to the far side of the roof before leaping into the air. He's quickly followed by the remainder of the patrol as I run, roaring, after them. Nearly taking off before I remember Robin.

She looks tiny. Arms wrapped tightly around herself.

I am entirely alone. My left eye is no longer functioning, either because I've been punched in it, or more likely...

When it hits me, I go down onto my knees. The searing pain in my head. As if I'm clamped back on the machine. Everything grows dim. Everything is pointless.

Even the soft hand on my shoulder and arm around my waist matters not.

The pain is back, and I'm going to let it take me.

Robin

Ayar curls up into a ball on the roof and moans like he's possessed, clutching at his head. My heart is wrenched into pieces at the sight and at my fear for Vypr. Other than the pool of blood and the dagger, we have no idea where he is, and the other Gryn have just taken off because, frankly, Ayar would have killed them.

I've seen him before, raging in the surgery at Orvos, but this is different. He's feral.

And we have no Vypr. No quiet, firm voice to penetrate Ayar's darkness. It's his constant companion I recognized when we were in the surgery. I have my own well of night. The one I kept hidden, the one which overflowed when I first found out I was on a planet full of male creatures.

The pool of agony I capped many years ago because it was easier not to feel at all. Not when caring got me nowhere.

Now I'm discovering if you let the heart rule your head, you can't turn back time. Instead, my chest aches as if I've been stabbed.

As if the pool of blood on the floor was mine.

Ayar whimpers. My feet of clay finally move me over to

him. He has his head buried in his hands, and I kneel, one hand hesitant over him. Blood which isn't his streaks his hands and forearms. The blood which does belong to him runs in long thin strips over his torso. Very carefully, I touch his hair, brushing it back from his face.

"Hey," I breathe, holding back any emotion I have. Ayar's distress is so strong I can almost taste it. Metallic and sour. "Ayar, my darling. It's going to be okay. We'll find him."

"Head," my poor Ayar moans. "Hurts. Need Vypr." He growls out Vypr's name.

I want Vypr too, very much. His quiet, dominant nature, one which only comes to the fore when we're alone together but sits at the very front of who he is within all three of us. We're not just missing him, but we're missing who he is inside us.

But it's Ayar's paralysis, it catches me in the gut, making it hard to think or even breathe as he stays curled up on the ground. My big, scarred warrior. A male who thought nothing of taking me to safety. He's laid low.

"What's going on?" A voice has me looking up. A large Gryn stands, his body against the light so I can't see his face.

Ayar is on his feet instantly, snarling like a beast. He pushes me behind him, claws scratching my skin.

"Keep back, or I'll end you." The words are hardly recognizable.

"Ayar, it's me. It's Syn." The warrior steps forward, and his features are clearer.

If Ayar recognizes him, he doesn't show it. His shoulders hunched, his wings outstretched. All he does is rumble a low growl.

"What do you want?" he eventually says.

"I was in the area and saw you here," Syn says with a shrug. "I saw the patrol leave."

I don't believe him for a second. There is most definitely

another reason this male has ended up 'coincidentally' in the same place as us.

"We were attacked by the lizard people, the Kijg," I call out from behind a bristling Ayar.

"Vrex!" Syn swears. "We've had reports of Drahon activity in this area." He stares at Ayar. "Why are you here? The mission to find the weapons is for the whole unit, not you and your..." His gaze wanders to me. "Mate?"

"Ayar and Vypr brought me here to see more of Ustokos." I step out from behind Ayar, hoping he's going to back down. I get a rumble, but he doesn't stop me. "We need to find Vypr."

"He's missing?" Syn queries, eyes lighting up with a strange sort of concern.

"Of course he's vrexing missing, or he'd be here, wouldn't he?" Ayar fires out. "And my head wouldn't be wanting to split open."

He snorts a painful breath, and I'm snagged by my clothing, a dusty wing enveloping me.

"My Ayar." I press myself into his bloodied side, putting a hand on his face and wincing as he flinches at me. "Maybe Syn can help? He could go and get the rest of the unit while we look for Vypr."

"We don't have time to get them," Syn says sharply. "If the Drahon have him, they'll be looking for a way to get him off Ustokos and into slavery as soon as possible. It's what they do."

"But the defense system?" Ayar says, one hand clutching his head. "That will stop them."

"Then they might not keep him alive."

"No!" Slowly, Ayar looks at me, his eyes clouded with pain, fear, and something I recognize only too well. Terror.

It's the terror which cages my heart. It stops me instantly. No one should ever be this terrified.

I am helpless. Again.

For all I tried to be who I knew I could be on Earth, in the face of a man who hated me so much he couldn't let me go. For all I wanted to be free of the confines of emotions. To be free to be who I wanted to be. I already know it's too late.

Ayar and Vypr have become part of who I am. They have snuck into my soul and taken over who I am.

But I don't know if I can carry Ayar's burden as well as mine. For all I recognize what clutches at his mind and fogs his senses, I hold it too. We both have to act, and yet, I'm not sure he can.

But without him and without Vypr, we are condemned to a half-life.

If Vypr is gone, so are we.

Vypr

My head feels like gak. Eyes seem stuck closed initially, and I'm aching all over. Whatever the narcotic was, it's done a number on me.

"Vrexing Kijg," I groan and attempt to move. Clanking alerts me to the fact my wrists are chained, and somehow, my wings are fastened behind my back in a way which means I can't move them.

And in such a way it's painful to move at all.

"Vrex." I blink my eyes, attempting to clear my vision and my head, which is stuffed with down. As my eyes adjust, I realize I'm definitely underground somewhere. There's a strong smell of damp and Kijg. Sitting above it all is the strong scent of the Drahon, foul and sharp in my nostrils. Although dark, the space I'm in is small, cell like, and lit with a single small artificial light above my head.

None of this is good. I get to my feet, using the wall behind me to heave myself up. My legs are nearly useless, and I sway like a drunken warrior at a party, my breath coming in ragged waves. My chest is painful, and I expect a couple of the

Kijg I damaged may have taken their frustrations out on my unconscious body. Cowards.

Regardless of the likelihood of the chains being loose, I pull at where I'm anchored to the wall. They are firmly attached, and I'm able to move around one body length. I remember Huntr telling me the Drahon were fond of chains and the control collar. I feel at my neck and find it, thankfully, free of any collar. For the time being at least.

As for my wings, any movement at all is agony. I attempt to look at what's holding them, but it's impossible.

There's a door ahead of me, and I shuffle along the wall, but the chains bring me up short. I end up back on my ass on the floor.

"Vrex it!" I snarl out as the action bumps my wings and sends spikes of pain shooting through me.

Not only am I captured, but I don't know what happened to Ayar and Robin. I have to hope they got away, that I was enough of a distraction for the Kijg. If I close my eyes, I can still see Ayar's handsome, scarred face, his little smile when he found something he loved, whether it was one of his pebbles or just a piece of rare cooked maraha.

And my precious Robin, a female. A gift neither Ayar nor I thought we would ever get or even knew we wanted. Her sweet face and even sweeter body. A body my Ayar is dying to fill with a youngling.

Something which, sitting on the damp floor surrounded by the sound of dripping water, I contemplate. I agreed to mate with Robin for Ayar's sake, but do I want a youngling myself? The strange weight in my stomach at the thought has lightened. When we are together, somehow, it seems right.

The cell door opens with a crash, and three Kijg leap in, stun sticks in hand. I don't move. Not only is it too painful, but given how terrible the Kijg are at fighting, I'm likely to flatten them, and until I know what they want from me, I'd rather get the information before resisting.

I will be escaping back to my mates. Because I'm not going to be a Drahon slave, and I'm not leaving Ustokos, whatever the vrexing Drahon have planned.

Grid ambles in. I know Ryak, our head of security, has had dealings with this particular Kijg, and he is not to be trusted.

"It's Vypr, isn't it?" he says, his words ending with a slight hiss around his long, slim tongue.

Chains clink as I fold my arms. I shake my head. "I don't have to tell you anything."

Grid steps a little farther into the cell, small black eyes dark pits in this dimly lit place, one of his three fingers touching his lips as he remains silently appraising me.

"No, you're right. You don't have to tell me anything, but I want you to." He drops his hand away, and one of his lackeys slams the stun stick into my side.

It burns intensely, sending hot rivers of pain coursing through my veins as I shake with the effort of not moving my wings.

"Torture, Grid? Is that all you've got?" I laugh as soon as I can un-grit my teeth.

He crouches down. "I remember you, Vypr. Believe me, if it wasn't for the information my master needs, you'd be facing much worse than torture."

"You were hardly pretty before you met the unit." I don't let my gaze leave his. "So I can't see you have any complaints." I cock my head to one side.

Grid snarls, his scarred mouth lifting to reveal small, sharp teeth. The finger lifts, the stun stick is shoved into my side, this time for longer.

This time, I can't stop my wings from moving, and I do everything I can not to cry out in pain. My chest heaves as I return my gaze to Grid.

"The Drahon killed my brother because of your *unit*. They don't take kindly to failure."

"That's a shame." I drop my gaze to my limp arms, heavy in the chains and after the stun has been applied. I contemplate my claws, just the tips appearing from their sheaths.

"Yes, it was a shame, *Gryn*," he snarls. "My brother was everything to me."

I lift my head and stare directly into the flat black of his eyes. "I didn't mean it was a shame your brother died. You chose to align yourselves with the Drahon, and I have no sympathy. I mean it's a shame because the Drahon are always going to fail if they have designs on Ustokos or its inhabitants."

Grid's mouth opens. I extend my claws. He shuts it again.

This time, the stun lasts even longer, and I end up on my side, panting, trying not to writhe.

"Do you like the clamp on your wings?" Grid seems to have gotten his voice back. He walks around me, and a pressure is put on whatever is holding them. The pain is intense, but I'm too stunned to react. "Designed by the Drahon as a way of keeping Gryn in check. They've had plenty of Gryn to practice on, but apparently your females were too delicate. You have a human female as a mate, don't you?"

He crouches down, staring intently at me.

I don't look at him.

"And you have a Gryn male too. I'd heard the Gryn were capable of nesting with both sexes, but I never thought I'd see it."

"You leave my mates alone." My voice is a bare growl, the words escaping my lips before I have a chance to stop them.

I can't let Grid know what matters to me more than anything because Ayar and Robin are still out there, away from the safety of the eyrie and the protection of the rest of the unit. And he can't have them. They are mine.

"I won't be touching your mates." Grid exposes all his teeth in the Kijg version of a smile. A nasty smile. "But the Drahon, on the other hand, they want Gryn, and with Proto gone, we're the only way they can get them. I find it hard to believe, but your warm-blooded species is very much in demand."

He takes in a deep breath and stands.

"Apparently, your nature makes you very good at doing the dirty work of the galaxy."

I reach out to swipe at him, but the chains hold me back.

"You don't touch my mates. No one does," I reply.

"You won't get too much of a say in what happens to them, but you may be reunited briefly, especially if the female is not with young." Grid puts a foot on my wing again, grinding the clamp into my flesh, and I suppress a roar. "But," he grimaces at me, "if you co-operate, maybe we might lose them. Maybe they might escape. Who knows?"

"Vrex you, Grid." I loathe the creature, and if I could stand, or move, he would be dead.

"Think about it," he replies, kicking me onto my back, and the pain in my wings intensifies. "You've got half a turn."

He pulls back his foot, considering whether or not to kick me. I brace myself for the blow. But he lowers it again, shaking his head.

"Mustn't damage the merchandise too much." He chokes out a laugh at the other Kijg. Turning, his long tail whipping the air, he stalks out of the cell.

A stun stick is poked into my back and unconsciousness beckons.

Ayar

Syn stinks. His scent invades my senses and makes my headache pound all the harder. He's the reminder of everything I loathe. An insolence of the Gryn which has led us to the point where we still trust the foul, vrexing Kijg because we are *better*.

We are nothing. Not without each other.

I thought I saw Vypr on the edge of the roof, beckoning to me. Except it wasn't him, it was Syn, and I hate him all the more for it. He wants my mate, my female, and he wants to take Vypr's place in the unit.

He can't have them. He can't have anything from me.

"Vrex the mission and vrex the unit," I snarl.

"I guess that attitude answers the reason you're going to end up off the unit and back where you can't cause chaos." Syn cocks his head to one side as if he's contemplating my intentions.

"What do you mean?" I straighten slightly from my attack stance.

"You mean no one told you?" He hitches up the corner of

his mouth, as if he finds something amusing about the situation, and I want to rip him to pieces.

Robin tenses next to me.

"What did Vypr not tell me?" I ask her.

"That if you don't manage to control yourself, you're off the unit, and you become Fyn's problem, not the Guv's," Syn butts in.

I want to speak, but I can't speak. I want to roar, split the air with everything I have in my lungs. But they won't let me. My tongue is silent until finally, it comes to life, and I'm leaping for him.

Vrexer dodges my headlong rush.

"Ayar, please!" Robin calls out. "Don't!"

"Did you know?" I round on her.

She stands in front of me. Arms by her side and chewing on her lip. Her beautiful eyes, set in the prettiest face I've ever seen, fill with unshed tears.

She knew.

Vypr knew.

Everyone knew.

Except stupid Ayar. Vrexing Ayar, the liability. The warrior without control. A warrior who was about to lose his mate, his position, and his home because he didn't know.

A warrior who has lost everything anyway. My head wants to split open. Memories come tumbling out. Memories of the machine.

"Wait, Ayar! No!" Robin calls, but she's far away. Far from me as I'm in the air, knowing the machine will come for me.

It will take me, it will hurt me, and it will break me.

The bustle of the trading post fills every sense for a second, and then it's gone because I've found what I need. The air might be musty, but inside it's dark, small and the only place I can be. The hole.

The hole is safety. The hole is mine. The one place the machine is not.

Without my mates, I am nothing. Here, I can be nothing.

Robin

"What the fuck did you have to go and say that for?" I shout at Syn.

"Vrex!" He clutches his hand to his forehead. "I didn't think he'd react like that."

"No, you fucking didn't think." I watch as Ayar flies in an unsteady arc, descending down into an area which looks particularly ruined. "He was only just holding it together as it was."

"I thought Vypr would have told him," Syn says, the words catching in his throat.

I'm so angry I can barely speak. Anger at Syn's crass words and anger at myself for keeping the secret from Ayar in the first place. "You're a member of the unit. You probably know him better than me, and you thought something like that could just be said without consequence?"

"It's Ayar." Syn manages to at least look somewhat anguished. "Vrex!" He moves his hand from his forehead to his chin. "Vypr!"

The loss of both males comes in to hit me like a sledgehammer. We don't have any idea where Vypr is, or even if he's alive, and now Ayar thinks we both betrayed him. The two beings on which he thought he could rely.

This whole thing is fucked up, and I'm left dealing with the aftermath, along with my own churn of emotions I don't even know how to process.

How is it possible I've gone from investigating with two gorgeous males who had got under my skin and made me invincible, to feeling as if I've had my heart ripped from my chest?

"Vrex!" Syn says again. "I mean, we might not have always seen eye to eye, but I don't want to lose either of them from the unit. I'd prefer it if Ayar didn't blow everything up he comes into contact with, but I'd have him fighting by my side any turn."

"You should have told him that," I mutter, realizing immediately I'm just as bad.

Which doesn't help the horrible empty pit yawning in my stomach at the loss of Vypr and Ayar. Being abducted didn't change how I felt about relationships, given I've never been in one which wasn't heavily weighted to the other side, whether that was my family or him.

All I've experienced was take. Then I meet Ayar and Vypr. Two males who didn't want anything from me, other than my presence in their lives. Two perfect souls who needed me but on my terms.

I am empty and I am alone. My cheeks are wet. Tears I should have cried forever pour out of me. The last thing I want to do is cry, and yet, I can't stop. I'm standing on a roof of a decrepit building on a planet which is not mine, and I'm crying in floods, sobs wracking my body.

"I'm sorry, Robin." Syn edges slightly closer but keeps his distance in an odd but respectful way. "I'm not exactly a team player. Or a mated male." He twists his clawed hands together. "Let me help you, in whatever way I can."

Gone is the cocky male who squared up to Ayar earlier. Instead, he's contrite in the face of a female who has become all snot and water.

I want to be decisive. I want to be the professional I am, but there are two males who are missing from my life, and it's impossible to know what to do.

"Is what you said about Vypr true? Will the Drahon..." I swallow back bile which rises. "Will they hurt him?"

Syn's eyes widen, and he takes a step back, clearly worried about the onslaught of tears he might unleash with his answer.

"The Drahon don't care about other organics. They only care about themselves." His breath hitches. "They will probably torture him."

I feel like he's punched me in the stomach. My back aches and my head pounds, nerve endings jangling. I close my eyes, and the scent of damp fills my nose. Nothing is right.

"Robin." I open my eyes to see him standing close to me. "For what it's worth, they won't kill him. Ryak's sources indicate the Drahon feel Gryn are too valuable to destroy."

I close my eyes again. Syn is not helping, not in the slightest.

"We need to find Ayar," I say. "At least we know approximately where he is."

"I don't want to be unhelpful, but we'll need to walk," Syn says, and I open my eyes to glare at him. "If we fly, I'll put my scent on you and well, basically, Ayar will kill me."

As if things couldn't get any worse.

THIS PART OF THE TOWN IS ALMOST COMPLETELY destroyed, either with the passage of time or from a huge battle, but either way, I'm picking my way over what is, in essence, a pile of rubble.

"Where are you?" I say under my breath. "Give me a clue, Ayar." I don't want to shout out and draw any more attention to us than we've already had, given Vypr's disappearance.

"Do you not feel your mates?" Syn asks me.

I stare at him, narrowing my eyes. Are all Gryn obsessed with sex?

"In what way?" I fold my arms.

"In here?" He taps his head.

"Don't be silly." I turn away. "That's not possible."

"The other humans do," Syn calls out. "They feel their mates. You should try."

I raise my eyes to the heavens, or at least Ustokos' churning clouds. Nothing this male says makes any sense.

And then the pain spikes through me. Firing through my eye and down my left shoulder. I'm somewhere dark, somewhere which should be safe. Somewhere nearby.

When my vision clears, I'm looking directly at the entrance to a small hole. Feathers poke from it, dark slate gray and white.

"Go back," I say over my shoulder to Syn. "Go and get the others or whatever you need to do, just go."

Vypr

The Drahon male hits me in the chest again, and I hear a crunching which is probably a rib. If I have any luck left it will be his hand, but as pain spirals through my torso, it becomes pretty clear it's a rib. That can join some of the other bones in my body the Drahon have decided I don't need for the time being.

"Where is the controller for the defense system?" Grid asks again. He's sat in a comfortable chair, sipping on what looks like a tankard of cold var beer.

"What controller?" I spit out a mouthful of blood on the floor.

"Hoist him up again, see if that'll loosen his tongue," Grid replies, with disinterest.

I can only see out of one eye, but the Drahon reaches for the hook which hangs from the ceiling and hauls me to my feet by my wings. Pure white agony splits through me as he attaches the hook to the clamp holding my wings in an unnatural and painful position.

I can't give in, and I can't beg for mercy, because neither the Drahon nor the Kijg have any. There is no way I'm giving up any information about the defense system, as it will put all of Ustokos in danger.

"Wait." Grid drains his tankard. "I have a better idea. Get his mate."

"What?" I curse myself internally for reacting, but it's exactly what Grid wants. He bares his teeth at me.

"Did you not think we'd get them too? It was easy. They were looking for you." He laughs. "Now we have more Gryn and more leverage with your seniors." He leans in closer, knowing I can't move. I can't touch him, as much as I'd love to rip the other side of his face off. "We also have leverage over you."

He jerks his head at the Drahon, who shambles away, out of the cell and down a corridor. Grid stares at me, his gaze unwavering as I slowly spin, first one way, then the other.

My wings are numb, as are my legs. I'm just hoping beyond hope this is a ruse, that Grid is hoping I'll crack.

In the corridor, there is the rattling of chains, and the Drahon reappears with something small, covered in heavy sacking. The creature is about the same height as Robin. I go to inhale, but my cracked rib stops me from being able to breathe deeply enough to take in her scent.

To tell if it is truly my Robin, and if she also has Ayar's scent on her.

I long to scent them both. I long to have my arm around Ayar's warm, firm, muscled body and Robin sitting between my legs. To wrap my wings around them both. Once I get them back, I've already promised myself I'll never let them go again. Never. If I had any doubts a Gryn could love two mates, they have dissipated the longer we've been apart.

Robin completes me and Ayar. My heart bursts with all I have for them both.

"We have your mates," Grid says. "If you want them both to survive, you will tell us where the controller is."

He nods at the Drahon, who pulls a dagger from his belt and plunges it into the figure, who crumples to the floor.

"Robin!" It's a howl, not a word.

We are destroyed. I am destroyed. In one moment, I've lost everything. Ayar will never be the same again, not if she's gone, and without him whole, I am ended.

"You fool," I growl at Grid. "You'll get nothing from me. Not now, not ever."

"I'll get exactly what I want, or your other mate will get the same treatment as you. Only I won't stop. Not until his wings are wrenched from their sockets."

I stare at the crumpled form. I shut my eyes.

I die my own death.

Robin

I approach the hole carefully. As I get closer, the pain gets greater, only somehow, I know it's not my pain. I bend down and peer inside. Ayar is crouched, perched really, arms resting on his knees. His head is bowed, and he almost looks like he's meditating.

Only I know he's not. He's in pain, and although he thinks it's physical, it's all in his poor mixed-up head.

"When the Gryn first found me and released me," Ayar says quietly, not looking up, "I couldn't stand the light. My eyes had been damaged, but I couldn't stay in the surgery either."

"I can imagine." I shuffle down until I'm sitting opposite him.

He lifts his head, long hair in his face but the tiny hint of a smile, sad but there, at the corners of his mouth.

"I used to hide. I would find places small enough that only I could get in them. It didn't matter where they were, just as long as they were dark." Ayar's chest expands, and he exhales as if he's trying to dislodge a demon. "Vypr would find me. He would always find me, and eventually, he showed me a place he had made, just for me. He lined it with furs, made sure it was hidden away from the rest of the lair, and if I went there, he would wait outside until I came out."

I'm not entirely sure I can breathe. My chest is impossibly tight as I reach for Ayar's hand, dangling off his knee. He offers no resistance as I take it in mine.

"I didn't have anywhere to hide," I say.

"You suffered," he says, and this time, he does lift his head, his dark eyes boring into me. "But you do not need to hide."

"Why?"

"Because you have me. And I have Vypr," Ayar says, simply.

"I would have done anything for you to have found me on Earth." A sob escapes me because I want him to be healed, all of him. The part in his head which causes him pain, the searing of his brain which scrambled all his thoughts. And I want Vypr too. I want it so much it hurts like I'm being torn apart inside.

"You make us complete, Robin. You are the key who locked our hearts in an eternal loop," Ayar says, his deep, dark eyes fixed on me.

I can't hold back any longer. I want Ayar more than anything in the entire universe, and I'm crawling into the space, into his arms, and shoving myself against his chest, drinking in his unique smell, one which comforts me just enough to stem the tears. He shifts on his side, curling up in the space to allow me to snuggle into him.

"We should have told you about the seniors," I say fiercely. "You should have known the truth all along. I know Vypr wanted to tell you. He just wanted to make sure you were healed first." I look up at him. "It was wrong. But it was all because he loves you."

"And what about you, precious mate. What do you want?" Ayar rumbles. I feel his heart beat, fluttering in his chest like the wings he uses to take flight. It's a heart which isn't whole, not without Vypr.

"We're two broken things, aren't we?"

"You are not broken, my Robin. You are perfect." Ayar nuzzles into my hair.

Perfection itself

"What did you say?"

"Nothing." Ayar holds me tightly.

My head fills with a dark cloud, tinged at the edges with blue. The calm around the storm.

Chaos held back by beauty.

"It's you." I pull away from him. "Syn said something about being able to feel each other, and I can feel you!"

Ayar's lips twitch a little. "Now you feel me."

"What do you mean?"

"I've always had you, Robin. In my head and in my soul, even when I didn't know it was you."

I shift position so I can touch his face, cupping his cheek in my hand. "You are an enigma, Ayar, and I'm not sure even you know it."

This time, he does laugh.

"You are the clarity I needed, where Vypr is my rock." He shuts his beautiful eyes, and when they open, they are clouded with all the horrors. "The machine Proto had me in was designed to kill me and revive me. It did that hour after hour, turn after turn. I've no idea how long it went on, only who I was before the machine eludes me. I just know I was someone else. Someone good. Someone you and Vypr have shown me I can be again."

And just like that, I see the male he wants to be. A strong warrior, ready for anything, unbroken and unbowed. He is my Ayar, my mate and my center, just as Vypr and I are his.

"Vypr needs us," I say, the words springing suddenly into my head and into the open. "He's not far. He needs us."

My back radiates a dull ache again, this time not because of my cramped position but something else.

"How is this even possible?" I query.

"Thoughtbond," Ayar says, pressing a kiss to my lips.

"Thoughtbond? You mean something psychic?"

Electricity sparks between Ayar and me as his lips brush mine, and I'm seeing, not the interior of a hole in the ground, but a cell. Lit by a dim light in the ceiling.

"I can see!" I grab Ayar's cheeks and thump my lips back to his, plundering his mouth for all I'm worth.

Mates

"He's near!" Ayar gasps as I release him.

"Hearts locked," I whisper.

"Hearts healed," he replies, scooping me into his arms. He unfolds himself from the hole, and we step out into the light.

Ayar

I may not know who I was before. My head might be full of pain, fog, and the visions which dance in my eyes on occasions, but when Robin kissed me it was as if I was joined in a circle of complete clarity.

And what's more, she says she connected with Vypr through the thoughtbond. My Vypr! He is alive, and we get to claim him.

Up until now, my life has been needs, likes, and dislikes because it was all my fractured mind would let me hold onto. But with Robin and Vypr together, I'm rebuilding. I'm everything I can be.

I am Ayar, Gryn warrior.

"My Robin." I hold her close to me.

"You feel him too?"

"A little."

"Then he has to be nearby, doesn't he?"

I stroke through her hair, silky and entrancing. It helps me put my disordered thoughts back together. "I don't know much about the thoughtbond, only that I feel you, I feel my Vypr, and sometimes I feel others too."

I've never admitted to anyone, even Vypr, that I can catch others' thoughts. Partially because, for a long time, I believed they were part of the hallucinations which plagued me after I was freed from the machine. Once my life became more stable, because I fell in love with my Vypr, he made me follow a routine with work and play, and I realized the voices and thoughts were not my own or my imagination.

Except, I found it frustrating. It was hard enough to deal with everything wrong in my head, let alone get random thoughts from others.

But, as I connect to Robin and feel both her pleasure at being close to me and her concern for Vypr, I can see how this thoughtbond might be explored and used.

"We need to find a Kijg," I say, inhaling her scent deeply, wondering how on Usokos I've ended up aroused in this situation.

Because I'm very aroused.

"Ayar?" Robin looks up at me, and I see I'm pressed against her. "There's a time and a place," she says, but I stop her mouth with a kiss, her human kiss I can't ever get enough of.

"I know, precious mate. I'd mate you right here, but there's no mating until we find Vypr," I say as I release her lips from mine. "Then we will both take you until you are unable to move." Robin looks up at me, her mouth open slightly. She blinks. I lean closer into her. "Because I know that's what you want, little mate."

I unfurl my wings and beat down, once, twice, rising into the air easily. I need to put my Robin somewhere safe and find a Kijg if we have any chance of locating Vypr.

The last thing I need is to lose her, not when I've found myself within her.

Robin clings to me, but not because she's scared, because she's searching the ground below us. I'm reminded she said she understood how to find out information because of what she did back on Earth. Looks like she's doing it now.

"There!" she calls out and points below us.

In between two reasonably intact buildings, I see a male Kijg hurrying along. Something about him looks suspicious, and I can see why he caught Robin's attention.

"Follow him," she adds, "but don't let him know we're up here."

"Easy." I laugh, setting my wings and gently weaving from side to side to maintain height and use the lift from the buildings beneath me.

The Kijg continues, its scurrying gait not helping my prey drive. If I didn't have Robin in my arms, I'd most definitely be dropping onto it, to enjoy the feel of flesh under my claws.

To revisit some of my rage on the pathetic creature.

Instead, Robin tugs on my hair and points to a reasonably intact roof of a building. I follow her direction, trusting her to keep the Kijg in view as we drop down and I land as quietly as I possibly can.

"Down," she says, flattening herself on the roof and crawling towards the edge of the building.

"I am a Gryn warrior, I don't do 'down'." I shake my feathers out. A small, strong hand grips my wing, and I'm yanked downwards in a movement I didn't see coming.

"Guess what, you're slumming it today," Robin hisses. "We need to keep a low profile, until we find out where Vypr is."

"I'll find out where he is." I'm back on my feet again and in the air.

My clever mate knows how to keep herself concealed which means I can take the action I want. In this case, it's spiraling until I see the Kijg, still hurrying along. With a couple of quick beats, I'm stooping down behind him, snagging him easily as I fire myself back into the sky.

He squirms, his scent hitting me. I almost gag. Kijg stink in a way I usually cannot stomach. But this one is important, so I clamp a hand over his mouth, to stop the vrexer from shouting, and spin around until I'm back on the roof with Robin.

She sits, arms folded, staring at me.

"What part of 'low profile' was that little stunt, Ayar?" she says, eyeing the wriggling Kijg.

"We need him, for information."

"We don't need our own captive, though. What are we going to do with him?" Robin huffs.

I raise an eyebrow, feeling a grin hitching my lips. "I know what I'd like to do with him." I hold out the wriggling creature, my hand still covering his mouth, and look him up and down. He squeaks with terror.

"We're not doing that." Robin is on her feet. "Because you're better than him."

"Ayar certainly is."

We both look up to see Syn dropping silently towards us, his wings hardly kicking up any dust as he lands.

"Did you get help?" Robin asks.

"Sort of," Syn replies. "What are you going to do with that Kijg?"

"Depends," I reply, addressing the now limp reptile. "On whether I fancy a snack or not." The Kijg moans under my fingers but doesn't even try to move.

"He doesn't know anything. He's a thief. I saw him in the trading post, taking things which didn't belong to him," Syn says, somewhat smugly.

"If he's a thief, then he knows everything," Robin replies. "Let him go."

Vypr

There's a blissful relief in my wings. The clamp has been removed, and although I can't move them, or much of the rest of my body, just knowing I'm partially free of the intense, burning pain helps concentrate my mind.

Until I remember the small figure crumpling to the ground and the threats Grid made towards my Ayar. Parts of me do not want to believe for a minute, an instant, I've lost my mates to the Kijg. A species which is tearing itself apart internally due to warring factions. Their lack of cohesion and their alliance to the Drahon will be their undoing.

It's the only thing I have to hold onto as I finally prize my eyes open and work out my surroundings. If not, grief will paralyse me. Half my heart has gone. Robin is gone, and I cannot let Grid, the Drahon, or the Kijg know how much it has affected me.

"Gryn is awake," the Drahon from earlier grunts.

"Where the vrex did you find this great lump, Grid? Is he all the Drahon could spare?" I say as Grid's ugly face swims into view. "Or don't they trust you around a more intelligent one?"

I look the Drahon up and down. Thicker, taller, heavier set than the slight Kijg, they would be imposing if their arms didn't end in rather small, pathetic, three-fingered hands with claws they always seem to keep shorn short. As if they don't like to fight. Although they like to torture, that much is clear from the enjoyment the creature took from my multiple beatings.

Ones which have left me with broken bones, one eye swollen completely shut, and the rest of me covered in blood and bruises.

The dumb Drahon snarls at me, raising his fisted little hand. He might be stupid, but he doesn't like to be reminded of it. Good. The more havoc I can cause, the more I can push the memory of losing my Robin out of my mind. A beating will help.

It's a beating I deserve. I couldn't protect her. And now I have to answer to Ayar.

"Don't," Grid orders. For half a second I think the Drahon is going to disobey, but then he lowers his fist. "This," he pats the side of the cylinder I'm in, "will get us what we want much quicker than blows."

"More narcotics?" I scoff. "You know they don't work on the Gryn."

Although, all the stuff he's shot me with has had some pain numbing qualities, some interesting hallucinations, and a feeling of having partied very hard, none of them made me feel like giving up the information he wants. None of which will take away all the pain on the planet vested in my heart.

"No more narcotics, Vypr. You're long past that point. Further methods are required," Grid says, his words dripping with hate as his skin flushes scarlet.

"More than killing my mates and threatening my fellow warriors? Unless you're going to bring the entire lair here and slaughter them, you know it won't make any difference."

My heart wrenches in my chest, the spike of pain coming from within. I want to roar Robin's name from the skies. I want to hold her body close to me, take the last vestiges of her scent within my senses. I want to go mad from her loss.

I need to be there for Ayar. To protect my remaining mate from any further pain. If I can find out what Grid has done, maybe I can get to him.

Thinking straight is no longer an option. I've lost too much and I'm only just holding onto the tiny tendrils of hope which are Ayar's survival. It's all I can do. The despair filling my veins at the loss of Robin, I had hoped I'd become numb to the constant searing pain of it.

But it's worse now than ever. All I can do is fill my mind with Ayar.

Grid chokes out a laugh. "Your mates are the least of your worries. We need your seniors, or at least one of them, and you will be the key to getting what we want."

I want to give up. I want to tell Grid everything, anything, in order to get my Ayar in my arms again. To hold him close, breath in his scent, and never be parted from him again.

Only it won't bring Robin back, and I'd have to explain why I stopped being an honorable warrior. His sweet, handsome, scarred face floats in my mind. Brows furrowed, he doesn't understand why. Why I would betray the lair, our Prime, our seniors, our Guv, for him.

Although Ayar would do anything for me, he would do everything to protect our world and our warriors. He wanted a youngling because he was thinking of the future, both our future and that of the Gryn. I couldn't see it, not when I was intoxicated by him. But I see it now.

I see what he wanted. He wanted a legacy for us both. For Robin. She was the completion of the circle of our love, not the beginning.

"The Gryn will never give up Ustokos." I grit my teeth,

trying to persuade my limbs to move, only now the feeling is returning, my inability to move has nothing to do with the damage inflicted on me and everything to do with the bonds holding me down inside the cylinder. "And Ustokos will never submit to the Drahon, no matter what the scaly vrexers think," I snarl.

"Yeah, yeah." Grid flaps a deep blue hand at me. "The Gryn think this planet belongs to them, but you're wrong."

"It belongs to the species which inhabit it, Grid. That's where we differ. All we want to do is make sure we can rebuild and become something better." I look away from him, not wanting to see his irritating face if I can help it. "Something you'll never understand because you don't know what better is. Not while you ally yourself to the Drahon."

The big male lifts his hand again, but Grid stays it.

"Leave him. The machine will make sure he tells us exactly what we need to know," he says, quietly. "Your masters will get their information," he adds. Just for a second, his eyes seem less sure.

He moves back, and I hear the sound of claws on a keypad. From the side of the cylinder, a silver covering emerges. Rolling up, over me, it goes rigid and clear.

I know where I am.

It's the machine. The one which haunts Ayar's nightmares and mine.

It hums, a sound I'll never forget, and it's joined by another sound. My voice, my roar, and my shriek as every atom of my being is pulled apart.

From deep down, I feel the rage. Ayar's rage. Born of fear and pain. I understand it all.

I understand him, and I'm never going to see my mates again.

Robin

I look at the shivering lizard man at Ayar's feet. An anger I don't think I've ever felt before rises within me.

It's not mine.

Ayar stares down at the Kijg. His stance indicates he'd end the creature if he could. I feel him burning through me.

All those times I wanted to understand someone better, to see into their thoughts, to spy into their soul. It seems the Gryn have developed an ability to do this.

It is glorious.

The link I have with Ayar, it's something else, something so delicate and beautiful, tears prick the back of my eyes. All I want is to be able to share it with Vypr too.

The time I spent stuck with Magnus because of fear, it melts away from me. Being bound to my two aliens is the most perfect, pure experience. Not because I need to know what they think and feel, but because I want to.

Right now, I want Ayar to calm the fuck down.

"Syn," I say to the big warrior with the permanent smirk. "Keep an eye on the Kijg."

I grab at Ayar's wing and pull. Initially, he remains planted, a solid mass of muscle I can't hope to move. Not until I let out a long breath and fill my head with thoughts of him.

Of what I want to do with him and Vypr when I get them alone.

And suddenly, easily, I have a male following me as I drag him over to the other side of the roof.

"We need the Kijg, Ayar, and I need you." I tap my chest, over my heart. "I'm breaking and I need you."

Ayar's breathing deepens, and I match it, holding him back, taking the swirl of his emotions and making him feel my own. I have fear, but I have hope. I have to connect with him on the same level as Vypr did. The way he could make Ayar understand, feel, and be the warrior he needs to be.

"Syn can get the Kijg to tell us what we need to know," Ayar says, eyes closed. "It's what he's good at, like Ryak."

"Ryak?"

"Our head of security. He was good at finding out things," Ayar rumbles as I step closer to him. "Syn can do it too."

"We can do the warrior thing soon, Ayar." I wrap my arms around his waist, snuggling into his warm body which smells of blood, metallic and sharp along his own unique spicy scent. "For now, we need to know what we're up against."

"I know, you're right. It's what Vypr would have done."

My heart nearly leaps out of my throat in my desire to reward him. He understands and he gets it. This crazy thoughtbond actually works!

I look over at the Kijg, still cowering under Syn's gaze. "How about we don't let on to the lizard man you understand?" I suggest.

Ayar frowns at me.

"I don't mean we should hurt him, just maybe make him think you would."

"I would," Ayar states baldly. "I really, really would."

"But not now, okay?" I pull his chin down until I can kiss him on the lips. "Let's get Vypr first."

Ayar closes his eyes and takes in my kiss. His pants bulge alarmingly. Now I have a calmer but more aroused male on my hands. I guess the thoughtbond will take more than a little time to master. Before anything more untoward can happen, I grab his hand and tow him back over to the Kijg.

Time for the alien version of 'good cop, bad cop.'

"Syn," I address the other male to a growl from Ayar. "Ayar has promised not to hurt this Kijg if he agrees to tell us what we need to know. As you know more about the situation than me, I thought you should ask the questions."

A pair of unblinking black eyes look up at Syn and stray over to Ayar, who has raised his wings and is looking particularly fearsome.

Some of which I don't think is an act.

"I don't know anything," the lizard man gibbers. "I'm a thief, just like he said." He jerks his thumb a Syn.

"Oh, don't talk to me. I'm just the female," I say and take a step back.

Syn finally cottons on, and he grabs the Kijg by his clothing, hauling the creature to his feet. He releases the male and dusts him off, forcefully.

Ayar snarls.

The Kijg gives him a terrified look. "Don't worry about Ayar." Syn smiles at the male. "He won't hurt you. Not while you're co-operating with us."

Ayar rumbles. I feel it in my chest.

So does the Kijg, who sways on his feet. Syn catches him by his shoulder. "All we want to know is where the Drahon base is. Then you can go and get on with, well, whatever it was you were doing."

There's a tinkle as a small gold colored bowl falls out of the lizard man's clothing and rolls away.

"After all, we're not part of the patrol and are not here to settle any disputes," Syn adds conversationally. "We're just looking for our friend and fellow warrior. And the Drahon. We're always looking for the Drahon."

"I don't..." The male shakes in Syn's grip, his hesitation still all too apparent.

Ayar extends his wings, beating them down once. He has his claws fully extended, and he's in the direct eyeline of the Kijg male.

"You don't what? You don't know?" Ayar says, although it's hard to understand him because he suddenly seems to have more teeth. He takes a step towards the Kijg.

"I don't think Ayar believes you," I join in, shaking my head sadly. "I want to believe you, though. Perhaps if you think harder. A little thief like you might have seen something useful."

"Useful to who?" the Kijg asks with a harsh laugh. "I'm hardly going to keep my head if I lead you to the Drahon, am I?"

"So you know where the Drahon are?" Syn asks quietly as Ayar seethes ever closer.

The lizard man doesn't know where to look.

"I mean, if you do know where they are, they won't know who told them. You can't be the only Kijg to know, right?" I add, looking to pile the pressure on. "On the other hand, Ayar one hundred percent knows you didn't tell us everything."

In response, Ayar releases a ferocious growl.

"Yes!" the Kijg yelps.

"Yes, what?" Syn asks, seemingly bored.

"I know where they are, just please, please don't let him eat me." He stares at Ayar, who has suddenly become a Gryn again. Feathers fluffed happily, claws almost gone, he flashes the sweetest grin at me.

"Where are they?"

"On the other side of the main square, there's an opening. It's heavily guarded, but it leads down. Underground. That's where the Drahon are, and that's where they took the Gryn."

"How many?" Syn asks.

"I'm not sure."

Ayar makes a sound like fabric ripping, only far more sinister.

"About a hundred. All that's left from those who were on Usokos when their ships got stuck outside the defense system."

Syn sucks in a breath.

"What is it?" I ask, sure he can't be worried about numbers. The Gryn have far more warriors than a hundred.

In a move I wasn't expecting from him, Syn slams his boot into the Kijg's head, and he goes down. He moves swiftly over to Ayar and grabs him around the shoulders. I see Ayar visibly flinch at the touch, and in an instant, I'm beside my mate.

"This Kijg shouldn't know about the defense system," Syn says in a low voice. "No one outside of the Gryn seniors and a handful of Mochi elders should know. This is bad. Very bad."

"It doesn't matter what that streak of gak knows or doesn't know," Ayar spits. "We need to go get Vypr." He attempts to squirm out of Syn's grip and get closer to me.

"It does matter because if the Kijg and the Drahon know Vypr knows the location of the controller for the defense system, we're all in big, big trouble," Syn says, gripping Ayar ever tighter. "And Vypr's in the most trouble of all.

Ayar

Being close to my Robin is the only thing keeping me from doing something, or someone, some damage. Particularly because Syn got to deal with the Kijg in the way I wanted to earlier.

Although, I notice he didn't get told off, not like me. I don't get to visit violence on the filthy creature, but Syn does. He also didn't get into any trouble for tying up and gagging the Kijg. None of which I think is fair.

Robin also made me hold back, and instead of flying to the supposed Drahon base, we've walked, taking a circuitous route which seemed like wasting time to me. Finally, we're on the opposite side of the square with the entrance to the base in sight. From our hiding place behind a crumbling wall, I see two Drahon guards, poorly disguised as Kijg, lurking near a doorway of a semi-ruined building.

It's taken everything I have not to just go. Especially when my Vypr is inside. But Syn says we have to wait, and Robin agrees.

"Are you sulking, Ayar?" Robin presses her hand against

my chest, and I look down into her beautiful, clear eyes. Her lips are deliciously full and red. She is eminently kissable.

"No," I reply, failing to take the sulk out of my tone. "Yes," I add. "I wanted to deal with the Kijg scum, and I want to get into the base, right now."

"You don't need to be the one doing all the fighting, you know. Sometimes you can work with others," she says, inclining her head to one side and making me want to run my lips down the curve of her neck.

"All I want is to protect you and Vypr. I'm not doing such a good job so far," I grumble.

"You've got me here and unscathed, haven't you?" Robin replies. "And we've found out where Vypr is, without the need to shed any blood. I'd say you're doing great."

She knows me only too well, especially because we're linked. I should keep her out of my head. I don't want her to know what worries me. I don't want her to see the things my brain makes me see. But I can't. It seems we have the bond, and I have no way of filtering it.

"I don't want you to filter anything, Ayar," Robin says, quietly. She delves her hands into my wings and strokes over my feathers in a way which makes me both want to melt and mate at the same time.

She laughs at my thoughts, the sound tinkling out over the crumbling roof of the building, filling every part of my being with light.

"Just stay being you, and we'll go get Vypr."

That's where she's wrong. I can't be me, not anymore. I need to be better than Ayar, the warrior with the laser cannon letting rip at anything which bothers me.

I need to be more like Vypr. Controlled, decisive, untroubled by visions, hallucinations, and a well of rage which goes to the center of Ustokos. I need to be more Vypr if I'm to ensure I do my best by my mates.

"We can't take on a hundred Drahon," Syn says.

"I'll take on as many Drahon as I need to," I reply.

"Two Gryn against a hundred Drahon. Interesting odds." I spin to see the speaker and find myself looking into the warm brown eyes of Mylo.

He has one laser cannon on his shoulder and another dangling from his fingers. The huge, broad warrior grins at me, sharp teeth on display. I immediately step in front of Robin, hearing the growl rumbling in my chest but at the same time wishing I could thank Mylo for being here.

"And you have your little female with you," Mylo says, leaning to one side to look at Robin, despite my obvious annoyance. "A crack shot and brave too." His grin widens. "You look like gak though," he adds, looking me up and down.

"Patrol," I mumble. "Bunch of vrexers."

"That 'bunch of vrexers' came and got us." Jay steps into our little group from an empty doorway, laser rifle slung over his shoulder.

"Well." Mylo extends his hand and tilts it one way and then the other. "Sort of."

"Okay, I caught them heading up to Ryak's office."

"Jay can be persuasive when he wants to be," Mylo says, huffing out a laugh. "Although we owe them more var beer than I think we'll ever be able to get."

"Why?"

"We persuaded them not to take the matter to the Guv but to let us deal with it. Unit business and all that," Jay says, studying his claws. He looks up at me. "Can't lose you, Ayar. You're the best part of the unit. Without you, we're nothing."

"Who else can we depend on to cause an almighty vrex up?" Mylo says as he swings a laser cannon towards me.

"Does the Guv know you're here?" Syn asks. Trust him to make things difficult.

"What do you think? Going to fly away and tell him?" Mylo snarls.

"No," Syn says, wrinkling his nose. "I shouldn't be here either."

"You're Ryak's little mochi-ka." I sniff. "He probably knows you're here."

"True." Jay cocks his head to one side. "But lair politics aside, we need to get you and Vypr back to the eyrie before anyone notices."

"So you all knew?" Robin interrupts. "About Ayar?"

I know what she's thinking. Her swirl of emotions is a cloud of dark gray anger. She's remembering the time back at the firing range when no one said anything.

"We knew, and we were never going to let it happen," Jay says.

Robin looks sideways at me, clearly worried how I might take the news that everyone knew about my imminent departure from the unit except me.

The thing is, I don't mind. Because, as it turns out, no one wanted me to go. They all wanted me to stay, and they're here to help find my Vypr.

I lift my wing and wrap it around my mate. "Good thing, too," I say to Jay. "I've saved your sorry wings more times than I'd like to count."

"You've tried to explode me just as many times." Jay bumps me with his wing, and this time I don't flinch.

Because I have Robin with me, and I know Vypr is close.

And now, I get to explode something.

Something green and reptilian, and all in order to save Ustokos.

Vypr

In the back of my mind, Ayar is...feathers fluffed. He's ready for something. He's ready to come and get me.

"Vrex!" I roar out as my lungs inflate again. Life returns to my body, and my brain registers all the pain, all at once. The dream remains, almost as if it were real.

I shouldn't even be able to function. The machine kills me and revives me over and over. Each time it does, I see Grid's foul visage peering in at me, and all I want to do is kill him.

Or for the pain to be over. It doesn't matter which.

And then, in the depths of my nightmare, I catch Ayar in my mind. But it's not a memory. He's actually here. Somewhere.

"Zarking Gryn." The cover on the machine folds back. "Why won't he break?" Another Drahon peers in. This one is slimmer in the face, more like a female.

"Gryn are tough. You know that." I hear Grid's voice. "You've trained enough of them."

"That's why the zarking worm had this zarking machine. It made them compliant."

"It made the ones from the camps compliant," Grid says. "These are warriors."

"Zark them," the Drahon says. "We don't have time for this. The portal isn't operational and the fleet is waiting. We need to secure the planet. We can't risk losing any more ships to the zarking defense system. Put him through another cycle, and if it doesn't work, find a Gryn it will work on."

"Yes, Bisgur," Grid says, and then bows at her sharp look, "yes, my queen."

My teeth grind together. I try to make a noise, but all that comes out is a hiss of breath because my body is too tense to do anything.

The Drahon peers in at me again. "Zarking Gryn. If they weren't worth so much, if this entire planet wasn't worth so much, I'd happily never see one or this zarking place again."

"The fleet will be staying?" Grid asks. "I thought you were just taking the Gryn?"

Bisgur makes the choking laugh of the Drahon. "You think we'd invest all of this effort for a few slaves? We're not just staying, we're taking. Ustokos will be ours."

What's left of the blood in my veins runs with ice. The seniors didn't think the Drahon were a threat, not with the defense system in place.

The Drahon are *the* threat to us all now Proto has gone. It's with creeping horror I see it all spread out. The Gryn might be honorable warriors, strong, true, and the best fighters the universe has ever seen. But without tech, we are at the mercy of foul creatures like the Drahon.

This is the way of the galaxy. We are foolish to think otherwise.

My body still won't respond. I'm helpless in the face of the Drahon, their machine, and their plans. I can't do much, if anything at all, but I can think about my Ayar. I can imagine his face, the feel of my hands in his feathers, and the gorgeous happy noises he makes as we bathe together, despite every protestation he makes before hand.

My Vypr. My eregri.

It can't possibly be Ayar? Can it?

The canopy closes. I'm not able to brace myself for what is coming because I already know this time it will break me. To die would be easy. It's going on with part of me missing that's hard.

Of the knowing Ayar and I would have to go on without her. The tiny precious human who made her way into our souls.

The canopy clicks into place, and the machine hums, the hum becoming a whine. The light within brightens, and each atom within me begins to suffer. The pain is at once there. All areas, all agony. It continues as all the air disappears, and I start to die.

As life is snuffed from me, I want to kill. A rage, a torrent of molten emotions rises. It is my desire for life, for love, for air.

For my remaining mate.

It turns to fury. Twisted with the searing death infecting my body. If I cannot live, I can die fighting. I will not let the Drahon take my need to be away from me.

So when I become aware of the explosions, I assume it's the last of my body giving in. My mind will surely follow.

Ayar

"Any chance you could stick to the plan?" Mylo asks me with a wing bump. "Because this time, it is a bit important."

"I always stick to the plan." I give Robin a sideways look. "If it's a good plan."

"If it involves explosions," Jay mutters.

We've moved into a position closer to the Drahon base, taking yet another circuitous route on foot because, after far too long watching for my tastes, Syn says they cycle the guards too regularly for us to be able to fly in.

"How will we know if Syn is in position?" Robin asks.

She holds my laser pistol as if she's had one in her hand her whole life. She did say she'd had some weapons training on Earth, although most handheld weapons are apparently out of bounds to humans in her country, whatever that means.

My inner warrior wants to protect her, wrap her in my wings, and never let her out. But seeing her standing alongside me, weapon in hand, quietens that warrior and releases a sense of pride. Unfortunately, the sight also awakens the other warrior who wants to mate, vigorously.

I have to keep taking long, deep breaths.

"You do know I feel everything, don't you?" Robin murmurs. "Including anything below your belt."

By the goddess, I want her to feel what's below my belt!

"I actually heard that, Ayar." I have a pair of blue eyes trained on me.

Robin looks very serious, until her gaze travels down my body. Then those eyes widen at the bulge she's causing.

"That is not me, it's you." She hisses. "Think about Vypr instead!"

So I do. I think about my gorgeous big warrior and all of us in our nest together, a tangle of naked bodies.

"Not like that!" Robin punches me in the arm, although she has a smile on her face she quickly hides.

She's right. I have to be serious, like my Vypr. After all, Mylo's given me the explosives, so it's my job to get us into the Drahon base, and then we'll find my mate and deal with the Drahon as we see fit.

If they've harmed one single feather on him, I will kill them all. String them up as a warning to any species who dares to hurt my mates.

A low, keening wail whips on the wind to where we hide.

"Syn is in position," Mylo says, giving Jay a shove. "Get out there and take out the guards."

Be more Vypr. Be more Vypr.

I hold back as Jay slinks away and instead concentrate my entire being on Robin. She has her eyes closed. It seems like she's trying to control her breathing, and for a second, I worry she's ill. Until she starts up.

"He's..." She suppresses a cry.

And I feel it too. Just for a moment. The point at which he tips from life into death.

Out in the main square, two laser bolts sizzle. The air fills with the scent of ions. I'm no longer Vypr. I'm no longer Ayar.

I am chaos, and it's all the Drahon deserve.

In the air, I see the downed guards. In no time, I'm by the doors, pressing the short time mines onto the metal and leaping to one side as the explosion forces them inwards with a groan of twisting metal.

"Go, go, go!" Mylo calls out. Both he and Jay are just behind me with Robin, and I don't need any further encouragement.

I grab her hand, tuck her behind me, knowing Mylo has my back, and head into the base.

"Good explosion," Syn says, appearing next to me as if he's made out of smoke.

I grin at him.

"What the fuck!" Robin calls out. "If you were already in here, why did we need to blow the doors?"

"Because the Drahon need to know we're coming for them," Syn says. "And what better way of doing it than using Ayar to announce us?"

I shake out my feathers and hold Robin close to my side.

"We have to get to Vypr," she says, her voice a whisper. "There's something wrong."

Our surroundings are oddly familiar. For a brief second, my heart rate spikes as I see a flash of silver in the interior, the color of Proto, but then it resolves itself into the reflection of a burning piece of debris in the steely dullness I've come to associate with the ancient Gryn bases.

"This is Gryn?" I fire out at Syn. "The Drahon have gained access to an underground lair?"

"It seems so, although this one was badly damaged at some point," he says. "It may not have had any security controls."

"But if they have access to your technology, doesn't that mean they have access to you?" Robin asks Syn.

He attempts to keep his face straight, but instantly, I feel him. He was always here on his own mission. That me, Vypr, and Robin turned up was something he's used to his advantage.

As I watch, he shrinks back. My anger beats in my chest like I'm flying for my life. It wants out.

It wants blood.

But I want Vypr and Robin more.

"Do what you need to do," I growl at him. "Take Mylo and Jay. I'm going to get my Vypr."

Robin

Despite Ayar wanting to keep a rather too tight hold on me, I manage to wriggle free in order to be able to walk normally. I have to admit, seeing him rise into the air and the resulting explosion was something else entirely.

Something damn sexy. At least, I think those are my feelings. Some of them could be Ayar, as it appears explosions have an interesting effect on him.

I'm not getting the hang of this thoughtbond at all. Most of the time, it seems I have Ayar in my head. If I try to tune him out, I miss him.

And the glimpses of Vypr? They send a chill to my very marrow. We have to get to him.

Something large and lizard-like looms out of a side passage. Without even thinking, I fire off the laser pistol, not even taking aim, and the creature thumps down, face first in front of me.

"My *eregri!*" Ayar exclaims, jumping closer to me to inspect the dead Drahon.

My stomach cramps and I feel queasy. I just killed something.

"*Eregri*?" He wraps a warm wing around me, his sweet, musky scent filling my senses.

"I've never...I don't believe I killed him."

"With one shot." Ayar grins at me. "You're more than just precious trouble. You're a perfect weapon."

His enthusiasm is infectious. I look down at the dead lizard. He holds a vicious knife in one hand.

"It was you or him," Ayar says in my ear, or is he in my head? "Make sure it's always you."

This time, my stomach squirm is something else entirely. Ayar believes in me. He wants me to be the best I can possibly be. He simply wants me, and he will protect me until the end of time. It fires something within my soul. A desire to be the best and make my mates proud of me.

I am not a feeble human female.

I am loved and I love. And I have Vypr to save.

"Where are we going to find him?" I ask Ayar.

"Gryn bases have a pattern," he replies. "There are four large chambers, all linked. They branch out into smaller chambers for barracks, nests, food halls, healing pools, and so on." Ayar taps a claw against his teeth, and I worry for his lips given how viciously sharp the onyx scimitar is. "If they're going to have him anywhere, it will be in the larger chambers. The other areas would give him too great an advantage."

He looks at me, and I can feel his deep seated concern.

"You're doing great." I run a hand down his wing, knowing it will soothe him. "Good thinking."

"It's hard. I need him," Ayar stumbles out.

"You don't have to tell me, sweetheart." I give him another wing rub. "I feel it."

The relief which radiates from him is palpable. As is his etched worry because we haven't heard from Vypr for a while.

"Take care, my *eregri*." Ayar begins to walk. "These corridors were designed for Gryn but not enough to allow us to fly, more's the pity," he grumbles. "Makes you wonder what the ancients were thinking."

I know what he's thinking, and the violence is at once fascinating and terrible. That he can be so sweet and yet so dangerous is almost intoxicating. I think it might be the reason I just blew a large hole in a lizard man.

And why part of me feels so incredibly empowered by being able to be a badass.

"You are a badass," Ayar says, tuning in on my thoughts. "What's a badass?" he asks.

"It's something I never thought I'd be," I reply. "I thought I'd aways be in the shadows."

"When we get Vypr and get out of here, I will always keep you in the light, little Robin." Ayar levels his deep, dark gaze. "Unless I have you under me," he goes on. "In which case, I will enjoy filling every inch of you."

It looks like Ayar is most definitely a creature of pleasure and not the creature of violence everyone else thinks he is. We're so close now to Vypr. Even though I can't touch his mind, it seems I can sense his presence.

All of which makes me wonder exactly what is going to happen if we all get out of here alive. I get snatches from Ayar of warm furs and bodies wrapped around bodies. It's something I want, so very much. I've just learned I don't always get what I want.

Unlike the feathered chaos in front of me, tripping along at a tremendous pace which means I'm running to keep up.

"Hst!" He holds up a fist and shoves me behind him, into an alcove, where I'm pressed against a wall with a face full of feathers.

Ayar!

"Patience, little mate. I'd rather we didn't draw attention to ourselves. I think we're close to Vypr," Ayar murmurs over his shoulder.

A frisson of excitement runs through my body. Possibly it's mine, possibly it's a sneeze I'm trying to hold onto.

Turns out it's a sneeze.

And not a quiet one.

"Vrex!" Ayar grinds out, stepping away to allow me to breathe. "Looks like we're doing this the old Ayar way after all."

He shoves me back until we reach another corridor. I can't see what's going on ahead of me because there is a feathery wall of fluff still in my face. Then the feathers are whipped away, and Ayar is facing me. He has me in his arms, and we're flying through the air as the most almighty explosion reverberates around us.

"What did you do?" I shout over the ringing in my ears.

"I made my own door." Ayar grins at me. "Let's go get Vypr."

Ayar

Two explosions! This is nectar from the vrexing goddess. Plus, Vypr is close and I have Robin. My instinct, my thoughtbond is going wild because he is both in my head and not. It meant blowing something up was inevitable.

The dust begins to clear, and the area is dotted with a few Drahon bodies. I steer Robin carefully through them, not wanting her to get as upset as she did when she shot the male earlier. My brave little female. I always knew she needed protection. I didn't know it was from her own soul, which seems to want to stop her from fulfilling exactly who she is destined to be.

As I expected, we've blasted into one of the larger chambers, and I gather Robin's hand in mine. I have to hope Syn and the others are keeping the rest of the Drahon busy because we've just made enough noise to wake the dead.

"What is *that*?" Robin exclaims, stopping dead and bringing me to a halt too as the smoke dissipates and we can see the entire cavernous room.

In the center, I see what she's looking at. The familiar cylinder. The low hum.

"It's the machine." I take a step back. "The machine."

My words are lost in a roar of ultimate terror. I thought I'd never see the thing again, not after Vypr rescued me. He took me away and promised me I'd always be safe. Then we destroyed Proto, and the machines were no more. Vypr made good on his promise.

But here is the machine. It's right in front of me, and my entire world contracts back to the point where the bots clamped me into it and the horror began.

I should move forward. But instead, I fall to my knees. There is nothing else but the machine and me. The noise it makes, a low, terrible hum rising to a whine, it's ingrained in my memory as something I can never forget.

When I died and woke and died again. My head full of the things which crawl out of the dark.

Out of death. Because death no longer became a release.

It became a prison.

"Vypr!" The name sears through me. A name I have to respond to, even though the lights are dimming around me. My mate. My heart. My everything. "Ayar—help, please help? He's in here, and I need to get him out."

Time hits me. The present slams my face like a fist, like a wing in a vicious fight. I see Robin frantically pulling at the canopy. Tears run down her face, and she is sobbing.

My mate. My heart. My everything.

"I can't...the machine..." I whisper. Paralysis complete. There are no more needs, no more wants, only the machine.

Only the machine.

I want my feet to move. I want all of me to move, to get to the machine. To get to the thing he promised me I'd never see again. Every night when I woke screaming and he held me. He promised.

"Ayar! Please!" Robin heaves out, her voice a desperate cry. "He's dying! I can't open it."

Something snaps.

She is my all. He is my all.

Feet, wings, arms. They work again, and I'm by Robin's side. With little effort on my part, the catch bursts open, and my Vypr lies inside, arms and legs bound. His face pale. His lips blue and his eyes closed.

"Get him out!" Robin's voice seems so far away. "We have to do CPR!"

I gather him carefully up, lifting him like the precious bundle he is, but once he's out of the machine, Robin pulls at him roughly, making me lower him to the floor. She tilts back his head, pinches his nose, and kisses him deeply, once, twice before checking over his chest. A strange sort of human ritual, for the dead maybe?

"Fuck it, Vypr! You're not going to die on me!" she yells out and thumps her fist on his chest, leaning all of her little weight into pressing down, before she goes back to her kiss.

My face is wet. I don't know why. But Robin doesn't stop. She presses on his chest again, going back to his lips.

And then he groans. His chest expands as he draws air into his lungs, filling them inch by precious inch.

"Shit!" Robin cups her hands around his face, staring into his eyes. "It worked! Vypr? Are you okay?" She stares down at him intently.

"My Vypr?" I can't believe it. The machine did not get a victim.

He beat it, just like he always promised we would. The machine is no more. It did not take him.

"Ayar?" He croaks. "Robin? Are you here?"

Robin throws her arms around him, and she's shaking hard as she kisses over his face. "We're here."

I reach out to touch him, to make sure he's real. His skin is warm. His scent is perfect.

"*Eregri*?" He pushes himself into a sitting position with a wince and reaches for me, pulling me to him, Robin in his other arm.

"You saved me," he murmurs in my ear. "You are truly my boundless flight."

"We are," I say, my heart so light it could fly away on its own. "We are all in flight, forever."

Vypr presses a kiss to my lips and turns to Robin. "Fate," he says, simply.

My face is still wet, and I don't care. I have my mates. Even as I look up, I no longer see the machine.

All I see is our future.

Vypr

Robin. She's alive.

Our precious little female is warm and scented as she holds my head, bright blue, caring eyes staring down at me. Just like she did with Ayar in the surgery. Her heart is pure and whole.

"I thought he'd killed you," I whisper, my throat raw. Every single part of me aches and burns. "I thought I'd lost you."

"I'm here," she says, her voice sweet and perfect to my ears. "We're both here. You know we'd never leave you."

A pair of huge wings looms over me, and my Ayar is next to me too, one huge, clawed hand on my shoulder and the other stroking back my hair. Like I always do with him.

I might be off the machine and have my mates in my arms, but I'm as weak as a youngling and the horror won't ever leave me.

My Ayar, my beautiful, scarred warrior. All those cycles where I held him, soothed him, this is what he was dealing with. This is what he has been unable to process.

"You helped me, Vypr," Ayar murmurs. "Without you, I'd never have survived."

"And without Robin, neither would I." I look up at the little female.

I might have thought my heart was full, that Ayar could take all I had to give, but now I know this tiny female is the heart in which we both sit.

She is our goddess.

"That might be taking things a bit far." She smiles at me, eyes twinkling with her tears and her mirth, both of which war within her.

Thoughtbond.

Of course, that's how she knows what I'm thinking. She knows what we're all thinking. Our thoughtbond is extraordinary. What else could it be?

"But you're welcome to call me 'your majesty' any time," she says with a soggy giggle.

I clutch both of them to me, wanting this reunion to last forever. "Precious," I say, "you'll always be ours."

Some of their warmth is beginning to seep back into me. "Have you got any weapons?" I ask Ayar. "The Drahon have a plan we've got to stop."

"Here." Robin hands me a laser pistol. "I didn't like it much anyway," she adds flippantly, although from the flicker in Ayar's thoughtbond, there's more to it.

"We need to get you back to the lair and to Orvos for treatment," Ayar says with what can only be described as glee in his voice. "You're not stopping any Drahon today."

"You're going to love doing putting me at the medic's mercy aren't you, mate?" I growl. "But we've still got a mission to complete, whatever state I'm in."

"You've just been dead." Robin tugs at my wing. "Mission's over."

"The Drahon have a fleet, just outside the defense system. As soon as they find a way through, they're going to invade and take Ustokos," I rush out. "This is our chance to deal with their threat once and for all."

"Vrex," Ayar spits out. "Syn, Mylo, and Jay are keeping them busy while we rescue you."

"All of us have knowledge of the defense system. We have to get out of here and come back with greater forces."

"Except." Ayar's eyes are bright as he looks around the destruction he's already wrought. "What if we took the fight to the Drahon? Took their fleet. Maybe then the seniors might let me stay with the unit."

"Gak," I mutter.

"Syn told him," Robin says apologectically.

"Ayar, I'm sorry, I should have said something, but..."

"I know. You were protecting me, mostly from myself." Ayar gets to his feet and helps me up.

My legs are like a newborn maraha calf's. It's only because I can cling onto Ayar I'm remaining upright.

"Ayar, after what I've been through, the fact you were able to function at all is incredible, and anyone who says otherwise will be going one on one with me in the training ring," I growl.

It earns me a warm squeeze from Robin. She's intensely happy we're all together in a way I'm not sure even the thoughtbond can convey. It radiates from her in the same way her delicious scent fills my nostrils. Mingling with Ayar's and proving hopelessly distracting.

"How would we get to the Drahon fleet?" she asks Ayar. "I presume they're in space, right?"

"It looks like the Drahon got stuck here the same time we found you and your friends," I tell her. "We already captured two of their ships because they can't get past the defense system into space. It follows they have more here."

"This has to be the reason Syn was here," Ayar says, a grin

stealing over his face. "You know that vrexer. He thinks he's Ryak, secretive and all knowing."

"He's going to be the key to getting hold of the ship," I reply. "Where are we going to find them?"

In the distance, there's a low rumble.

"I suspect following the sounds of explosions and general destruction is how you find any Gryn," Robin grumbles. "It's definitely what you're good at."

"The Drahon exploded the ship you were on, not us," Ayar says, attempting and failing to sound hurt. Because my mate loves a good explosion.

"I know." Robin slips in front of me to give his wing a quick stroke, and I find myself feeling somewhat jealous and annoyed his tone worked on her.

And I feel she might be prepared to explore any rivalry from the twinkle in her eye.

An unpleasant scuffling has Ayar turning. He shoves us both to one side and leaps into the air as a laser bolt shoots just under his left wing. He hits the ground, rolls over, and grabs his laser cannon, which he must have abandoned when he was getting me out of the machine. The thing whines as he flicks the switch and then lets rip with an enormous bolt.

"We should go," he calls over his shoulder. "Find the others and get out of here."

My Ayar. For once, he's not racing into the fight.

Robin

Vypr is pretending he's okay, but it's more than clear he's badly hurt by whatever that machine was. I've never been more pleased I kept up with my first aid training because when it really mattered, I was able to bring him back.

He died and I brought him back.

I have them both, in my head and in my heart.

It almost makes me want to laugh out loud in joy and at the incredible fortune which means I have not one but two handsome, glorious warriors in my arms. I am no longer the woman Magnus said was worthless without him. I am the woman who saved her mate and who shot a lizard man about to kill me.

I am so much more. Because I have Ayar and Vypr.

With Ayar on one side, holding Vypr around the waist, the echo of debris falling around us, we race from the cavernous space into a corridor. Ayar props Vypr against a wall and peers back the way we came. Vypr's breathing is ragged from the movement.

"I'll be okay," he says, putting a hand on my shoulder and touching my hair. "I just need some time."

"You're not okay," I say, and he holds out his hand flat, trying to quieten me.

"Don't let Ayar know."

"There's been enough secrets, Vypr. And anyway..." I tap the side of my head. "Thoughtbond. He knows." I put my hand on his chest, feeling for his heart. It bangs against his ribs, the rhythm not quite right. "He's always known. He's just not been able to tell us."

Scuffling around the corner has Vypr raising the laser pistol, and as the Drahon shambles around the corner, he lets rip, the reptilian falling to the floor without even a sound.

"I'm not dead again yet, sweet Robin. Don't write me off."

"You need the medic, my mate." Ayar is by our side again, laser cannon on his shoulder. He cups Vypr's chin in his clawed hand. "And I'm not losing you," he looks at me, "either of you again. To the machine or to the Drahon."

At the look on his face, his jaw set hard, his eyes glittering with determination, it slots into place in my mind. His terror in the chamber, his paralysis until I screamed out Vypr was dying.

"The machine," I whisper. "It was your machine."

"It's just a machine," Ayar says. He shifts the cannon, turning back to face the entrance, and the cannon discharges once again. "And it won't hurt any Gryn ever again."

Relief washes through me, not just my own, but that of Vypr too. Ayar has faced his demon and done the only thing he ever would. He has obliterated it.

I watch him as a smile curls around his lips. A genuine smile, not one bourne of his fears. Ayar is happy. A happy male and the warrior Vypr and I knew he always was.

And now he's entirely fearless.

"I need to get my mates to safety so they can be healed." He puts his arm around Vypr's waist. "Healed enough we can go back to our nest and stay there." His eyes glint with meaning, and the images which fill my head are, to put it mildly, X-rated.

"Ayar!" Vypr groans. "You will be the end of me, mate."

"He's been like this ever since the thoughtbond," I say, adding my own smile to the mix. "I try to tell myself he can't help it." I look at Ayar, who grins wildly. "But I'm pretty sure he can, he just doesn't want to."

His eager nodding has both Vypr and me rolling our eyes. It looks like I'm going to have my hands full in the very near future, and that will be with only one male.

I already know the hunger which burns inside Vypr. These males are absolutely going to be a handful.

A set of smaller explosions somewhere in the underground base draws Ayar's attention. "Mylo," he says, head cocked to one side. "And Jay."

"All the unit?" Vypr queries.

"Not all."

"Not quite all," a voice rumbles from somewhere in the darkness behind us.

A huge warrior steps into the light, one I recognize from my brief meetings at the eyrie.

"Huntr?"

"I heard there were Drahon who needed killing." He shifts a laser cannon easily on his shoulder. At his belt are a vicious knife and axe, both of which are covered in black blood. "So I came."

"The Drahon have a fleet massed just outside the defense system. We have to clear this base and make sure none of them get a message out," Vypr says.

Huntr looks Vypr up and down. "You're pretty vrexed," he states. "I'll do it."

With that, he turns on his heel and stalks away.

"Weird. Is he always like that?" I ask as more explosions

sound off in the distance. And not in the direction Huntr took.

Vypr attempts a shrug which turns into a wince.

"He's been both in Proto's clutches and the Drahon's," Ayar says darkly. "He has much to deal with."

And the lightness flooding my mind comes directly from Ayar. Joy fills him, joy at being together with mates he loves.

He pulls Vypr's arm around his shoulders and touches me gently on mine. "Time to go, little Robin."

Vypr

I feel as if something has hollowed out my insides and then stuffed them back but not in order. Every step is agony, but Ayar is carrying me far more than he should as we make our way towards the sounds of a battle.

"Is this an underground lair?" I ask as we pass what looks like a barrack room, only without any ledges.

"Yes. Syn says it was damaged somehow, which is why the Drahon gained access."

"It looks like it was damaged before the Drahon got to it," I say as we pass another room which did once contain healing pools.

Ayar lifts his head and inhales. "Kijg," he says. "They were here first."

"Vrex it." Ayar's always been right about these sort of things, as if the damaged portion of him enhanced other areas of his faculties. "If they've had any chance to find out what is in these bases, we could be in trouble."

Robin comes to a halt and looks into another room. All the walls are blank. "What is this for?" she asks.

Ayar gently takes my arm from around his shoulder and holds me upright while he steps through the doorway.

Immediately, the room lights up, and Ayar practically jumps back into my arms.

"Welcome, Ayar of the Gryn."

"Proto!" he says through gritted teeth.

"It's the lair, Ayar," I say, kindly. "It recognizes us. You know it does. We've been in enough of these lairs."

Ayar shakes out his wings. "I knew that," he says, although he remains suspicious.

With some effort, I shuffle inside the doorway.

"Lair. Have you been compromised?" I ask, staring around at nothing.

"Only Gryn may access the lair," it says.

Very vrexing helpful. Especially when it's something I already know. Vrexing lair.

"Ask it when the Gryn last accessed the lair," Robin says from beside me, her hand in my feathers.

"Welcome, Robin of Earth," it says. *"The Gryn last accessed my data one hundred and thirty two cycles ago."*

"The Kijg and the Drahon haven't got anything," Robin says, looking up at me. "No one who could have used this place has been here for a very long time."

"Grid wanted me to give up details of the defense system. I expect if I'd done what he asked, he'd have used me to access the lair, too," I say.

"Good thing we've got the little bastid then." Mylo's voice booms down the corridor.

Ayar hoists my arm back onto his shoulder as Mylo, Jay, and Syn walk towards us. Grid dangles from Mylo's claws, his legs dragging on the ground.

"Where's the Drahon ship, you vrexer?" I snarl at him.

Grid curls his lip. It looks like the other side of his face is blackened to match. He hitches up his mouth to reveal his teeth in a long hiss of breath. "I won't tell you anything."

"Oh, in that case, I guess I can just kill you now," Mylo says, sounding bored. He slams a set of claws into the area between Grid's legs. "I enjoy eviscerating Kijg as much as Drahon."

Grid screams as the claws enter his body. When Mylo doesn't move, he pants, his eyes, black and dull, starting from side to side.

"The Drahon need access for the fleet. The queen and the others were left here when you activated the defense system," he rushes out, clearly having second thoughts about keeping quiet. "I thought they just wanted the Gryn and I was happy to give you up." He snarls and Mylo digs his claws in just a little deeper. Grid moans. "I didn't know they wanted to take the planet as well."

"You didn't care, you mean," Syn says. "I bet they promised you riches the like of which you could only imagine."

"What do you think? That I want to spend the rest of my life scratching a living on this pathetic space rock? You Gryn have everything, all the power, all the tech." He narrows his eyes and stares into the room with the lair computer, all lit up. "And you don't even know what you've got. The Drahon do. They promised to share it with me."

At a nod from me, Mylo withdraws his claws.

"Why the vrex would they share anything with *you*?" Syn asks.

"The Drahon and Kijg are kin. What's theirs is mine," Grid says, but as the words come out of his mouth, I feel a flicker of something.

"You don't believe that for a second." Robin steps toward the injured Kijg before either Ayar or I can stop her. "I know you don't. You started helping them to serve your own desire for revenge on the Gryn, and now you don't know how to stop the Drahon."

The thoughtbond. It flares into life, stronger than I've ever felt it before. Ayar stiffens next to me because it's not just my thoughts he can hear.

Like me, like Robin. He can hear everyone.

Mylo is hungry. Jay wants to deal with the Drahon and get back to his mate. Syn wants glory.

Grid expects death.

The noise is overwhelming, coming in at us in a sudden rush. I close my eyes to separate out my mates' thoughts and feelings. Gradually, the boom of everything lessens, fading into the background until it's gone.

Ayar stares down at Robin, who seems frozen.

"Robin?" Her name is a whisper on his lips. "She knows."

"What? What?" Syn demands, stepping in front of us, bristling with anger. "What does she know?"

Ayar and I look at each other. With a huge intake of breath, I pull on every element I have, every last drop of my reserve.

"The Drahon queen. She's here, in this base," Ayar says. "Close by."

"And she must be stopped," Robin breathes.

Then she takes off at a run, slipping past the others as we shoulder them aside and I grab a laser rifle from Jay.

Their protests, their queries, fade into the background as we follow our brave mate into the lair. She will be protected at all costs.

And we will deal with the Drahon once and for all.

Ayar

Every single part of me sings with the delight of the chase. I felt the queen in my head as much as my mates did, her blackened mind an infection which nearly killed my Vypr.

Together, we are unstoppable. It's not long before we catch up with our swift mate, and we're dodging debris from the unit's earlier firefight with the Drahon.

"Where is the queen?" Vypr gasps as we slow our pace. I think he caught the very last of the bond connection between Robin and me.

"She's preparing to leave. They want to get to another hiding place and see if they can continue to torture Gryn until they get what they want," Robin says through gritted teeth.

I'm pleased she said it. I don't want to revisit the mind which was so full of hate it made my guts hurt.

"This base has an added area, unlike the others," I tell Vypr. "It has a launchpad."

"The reason the Kijg broke in," Robin adds.

"We're not going in there, lasers at the ready. We need a plan," Vypr says. "And it doesn't involve you, Robin."

"Oh, I think it does. You're not relegating me to the sidelines, Vypr," she says evenly, spinning the laser pistol she holds in her hand with a practiced air.

I could mate her where she stands. Such a beautiful female, hair tangled, silky strands begging to be touched, caressed. Lips which need to be kissed until they are swollen with need.

"AYAR!" both my mates bellow.

I shrug. "I like mating. What can I say?"

Vypr stalks forward, grasping me around my neck and placing his forehead on mine. "We go together, check out what's in there. If the unit has done a decent job, we'll meet minimal resistance." He closes his eyes, trying to calm himself, to blanket his pain and his worry with the need to get the mission completed. "Robin can stay here. The unit is not far behind. She'll be safe."

Robin huffs.

"Robin, my precious, perfect mate. If Ayar and I are not worrying about you, we'll be much safer." He croons at her. "And anyway, we need someone to watch our backs."

He is love incarnate, for her and for me. I know we do all of this for love. For each other as much as for Ustokos. Without it all, we cannot be.

And we must be. I faced the machine to be here, for them.

My head is clear. I know what I want. It's as if the mission all along has been to find the clarity I sought but didn't know where to find.

I love this mission!

"Okay." Vypr straightens with a wince. "The others will catch up with us shortly. Robin, you stay here and cover us. Ayar, with me." His tone brooks no argument.

"Yes, sir!" Robin grins from ear to ear. Vypr narrows his eyes.

"Yes, sir!" I echo, and he rolls them, muttering about trouble.

Lifting the laser cannon onto my shoulder and with Vypr by my side, we follow the corridor through to the light at the end. I check to see Robin standing behind us, her arms by her sides, her mind a blank, just before we walk out into the enormous chamber.

It's big enough for us to get in the air if we need to, although I sense Vypr would struggle. He's only just holding things together as it is.

Squatting on the landing pad is a Drahon ship, all silver and hissing steam. I let rip at the entrance ramp, rolled down onto the ground where around half a dozen Drahon males are gathered.

"Ayar, we need that ship," Vypr cries as the Drahon are thrown in the air like leaves.

"It's not damaged," I say. "Jay's not the only Gryn with a good aim."

Vypr laughs as he sees the ramp and ship unscathed. "What do you reckon? Are we going to make it through a mission without something being blown to the goddess?"

I incline my head, frowning at him, attempting to be serious, despite the blood singing in my veins.

I am with my mates. I am on a mission. My head is clear.

"Let's wait until it's all over before making that call." I grin.

"I want the Drahon queen. She's needs to pay," Vypr growls, his shoulders hunched as he attempts to push through the pain. "And the Drahon cannot be allowed to take Ustokos, for our younglings' sake."

"Our younglings?" I query, my chest tightening.

"Our younglings," Vypr says firmly. "I want a youngling as much as you do. I want to see Robin round with a little one in her belly. Yours or mine, I don't care. I want it."

"Then what the vrex are we waiting for?" I spring into the air, hearing the engine note on the ship begin a steady rise in volume. "I want this mission to be over because there's a nest calling our names."

"Robin is right. You are trouble, mate," Vypr calls up to me as he begins a lumbering run, laser rifle in hand as he lays down covering fire for me.

"Engines, engines, engines," I chant to myself, remembering something Syn said once about how they can always be rebuilt.

If I can get a laser bolt into them, we can deal with the Drahon at our leisure.

A thin cry rises from below me. Spinning in the air, I look down to see Robin between two Drahon males. She's fighting the best she can, but her laser pistol goes skittering across the ground. Across the chamber, I see the rest of the unit arriving, but she's a long way away from them.

The Drahon ship lifts, wobbling from its position. If it gets away, it's mission over.

'Don't do it.' Vypr's voice reverberates around my brain. *'Get Robin.'*

He's doubled over in pain, rifle dangling uselessly from his hands.

A laser bolt hits one of the Drahon holding Robin, and he drops to the floor. The other turns towards where Jay is resting his rifle and pulls her in front of him.

He's using my mate like a shield as he backs towards the now hovering ramp of the ship.

When it cracks open, my anger is like the white heat of a forge. Molten and destructive. I am not going to let them take my mates. Not now, not ever. I fire off the cannon at the ship multiple times. It won't leave, not with Robin on it. It won't leave ever.

The engines stutter, the whine decreases. But inside the ship, there is an ominous rumbling.

I think we're unlikely to get away without destruction this time.

Robin

The fucking Drahon won't let go, no matter how hard I kick the scaly bastard. There's no point biting them—their skin is as thick as an elephant, I know. I tried it once before.

I still can't believe I let the two stupid lizards creep up on me. I was too busy trying to locate the Drahon queen using the weird bond. The longer Vypr, Ayar, and I have spent together, the stronger the psychic power we're developing is getting.

But I never expected it to allow us to read others so completely. It was odd enough when it was just the three of us, but an overwhelming amount of information hit me just before my brain seemed to engage some sort of filter and it shut down again.

All but the queen and I was attempting to see in my mind's eye if she was on board the ship or nearby, when a pair of arms encircled me, lifting me off my feet, into the disgusting fleshy chest of a Drahon.

Even though one of them has been hit by the Gryn, I can't

seem to get this one to let me go as I'm dragged inexorably towards the ship.

And I know one thing. I will never, ever get on a spaceship again. Especially one with Drahon on it. I bear down on the Drahon with everything I have, hoping he'll decide I'm not worth the trouble. Above me, I hear a laser cannon discharging over and over, until there is silence.

Which is broken by a long, low groaning sound, like a creature rising from the depths of an ocean. A creature full of hunger which intends destroying and devouring everything in its path. It's not a noise you ever want to hear coming from a spaceship.

The Drahon drops me, staring up at the ship which has started to list. I take the advantage and scuttle backwards on my bum until I can scramble to my feet. Ahead of me is Vypr. He's clearly hurt as he's crouched down, one hand on the floor and feathers pooling around him.

A shrieking, wrenching noise rends through the air, and I check over my shoulder to see the ship is falling, toppling, almost in slow motion, towards the ground. Whatever happens, when it hits, it's not going to be good. Not at all.

I reach Vypr and throw my arms around him, doing my best to shield his broken body from whatever is coming.

"There is no need to sacrifice yourself, my sweet *eregri*," he murmurs in my ear.

"There is every need. You and Ayar, you belong together. I always want you to be together," I shout over the screeching of metal against metal.

"We three are one, little Robin. That's how it has to be." Vypr's eyes are clouded with pain, but his words are clear. "Make your nest with us. Let us fill you with new life. Let us set you free."

His words are almost inaudible over the

crash/wrench/thump of a spaceship in its death throes. My back is scorched by a searing heat, and just before I close my eyes for the final time, I feel myself hit with the rushing wind of the last explosion.

"I don't want to stay."

"You're staying until we're discharged. You know that, Ayar."

"It smells funny in here. I want to be back in the eyrie."

I feel my brow furrow at the oddly familiar conversation. My entire body feels like someone ran over me with a train. Only the pain isn't concentrated in my arm or ribs. It's everywhere. In particular my back. It feels sort of sticky and hot.

"Robin's awake, look!" There's a rush of wind over my face and warm breath on my cheek. My hands are being held in soft, warm flesh.

"Ayar?" My voice is a croak, cracking with lack of use. "Don't give Orvos a hard time, okay? I'll get up in a minute and help." I prize my eyes open, one at a time.

The familiar ceiling of the surgery has been replaced by two pairs of dark, concerned eyes in impossibly handsome faces.

And, in Ayar's case, slightly singed hair too.

"You don't need to help me, sweet mate," Ayar croons. He looks over at Vypr. "I think she thinks I need looking after like before."

"It's our turn to look after you, precious Robin." Vypr runs a knuckle down the side of my face, and Ayar leans in to give me a slightly wet kiss on my forehead. "Because you are ours now."

"She's mine until I say otherwise." I hear Orvos's bossy

tones, and I'm not able to stop the groan escaping from my lips.

Ayar snarls, his head wrenched away from where he was staring down at me.

"Vypr!" Orvos says, his voice slightly higher pitched. "What did I say about Ayar being in the surgery?"

"He was injured like us, Orvos. Where did you want me to bring him?" Vypr hasn't stopped looking down at me, his hand folded in mine. "There was no way he would leave our Robin." He hitches up the corner of his mouth, exposing a sharp canine.

"How...what happened?" I whisper, throat raw.

"The Drahon ship blew. Ayar grabbed us both, but not before we were hit by the initial blast. You've been here for the past three turns." Vypr's eyes are liquid with his concern.

"And the queen?"

"The seniors are dealing with her. You need to rest though."

"You all need to vrexing rest, but I'm not having him in here if he can't control himself," Orvos snarls.

"Does that mean we can be discharged?" Vypr finally tears his eyes from me. "Go back to our nest?"

Orvos oscillates. He stares hard at Ayar, then at Vypr. Finally, his eyes are on me. He walks over to my bed. Ignoring Ayar's throaty growls, he drops down next to me, running his hand over my face.

"If they promise to take good care of you, you can go..." Orvos says, quietly, and I open my mouth to agree. "But," he holds up a finger, "you have to take care of them too."

"I think we can manage." I smile up at him, and his eyes twinkle with fatherly joy.

"Then you'd better get out of here before I throw you all out," Orvos intones, rising to his feet and rattling his feathers at my mates. "And don't bring him back unless he's properly injured next time." He growls as I'm loaded into Ayar's arms, and he beats a hasty retreat from the irritated medic.

"Time to go nest." Ayar grins at Vypr. "If you think you can make it?"

"For you, I'll make it," Vypr replies, his face wreathed in a grin of epic proportions as he unfurls his huge wings.

Vypr

Ayar took a beating in the resulting explosion, but he was still in better condition than me, even if he was somewhat crispy around the edges. Which is why he gets to carry Robin up to the eyrie and straight into our nest, even if it's what I wanted to do.

But as soon as we arrive, it doesn't matter anymore. Seeing my two mates together, I slam the door closed behind us and drink down their scents like a Gryn possessed.

Ayar, all musk, all male, all need. Robin, sweet like ambrosia with the hint of warm sun.

"Vrexing perfection," I say, stalking over to them.

Ayar gently puts Robin on her feet, and she sways slightly.

"How do you feel?" I ask her.

"Like something chewed me up and spat me out," she says.

"You were a bit burned." Ayar is biting back a groan. "I let Orvos put you in his machine because it heals and doesn't hurt."

"Ayar watched the whole time, didn't you, mate?" I run my hand down the shoulder of Ayar's wing until I reach his neck, spanning my claws over it and enjoying the feel of his warmth against mine.

He vibrates under my touch, his eyes closing. "I watched. I like to watch." He groans.

"What do you like to watch, my *eregri*?"

"I want to watch you and Robin," he breathes. "I want to watch you take her." He shivers, all of his feathers shaking with his desire.

"But don't you want to mate, my love?" I murmur in his ear.

"Only when you take me, too."

"Vrex!" I'm so incredibly hard, it's painful.

He's holding back because he wants me to bond with Robin and just the thought makes me want to spill my seed immediately.

"Strip," I demand. "Robin needs the healing pool, and you need a bath," I tell them. Because if we don't take this slowly, our healing bodies might give out before we even get the chance to pleasure each other.

Robin sucks in a breath, and I turn her to me, tilting her head up by lifting her chin with a single finger. I gaze down on her. Her lips part, ruby red and willing. I want to see them wrapped around my cocks. Two red spots make her skin look absolutely perfect and her half-lidded, crystal blue eyes are begging me to deal with her appropriately.

"Is this what you want, Robin? To be taken and mated by Ayar and me? We can't be gentle, not once we start. You have to be filled and filled thoroughly. We have to ensure our seed takes root in your womb. There can be nothing less."

Her bottom lip trembles, delicate eyelashes beating on her cheeks as her breath comes in short bursts, and the aroma of desire fills the room. It's so strong, I could almost touch it, just like I want to touch her, everywhere.

"Bath," Ayar moans.

He's stripped naked, his enormous cocks jutting up and spurting pre-cum.

"Help me with our little female. She needs to remove her clothing," I order him.

"Rob-in," Ayar says, singing her name. He moves closer, bumping his obscene members against her, and she makes a grab for them.

"Naked first," I warn, batting her hand away and gently peeling her medical shift over her head.

She stands before us completely bare and completely edible. I know I want to feast on her, but the healing pool is calling us, and it will be the best place to consume our female before we take her, mate her, and fill her belly with a youngling.

Robin takes a step forward, looking me up and down, boldly for such a tiny scrap of a thing, sandwiched between two huge warriors. Her look is one of pure hunger.

"You are not naked, Vypr. And I believe you should be if you want me and Ayar."

She pulls away from me and wraps herself around him, her tiny hand working his huge cocks, cocks I can't even believe he got inside her, let alone were allowed to swell as he gave her the contents of his second cock. Ayar throws his head back. She runs her hand up and down his shaft, her eyes not leaving me, teasing us both.

I'm not sure I've ever removed boots and pants as fast in my entire life.

Robin licks her lips, and my newly freed cocks jerk up as Ayar reaches for them. His rough hand tightens as he strokes me just the way I like, and I'm groaning out loud at his touch.

"Mate, I will spill my seed if you continue," I rasp, my self-control on a knife edge.

He releases me, just in time. Robin smiles at both of our naked forms, then she turns, and we follow her beautiful ass, all delicious globes I could sink my teeth into (and probably will soon), through to the pool.

The water churns and steams as she dips in a toe, looking at both of us under her eyelashes, pert breasts with peaked nipples teasing us as she slowly lowers herself into the water, hissing as it touches the tender skin on her back. With an impressive splash, Ayar is in the water helping her until she is seated under the surface.

I wade in, up behind my mate, running my hands through his feathers, where the base of his wings meets his broad back and letting my claws trip over them until he leans back into me. I wrap my hand around his throat, pulling him until he's sitting on my lap under the water and I'm able to rock my shafts against him. His musky scent only gets stronger the more aroused I make him, and I want him very, very aroused for what I'm going to do next.

"I'm looking forward to you watching, Ayar," I growl in his ear, wrapping my hand around his cocks and pumping him hard as I thrust up between his cheeks. "But I don't think you can wait for me, can you?" Ayar makes a guttural sound which is a cross between a groan and my name. "Such a needy mate," I croon, as I slide my fingers down his cleft and circle his tight little pucker.

I look over at Robin, and she's watching us intently, her legs parted under the water and her fingers between her folds.

"Who said you could start without me, Robin?" I lift my lips to show my sharp teeth and all the wanton little mate does is throw her head back and dip her fingers deeper.

It's no use. There is no way any of us are bathing, not while there's mating to be done.

Ayar

All power of rational thought has left me as I watch Robin touching herself, one hand on a tight nipple and the other deep within her.

Vypr's huge cocks are pressed up against my back, his hand wrapped around my shafts. It's almost too much. I can't possibly think through the pleasure or my seed will erupt.

This is all I've been dreaming of for days. Waking up Vypr in the surgery with my moaning. Meaning he's had to provide me with relief while my body healed.

Just because Robin went on the machine, it didn't mean I was prepared to give it a try. I settled for simpler remedies to my burns.

Vypr was just pleased my dreams were more of mating than anything else.

I think I'm always going to dream of mating from now on, especially as Vypr cannot keep his hands off me, even when he told me I could only watch. His cocks press hard against my butt cheeks, and I grind myself against him under the water.

"Vrex you, Ayar!" he roars, heaving us out of the pool until we're on the side, as he lifts me and impales me on his main cock.

I sing out with pleasure and with the burning, delicious burning, of being filled by him. My cocks pump out more pre-cum, soaking my abdomen with it.

And Robin still watches, her eyes wide as he begins to plunder my body, holding me, cradling me against him as I'm being pounded by his main cock, his secondary cock sliding up through my balls, and I'm stroking at it along with my own members, making Vypr groan with utter delight.

And then there is a second hand, working at our cocks, a small, clawless one. A pair of blue eyes looking up at us.

"Let me," she whispers, and her lips are around me, tongue lapping at my slits. It is the most vrexingly intense feeling I've ever had.

I'm so full, so incredibly aroused, Vypr drives himself deeper into me, and I can feel my climax rising, but I don't want to waste my seed, even if it might be barren.

"Robin," I moan. "I need to be inside you." All intentions are gone. All I want is to be closer to her, inside her, filling her, while Vypr fills me.

"If that's what you want, my Ayar." She lifts her head from her work and sees the need in my eyes.

"Mate him, Robin." Vypr continues to thrust at me. "Mate him and let him seed you before I do. I want your precious cunt running with his cum when I take you."

Robin rises, wiping her mouth with the back of her hand as my cocks jerk towards her. She straddles me, slowly, slowly lowering herself down as Vypr swivels his hips, making sure I feel every single inch of him while my cocks ache to be inside my sweet, perfect Robin.

"Are you wet for him?" Vypr demands. "Test her sweet pussy for me, Ayar?" he says as she descends.

I trap her waist, sliding one hand around her thigh and

down to her mound where soft, curls hide what has to be the sweetest entrance on all of Ustokos. I dip in my finger.

She is soaking, soaking. It takes all the effort I have not to come. Vypr buries his head in my neck and groans.

"Mates, you will be my absolute undoing. Ayar, take her, take her now!"

I thrust up and bury myself in Robin's sweet, perfect cunt with a groan which rattles my feathers.

As she settles, I can feel she's also taken Vypr's secondary cock inside her. He can too, and he rumbles against me. One hand across my chest, lips on my neck, he grinds himself inside me and inside her.

"So full," Robin moans as I palm her breasts and shift my hands down to her waist.

She is light, light as a feather, as I lift her from my cocks and lower her again. She rocks, placing her hands on my chest, her beautiful breasts pressed together and swinging as she gathers her rhythm.

Underneath me, Vypr thrusts, plundering me, making every part of me spark and shine. I want to come so much, but I know I have to wait for my mates, ensure their pleasure is as great as mine is at this very moment. I'm sheathed tightly in Robin, the mate who wants my seed, who will take it and make it into a youngling.

Our youngling, one we will raise together. The very thought brings me right to the cusp as Robin increases her movement.

"Ayar!" My name is on the lips of both mates as I am unable to stop my mind reaching theirs.

Vypr loses control first, his thrust irregular as his climax hits, and he explodes inside me and in Robin. I get the relief I crave just as she convulses on me, her hot, tight channel sucking at my cocks, taking in every single drop of seed she can as I erupt within her. My hot seed filling her, my cocks jerking, spasming as my body is consumed by my mates.

My fates, my boundless flights. They make me feel alive and whole. Not broken and abandoned. With them, I will always, always be the warrior I can be.

Vypr

My mates slumber next to me. Ayar's flat out on his back, gentle snores rising from my battered warrior. Being able to touch his mind through the thoughtbond is a delight. Robin is curled next to him, one hand on his chest and her feet touching me. Her lush curves are covered, just, by a single small fur.

I'm finding it hard to believe I was ever worried she'd come between Ayar and me. Instead, she has enhanced what we had, and now, it's hard to think of a time without her.

Ayar snuffles and rolls onto his side. Squirming to get his wing from under him, he grunts in annoyance, until he snags Robin by the waist and she too rolls over, shoving her butt into him as a smile creeps over his sleeping face.

And I have a pair of bright blue eyes upon me.

"You're thinking about us," Robin says, her voice quiet.

"How can I not? You are my mates. We all nearly died."

"Drama queen." Robin laughs. "Ayar was always going to save us. And you know it."

In his sleep, Ayar wrinkles up his nose and one wing flaps.

He looks the least ferocious I've seen him, and my heart thumps.

"He was always going to save us, wasn't he?" Now I'm whispering as my fear is suddenly, beautifully absent. "Because of you." I cup her little face in my hand. "You were the key to unlocking him."

She takes hold of me, tiny pink fingers curling around my clawed ones. "No, Vypr. You did that when you saved him. It just turns out both of you needed to be loved."

"And you, my sweet *eregri*, what did you need?"

"She needed two proper warriors to mate her and prove that males are not the same the universe over," Ayar rumbles, eyes still closed. "And now, unless you propose we mate some more, I believe it's time we all got some rest."

Robin smiles widely, her eyes dancing with pleasure and desire. She doesn't let go of my hand, instead guiding it up and over her body, onto Ayar, and as I shuffle closer, enclosing both of them within my wing, she sighs happily.

Our thoughtbond resonates with the swirl of blue and green, of mates who are waiting for the next round of mating. My mind relaxes. I am content.

"It looks like you vrexers can survive anything!" Syn wing bumps me as all three of us walk into the food hall.

I've left it late, in the hope the usual melee will have died down, but it's still pretty busy. Beside me, Ayar struts, feathers fluffed. He is the very definition of a confident male.

So much so, he wing bumps Syn back, albeit in such a way the other warrior has to take a pace to steady himself.

"Can't kill us off, Syn. No matter how hard you try." He

grins at the male, taking Robin's hand. He heads towards the food, one thing on his mind.

Well, maybe not only one thing, given what's just reached me through the thoughtbond and is extremely distracting. Or it would be if Syn hadn't stepped in front of me.

"You have a meeting with the seniors later, don't you?"

"Yes." I'd been trying to forget what we've been summoned to attend.

Ryak and Strykr, the Prime and Command, along with the rest of the seniors, want us in szent, a big meeting in their intimidating meeting room. I know it's going to be about Ayar and the destruction of the Drahon ship.

Even if the rest of the unit did capture the Drahon queen. The female who had already decided my life wasn't worth much. She's somewhere in the bowels of the lair while plans are being made to deal with the fleet hovering on the edge of Ustokos' space. Plans I know Syn is party to.

"I had a chance to look at the machine you were in," Syn says. "It's the same as the one Proto put Ayar in, isn't it?"

"Those vrexing things need to be destroyed," I growl at him.

"Except they are not instruments of torture, or at least they were never designed to be." Syn grins at me. "It looks like you've found the very machines which provided the seniors with their enhancements. Ones which can make all the Gryn invincible."

"Good for you. I'm not going back in one again," I reply. "I guess it means promotion?"

"I suspect there will be a promotion." Syn shakes out his feathers.

He shifts on his feet, moving enough so I can see my mates behind him. Ayar points out his favorite foods to Robin and piles a platter with the sweet pastries I love. An aura of pleasure surrounds them.

"I vrexing hope so. I've just put my life on the line for the Legion, and I expect it to be recognized," I reply.

Syn grins, wider than ever. "I hoped you'd say that. We're going to need all the seniors we can muster for the coming fight. That means you and Ayar."

"What do you mean? We're not seniors," I reply, folding my arms and frowning at the strange Gryn.

"If you've been on the machine, you will have some attributes, something to set you apart from us all already. The enhancements improve with time and depending on the warrior, some will have many more enhancements than others." Syn looks me up and down, before looking over at Ayar. "You're both prime candidates. I'll be making sure the current seniors know."

A warmth spreads through me. My knees feel weak. This piece of news, the knowledge damage has not been done to Ayar or me, that we can protect our Robin.

And she can be the calming influence in our lives.

"Much appreciated, Syn." I wing bump him. But he's already distracted by the orange-haired human female who's just entered the dining hall, accompanied by a dark-haired one, the one who smells of Huntr. "Looks like you have your own mating to deal with."

"What?" He turns back to me. "We're just *friends*." He says the word as if it's a piece of gak he wants to remove.

I raise my eyebrows at him, and he scuttles away.

Come and get some breakfast

The feeling, the desire, the words, they flow through me. My mates want me. Across the hall, Ayar waves, and I see Robin's sweet smile.

The food hall buzzes with life, mercs surround them all, but they are the only two beings I can see.

My perfect mates, my completed circle. My boundless flights.

Ayar

The food hall is full of mercs, but despite my instinct wanting me to protect my mates, Robin's reassuring concentration on getting our breakfast grounds me. Not a single snarl escapes my lips.

Syn, of course, grabs Vypr's attention as soon as we enter. He's got his own agenda, I know now my mind has cleared. Through the prism of my mates, I see him as a male who is desperate to win the affections of a mate.

A very stubborn mate.

A bit like my Vypr. He's a male who took care of me, refused to let anyone or anything hurt me. It was a shame all I did was sabotage him. But the upcoming szent is a chance to change things, for him and for all of us. It's time for the seniors to know what the Gryn are and what we can become.

Because I felt it, in my bones, from the moment we collapsed in the surgery, next to an unconscious Robin, both hoping beyond hope she would survive. I had no option; I had to face it. The machine in the back room.

And there was no fear.

Not one iota.

I let Orvos treat my Robin, Vypr by my side, our hearts only beating again when Orvos pronounced she would be fine with a little rest.

Then Vypr lifted her from the machine and handed her to me. I took her through to the surgery, settled her, and returned to watch over him as he was healed. Then I remained with my mates, quietly, until they woke.

The serenity which filled me then stays with me now. Behind me, Vypr talks to Syn, and his strong, steady presence is so much more than a protector. He is my world, as is the little female by my side.

The delicious, scented female who wants to eat, and I want to devour.

"Ayar!" I get a soft slap on my hand and a pair of bright eyes dance with mirth and repressed lust.

This scrap of a female is as insatiable as me.

"So what if I am?" She laughs. "We still need to eat."

"Eating or mating," I rumble. "If only there was a way to do both."

Her laugh stutters in her throat, becoming a low growl. "And what would you propose could be eaten while we mate?"

I sweep my hand over the food in front of us. There are sweet pastries which could be licked, rare, warm maraha which could be nibbled from fingers. A pot of ambrosia, which is out of bounds for humans but could easily be drizzled over pert nipples and aching cocks.

"Stop!" Robin cries out, looking over her shoulder at Vypr as her cheeks redden.

"These thoughts are for you, my Robin. Vypr is busy."

"You can control it like that?" She looks up at me as I take a platter and begin to fill it with food.

"So can you, if you try."

"You don't want me to try. You like getting me hot and bothered in public."

I incline my head, giving her a searching look. "I'd get you 'hot and bothered' anywhere, sweet Robin."

She slides an arm around my waist, and I feel her longing for Vypr to be with us like a long strand of golden thread.

"Good," she says. "Let's eat."

The platter is full. I've plenty of the treats he likes and those Robin pointed at. I check on my mate. He seems to be done with Syn, whose attention is taken with a female who has just entered.

The exact one I saw in my mind, captured in his arms, entwined with him. Everything he wants. Everything she doesn't.

I wave at Vypr as I smile at Syn. I might have had battles with my own mind, but he's got a much, much harder struggle in store. That is a female with an agenda, and something tells me it's much greater than his will ever be.

And she will be his undoing.

My handsome mate strides over to where we wait, and he takes the platter from me.

"Good choices." He smiles, and I run a hand through his wing feathers, reveling in his slight shudder against me.

"What did Syn want to know?" I ask as we settle down, Robin at my side, Vypr on the other side of the table, opposite me as he gets stuck into the food.

He licks his fingers wantonly at me. "He says the machine is not for torture but for enhancement. He thinks it will make us invincible."

"We're already invincible." I shake my feathers. "Machine's not needed. That's what got us into this trouble in the first place."

Vypr stares at me, tongue halfway out of his mouth. "Yes," he says. "Yes!" he adds, a little louder. "Proto."

"Anyone want to tell me, *in words*, what's going on?" Robin says as she sips on a cup of cala.

"Proto. It was a sentient AI system. It didn't start off as a worm, it started off as a climate control system under the control of the organics on Ustokos," Vypr explains.

"Worm?" Robin's eyes are wide.

"It is believed that, at some point, the system was infiltrated by an organic being, which manipulated it to its own ends. The thing we called Proto." I contemplate the information we have. "Its entirely possible the machines might have been made by the Gryn originally and their function twisted by the worm into something else."

Vypr's hand finds mine across the table. "Ayar, you are truly a miracle." His eyes shine. "It might explain why the Gryn are different now from those who built the underground lairs." He presses a kiss to my lips.

"I found a way to see." I take Robin's hand. "With my mates and hopefully a youngling soon."

Robin colors as I use the thoughtbond to tell her what I intend doing to various parts of her anatomy, very soon. Images which are joined by those from Vypr.

"Some things never change, my Ayar," he rumbles. "You'll always be a force to be reckoned with."

"As long as I have you both, my force is contained within me. There is a battle coming and one we will win." I grin at the pair of them, and the warmth which radiates out, it fills me with a deep and unrelenting joy.

And I don't just like it.

I love it.

Robin

I've heard about the szent room from Vypr and Ayar, but even all their descriptions (Ayar's—dismissive, Vypr's—stoic) haven't really made me ready for the size of the table made from all the parts of robots the seniors destroyed in the war against Proto and the chairs of similar size and intimidating presence.

And talking of intimidating presences...Jyr, the Prime of the Gryn sits in the biggest chair. He radiates power. Standing on either side of him are two other massive Gryn warriors. From his blue eyes, I've been told the one on the left is Jyr's second in Command, Fyn, and from the streaks of black covering the torso of the other warrior, he has to be Myk, the lair's weapons master.

But I have Vypr and Ayar. They stand on either side of me, huge, warm, scented, and my rocks. They ground me.

I am not afraid because they are not afraid.

That's how the thoughtbond works. We take our strengths from each other. And I'm not going to lie...it makes the sex, the mating, incredible. Frankly, it's amazing I can walk given how much mating we've been doing since we were discharged from the surgery.

But I can walk, and we've all recovered. Which means we've been summoned before the seniors. Apparently, what happened can't be dealt with by Strykr or his boss, Ryak, who lurks at the side of the room. He is, according to Ayar, a 'secretive bastid,' so there's no real knowing what's going to happen.

Only I can feel the room. As much as I can touch my mates' minds, Vypr's rumbling with calming thoughts, Ayar's...thinking about mating. What a surprise. I mentally roll my eyes at him and hear his grunt of naughty pleasure in return. But the room filters in too. Jyr's strength, his need to be strong for all the Gryn. Fyn's utter devotion to his Prime.

Little one.

The voice in my head is not mine, not Ayar's or Vypr's. My eyes trace over the faces of the others in the room, and I see Myk's dark gaze on me.

Your bond is strong. His words drop into my head. *You have the gift.*

What gift? I project. Somehow, I know my mates are not party to this conversation.

The gift of the sight. Ayar would have it too if he had not been so damaged. He gave it to you instead.

I look up at my sweet Ayar. His handsome, scarred face for once giving nothing away.

They saved me, Ayar and Vypr. I don't deserve anything more.

Myk's face shows the hint of a smile. *All Gryn are warriors. They simply won your heart, little female. As all good warriors should do. You cherish them and they cherish you.*

The bloom in my chest when I think of my males is warm, like a summer's day, it increases until my chest aches. Aching with my love for them.

Please don't punish them. They've been through enough.

Ayar knows what to do, Myk replies cryptically.

I know now, I will do anything for the two males whose reassuring presence calms any fears I've ever had. Myk's mind goes silent as Jyr unfolds himself from his chair.

He is huge, taller even than the enormous males surrounding him. He's a Prime for a reason, and it's not hard to work out why.

"Ayar, Vypr." He shakes his head. "Why does this unit plague me so?" He looks back at Fyn whose mouth is set in a thin line of annoyance. "If there's something you can explode or break, it's usually you two at the bottom of it."

He plants two spade-like hands, tipped with vicious claws, on the table in front of him and sighs deeply.

"My Prime." Ayar steps forward, even as Vypr reaches for him and misses.

"What are you doing?" he hisses out, but Ayar ignores him.

Jyr lifts his head and stares directly at Ayar with a look which seems to drill into my soul.

"You were the Gryn who showed us the way. Made us believe in fate and in the goddess once again. Fate is never wrong, Prime. Fate is prepared to put our *eregri*s in our path regardless of when we are ready for them."

Ayar looks over his shoulder, between his wings, at Vypr and me, then holds out his hands to us. I don't even look at Vypr. My heart beats so hard in my chest, I think it might burst free. I take his hand, and he draws us both forward so Jyr's gaze is on us all.

"Here are my *eregri*s. What I do, I do for them as I do for all the Gryn. We survive and thrive. There is an entire Drahon fleet above us, waiting to be conquered. And we will conquer them because I have my mates, my fate and my boundless flights, by my side, always."

"Ayar..." Vypr says, and then he has his arms around our

big, beautiful mate, as do I. Luxuriating in their touch, their scent, all of them.

"It was always you," I hear myself whisper. "Always. Both of you. My stars and my moons."

Ayar makes a happy sound, wings enclosing all of us as Vypr remains uncharacteristically quiet. It's only then I see he weeps silently. Tears rolling down his cheeks as we hold him tightly.

"You made me whole, my Vypr." Ayar nuzzles at his neck. "And Robin completed us. You need never fear again."

"Which means," Jyr intones from somewhere outside our huddle, "I expect you all to be banded as soon as possible. Ayar and Vypr will be given their own command, providing they stop blowing things up."

Vypr unpeels himself from us.

"With all due respect, Prime. While I wish to band my mates immediately. I cannot agree to the condition." He grins at Jyr with a smile I think I've only ever seen on Ayar's face. "As explosives expert, I will use my discretion, but it's likely something will explode at some point, especially where the Drahon are concerned."

Jyr runs his hand over his face and shakes out his wings as Vypr holds his gaze, moving in front of Ayar and me protectively.

"Could Ayar...?" he says.

"No," Vypr cuts him off.

"By Nisis!" Jyr slams a fist down on the table, and I jump. "You are as stubborn as me." He looks up at us all with a grin a mile wide. "Very well. You've brought us close to victory, so I will indulge you."

I feel Ayar relax behind me, which is a relief.

"Providing..." Jyr holds up a clawed finger. "You put on a banding ceremony to rival my own. It's not every day three mates are banded, and I need to be involved in that party!"

"Oh, it will be a party to remember," Ayar says enthusiastically as he wraps his arms around Vypr and me again, nudging his head into Vypr's shoulder. "And the mating after..."

He fills our heads with thoughts, positions and sounds which momentarily have my knees going weak.

It looks like I've found everything I ever wanted. My entire being is full to the brim of these two males. My Ayar and my Vypr.

My heart is entirely theirs.

Epilogue

Robin

Ayar lies at my side, his dark eyes looking up at me with unadulterated love. I'm flipping huge, and Orvos reckons I should be giving birth in the next two weeks. Ayar runs his massive, clawed hand over my stomach, marveling, once again, that there is a baby inside me he will soon be meeting.

Vypr sits on my other side, his dark eyes ever watchful for both of us.

I'm not sure whose baby I'm having, but it doesn't matter to them or me. I have a sneaking suspicion the little wriggler in my belly is Ayar's though, even if he doesn't think it is.

"Robin?" Ayar murmurs into the skin of my neck. I absolutely know what he wants. If I thought his insatiability was bad before I started to show, it ramped up to eleven once my bump became evident.

"You want to mate again, mate?" Vypr rumbles. "I think Robin has had more than enough mating for today." He stands from our bed of furs, stretching out his wings and drawing attention to the bulge in his pants. "But wicked males who can't help themselves will be mated thoroughly."

A low, deep growl emanates from the back of Ayar's throat. He knows exactly what's going to happen and so do I. In fact, my knickers are already drenched.

"Come, mate," Vypr demands. He drops his pants, and his cocks spring free, thick and erect. He strokes them as Ayar crawls off the bed.

"What do you want from me?" He lifts his wings and sheds his clothing, his obscenely large cocks dripping with pre-cum.

Vypr winds his hand around Ayar's head, clawed hand in his hair.

"I want you," he growls. "I want your mouth round my cocks before I mate you." His words are more of a snarl of passion, of desire, as Ayar descends on him, gobbling him up.

My, that male has a talented tongue, and don't I know it! I shuffle down on the bed so I can watch, slipping my hand to touch my hot little nub as I enjoy the sight of my mates pleasuring each other. Vypr's hips jerk at Ayar when he sees what I'm doing.

No matter how masterful he wants to be, seeing me watching him and Ayar always tips him over the edge, and this time is no exception. He pulls free of Ayar and spins the male over, pushing him into a crouched position. He lines himself up and slams his cocks inside. Ayar groans loudly with pleasure.

"Delicious mate." Vypr clutches at him, withdrawing to pound back in, circling his hips and panting with delight.

Ayar's wings flail. He's lost all control, his breath rasping in his chest. Vypr slips an arm around his chest, pulling him up against his wall of muscle. The other hand snakes around to grasp his cocks.

"Do you like being impaled on me, Ayar?" he murmurs in his ear, stroking the full, heavy lengths. "Are you going to take everything I have, then mess all over the furs? Am I going to be locked inside you?"

I'm not sure I can hold any longer, my fingers working furiously at my clit while Ayar gazes at me, eyes half lidded. He reaches out a hand, placing it on my belly.

"Take me, Vypr. Take all of me."

Vypr pumps at him, once, twice, and shudders, his heavy, muscular body vibrating against Ayar as he fills him, hands still working at his shafts. Ayar moans out loud, his cocks fountain their cream, and my entire body explodes in an orgasm I didn't even think was possible.

It shouldn't be possible.

I think my waters have broken.

"Help!"

"Well, that was an experience." I look down at the tiny bundle in my arms. Happily feeding, his pudgy, clawed fingers, thankfully soft, knead at my breast.

Tiny-ish. He's a Gryn baby, so he's not really so little. He's also the spitting image of Ayar, my handsome warrior who is currently face down on one of the ledges in the surgery, snoring gently.

For once, he's in the surgery by choice, and he isn't sedated. He's simply worn out with excitement. I'm worn out with giving birth to this big baby, but I'm ever thankful for Ayar's constant, upbeat enthusiasm and Vypr's reassuring presence throughout the entire process. Having them by my side every second was both perfect and an experience.

Vypr perches next to me, one arm around my shoulder as he stares down at the new life we've created with awe and delight.

"The next generation," he murmurs. "I never thought I'd see it."

"You knew you would, and I'm sure we'll see many more." I look up at him and then across at Ayar. "If he has anything to do with it."

"And me, my mate," Vypr rumbles. "I love to fill your belly as much as he does."

I shift on the bed as the baby nurses. "Mating will be out of bounds for some time."

"Robin, you know we only do what we all want when we're all ready," Vypr says. "And with Ayln to look after, mating will have to come second."

"Ayln?" I query. "Is that what you want to call him?"

"I do. It was my father's name," Vypr says quietly. "Ayar can't remember his family."

I already know I don't want to name my baby after any of my family. Because I have found my family, here on this alien planet with two males who didn't even know they wanted me until I arrived, and who have made me theirs completely.

"I love it." I smile down at my baby, gently tracing a finger over his sweet face, dark eyes staring up at me with the same look of love I get from Ayar. "Hello, Ayln. Welcome to Ustokos."

Book 4: REBEL: A Sci-Fi Alien Romance releases in September 2022. Read on for a taster of Syn and Diana's story!

Sign up to my newsletter for a free sweet/dirty bonus scene

where Ayar makes his first nest for his mates. You'll also get sneak peaks, cover reveals, exclusive content and giveaways.

So if you want all of the above, sign up HERE

You can also sign up on my website www.hattiejacks.com

And you can follow me on Bookbub, Amazon or even join my Facebook group - Hattie's Hotties!

REBEL

A Sci-Fi Alien Romance

Diana

"Excuse me!" I reach under the huge, winged warrior's wing to grab the last pastry from the table just before he snags it with his claws. "Thank you very much." I stare up at him as he attempts not to glare.

Then I lick the pastry.

He snorts.

I grin.

He flicks out his wings and stalks away. Females are a precious commodity on this alien planet I've been told. Certainly, females who are compatible with the Legion of the Gryn, the species who rescued me and several other human women from the clutches of our abductors, the Drahon.

Scaly, horrible lizard men. I still shudder at the thought of their ship and the way they pushed us around.

But because we're so precious, females are not allowed to do much around the eyrie, the sky-scraper style building in which we're housed. Which is fine because I have my own plans. Plans which involve teasing as many of the male warriors as I can, plans to investigate their history, but mainly I plan to get the hell out of this place and find my sister.

I take a big bite of my pastry which has an interior scarily similar to chocolate; although, as the Gryn have a human female as a chef, I remain eternally grateful for her chocolate-based input into their society.

After all not much could be worse than being abducted by lizard aliens, but a lack of chocolate on the menu forever? Nope. I'd rather have stayed in the exploding spaceship than face a life without chocolate. One hundred percent.

Before any more warriors can approach me, I pile up a plate and head back over to the table where my friend Jen sits, looking miserable. We're up late today, which means the food hall where all our meals are served is relatively quiet, but also the pickings are sparse.

"Hey." I sit down next to her, and she gives me a watery smile.

Jen is obsessed with the Gryn warrior I dubbed the 'monster in the cupboard' on board the lizard men's ship. He's called Huntr, and he's got an attitude problem to rival all of the males on this planet.

I know they both want each other. Tearing each other's clothes off type of wanting, but for reasons I can't fathom, neither of them is prepared to make the first move.

"I got the best I could from what's left." I plonk the tray down in front of her but swipe the half-eaten pastry. "Last one." I explain. "Had to lick it."

The comment at least elicits a genuine smile from Jen.

"Sounds like my life." She sighs.

"What have you been licking?" I say through a mouthful of crumbs and with raised eyebrows.

Being abducted and then stranded on an alien planet might have been an ideal time to start a diet, but it seems all I crave is carbs. As we live with a whole load of males, all we get to eat is carbs and protein. It means I've had to up my exercise regime. Doing burpees, sit-ups, press ups and jogging to every day. But there's the upside of being stuck with seven-foot alien males. I've always been taller than average, but next to them I'm tiny. They make me feel like a little doll.

It. Is. Awesome.

Jen sighs. "You know what I'd like to lick."

"That sort of thinking will get you into trouble." I stare at her.

I am sympathetic, but at the same time I wish the pair of them would get a room and scratch whatever itch they have. Especially as all the other human women on this planet have done something similar and most of them are very pregnant as proof of what can be done with a Gryn.

Shag-tastic.

"You want to get into trouble, too." She gives me the worst stage wink ever.

"I do not." I counter. "I'm perfectly happy on my own."

"I meant finding Freya." She says, although I absolutely know that's not what she means at all.

"My powers of persuasion are legendary, as you know." I say. "I think I might have managed to hitch a ride the next time they all go into space."

Jen's eyes widen. "You'd want to do that? All their ships look like they're held together with duct tape and string."

"Hell yes!" I already feel my veins flooding with adrenalin. "I once hitched a lift over the Sahara with a bunch of half-drunk soldiers. Going into space with the Gryn can't be much worse."

"Exploding in a ball of flames? No thank you." Jen says primly. "Anyway, you know they won't let you go."

"Fucking Gryn." I grumble a little. "I don't mean that." I add soothingly. "I appreciate what they've done for us, but sometimes it feels like we're only here for one thing."

As if to answer my question, Kat, one of the other humans here on Ustokos walks into the hall, her baby bump bulging.

Jen squeaks a little into her hand, and I roll my eyes at her, getting to my feet.

Kat is only one part of my plan. She is mated, as the Gryn call being in a relationship—or possibly married, it's not easy to tell—to Strykr, one of the more senior of the Gryn hierarchy. I need all the Gryn on my side, but I'm sure Kat can put in a good word.

Her little robot, Ike, buzzes over her head, shouting her name.

"Late start?" I ask.

"Myra kept me up quite late." She yawns. "She wouldn't settle and then this one," she pats her stomach, "decided three a.m. somersaults were a good idea." Kat gives me a wry smile, one I recognize of old. "Maybe you'll be finding out yourself soon enough."

"Maybe." I laugh and then put on a very serious face. "Maybe never."

Kat blinks at me.

I stare at her.

Then I grin. "I'm joking." I pull her into me for a hug. She's pregnant squashy. I feel a pang of guilt I'm in a safe, comfortable place but I don't know where Freya is, if she's okay, or even alive.

Her face is etched in my memory, her mouth open in a silent scream as she was dragged away from me, our fingertips touching until the last possible moment.

She wouldn't have even been at the dig on the Syrian borders if it hadn't been for me. Answering my cry for help like she always did, only I had an ulterior motive to have her by my side.

Then I went and got us abducted by aliens. Way to go big sis.

"I know what you want." Kat says, as Ike lands on her shoulder and burrows in her hair. "You know what the seniors think of letting you go anywhere. They believe it's their job to protect us."

"I appreciate it, I really do, Kat." I try my best, sympathetic smile. "I just know my sister is out there somewhere, either somewhere on this planet or nearby."

Kat embraces me again, tears in her eyes. "I'm sure they will find her if she's here."

"But," I say, carefully. "If she's not on the planet?"

"I'll ask Strykr again for you." Kat sighs, "but the answer will be the same. They're not going to let you go off world. In any event, they've got a big assault planned, and they're going to be too busy to do any sort of search and rescue. There's a Drahon fleet in orbit around us and the Gryn intend on taking the ships for their own."

"Sounds exciting." I say. "But I understand." I link my arm with hers. "Come on, I'm sure there's something left for you and this little one." I put my hand on her stomach. "Can't have mama getting hungry."

And I've got just what I needed. Information I can use.

Syn

The Drahon male droops his head between his arms, strung up above him. I hook one claw under his chin and lift his gaze to meet mine.

"See? That wasn't hard, was it?" I stand back a pace and look him up and down. "You're hardly damaged at all *and* you've given me the information I asked for."

"Zark you, Gryn!" The Drahon says, with the last piece of fire he has in him.

"The thing is," I lean closer to him in a conspiratorial manner. "The Gryn are honorable. We don't enslave other species and sell them to the rest of the galaxy, which means this is probably as bad as it's going to get for you."

His eyes brighten from their matte black dulled by pain.

"I mean, we'll probably just dump you in the waste seas." I release him and gently scratch at the shoulder of one of my wings. I have a knot there I can't quite get out on my own and it's irritating. "I suspect you'll end up eating each other, because there's nothing else to eat, but you won't be slaves." This time I lean back into him, all five claw points up against his skin, slowly piercing the green and allowing his black blood to flow. "You'll be free, unlike all my brothers you sold."

I could rip his throat out. I could eviscerate him easily. Happily. But we need information, and, as his bladder gives out, he begins to babble out the real information I've been tasked with obtaining.

The information which will gain the Gryn the advantage when we go to take the Drahon fleet in orbit around Ustokos.

As I leave the cell, I wipe my hand on a rag. "Clean him up and toss him back with the others. He's done." I say to the two guards outside. Young mercs, they're easy to please, and they rattle their feathers with the chance to 'have a go' at the enemy.

They're young enough, they probably never had to fight Proto, the sentient AI which ruled over our planet for as long as most of our memories stretch back.

Except, now it's been routed, now we have Ustokos back, there's a whole lot more to concern us than a bunch of bots wanting to kill or capture us.

I head through the basement levels of the eyrie, the large building the new legion of the Gryn has repurposed as a second lair. Here the lower levels go on a long way and were designed to accommodate a more war-like Gryn.

The Gryn we became just before our empire fell to Proto.

The Gryn Proto wanted to enhance and sell to the rest of the universe as mercenaries and slaves.

I've found myself a reasonable sized room out of the way of the rest of the weapons stores, cells, training pits. It's here I've been gathering tech and attempting to work out what happened to the Gryn in the Proto wars.

Because it's become pretty clear we didn't start out as big, muscular, or tall as we are now. We didn't have claws either, that much is clear from the touch screens our ancestors used. Claws just get in the way.

The more I research, the more it becomes clear to me that the Gryn were developing a fighting force of some kind. They were artificially enhancing the stronger members of the species into something else. Something vicious, something blood thirsty. We were to be stronger, faster, with improved healing abilities.

Or at least, that's my theory. I'm certain at least two of the elite unit have been subject to an enhancement pod. The problem is the unit doesn't trust me much, and the two warriors, Vypr and Ayar are not exactly the easiest specimens to handle. Even though I've told them about my theories, neither have given me any indication they're prepared to submit to even a little testing.

While I'm certain all the seniors were enhanced in the same way, walking up to the Prime and asking him if he wouldn't mind being examined is likely to earn me a beating and a very long time working in the laundry.

Which means I'm stuck looking at a bunch of bot parts, half of a pod I've managed to salvage, and a whole load of theory—none of which I can take to any of the seniors.

I grab my vectorpad and fill in the details I got from the Drahon drone. He's given me a couple of pieces of information we didn't already have, but the one Drahon who we need to get talking is the queen.

And she isn't talking.

Having filled out my report, I go up two floors to where my commander has an office. As usual, he's not in it. Strykr hates being tied to a desk, just like the rest of us. Instead, he's watching Huntr and Ayar spar in the training pit.

"Report, Guv." I hand him the pad, using his familiar title, even though it still grates on me.

This unit is everything I'm not, ill-disciplined, constantly fighting and partying and, more recently, mating. So many of my fellow warriors have claimed their mates from among the rescued humans. They're nesting. Younglings on the way, or already here.

I shouldn't be jealous. I can get mating action any time I like from the Mochi caravans which travel throughout the territory. But I don't want to mate the feline females, however accommodating they can be for Gryn warriors.

"Excellent work, Syn." Strykr says after skimming the report.

"Has the Drahon queen said anything yet?" I ask, more in hope she hasn't.

He shakes his head, and I quell the feeling of triumph inside. Strykr's dark gaze doesn't leave me. We didn't see eye to eye when Ryak first put me in his unit. The Commander didn't like having another troublesome Gryn foisted on him.

And I have been trouble. I got into a fight with the Prime of the Gryn's second on my first day out of my camp. Fyn took exception to me poking around where I shouldn't be, and I found out first-hand how much the seniors have been enhanced when he knocked me clear across the supply depot.

It sort of set the tone. I don't fit. I've never fitted. But I'm vrexing good at what I do.

Strykr rubs at his chin. "Have you been in with the queen yet?" He asks.

"It was deemed the pleasure was only open to more senior Gryn." I reply, turning my head away to look down into the pit, seemingly uninterested.

"That's Ryak for you, he's a secretive bastid." Strykr barks a laugh. "I think he could do with your help. The queen won't crack, and we need her codes if we're to surprise the fleet."

I shrug, my feathers shifting and the knot making itself known. "He hasn't asked."

"Well, I'm asking." Strykr says and he claps an enormous hand on my shoulder. "After you've gone a round with me in the pit, we'll go and see him."

I do my level best to keep my face straight. It seems what the goddess gives with one hand, she takes away with the other, and I'm going to have to face our senior commander covered in bite wounds from a Gryn who takes fighting dirty to a whole new level.

Want to see if Syn gets what he wants?
REBEL will be released in September 2022

Also by Hattie Jacks

ELITE ROGUE ALIEN WARRIORS SERIES
STORM
FURY
CHAOS
REBEL (Coming soon)
WRATH (Coming soon)

ROGUE ALIEN WARRIORS SERIES
Fierce
Fear
Fire
Fallen
Forever

SCI-FI ROMANCE ANTHOLOGY
Claimed Among The Stars includes:
Fated: A Rogue Alien Warriors Novella

HAALUX EMPIRE SERIES
Taken: Alien Commander's Captive

Crave: Alien General's Obsession
Havoc: Alien Captain's Alliance
Bane: Alien Warrior's Redemption
Traitor: Alien Hunter's Mate

Just who is this Hattie Jacks anyway?

I've been a passionate sci-fi fan since I was a little girl, brought up on a diet of Douglas Adams, Issac Asimov, Star Trek, Star Wars, Doctor Who, Red Dwarf and The Adventure Game.

What? You don't know about The Adventure Game? It's probably a British thing and dates me horribly! Google it. Even better search for it on YouTube. In my defence, there were only three channels back then.

I'm also a sucker for great characters and situations as well as grand romance, because who doesn't like a grand romantic gesture?

So, when I'm not writing steamy stories about smouldering alien males and women with something to prove, you'll find me battling my garden (less English country garden, more The Good Life) or zooming around the countryside on my motorbike.

Check out my website at www.hattiejacks.com!

Printed in Great Britain
by Amazon